At ten-thirty a Messerschmitt 109E seemed to come floating up the wadi. It went lifting over the top of the escarpment, came round in a wide circle, and the next thing the sleeping men knew was that bullets were raking their sangar.

The Messerschmitt called up the other aircraft; a radio message flashed to Rommel in Tobruk—'Found!'

The five Messerschmitts came in line astern into the attack. Yeats-Urley thought, 'No good pretending we're not here and they'll go away,' and gave the order to fire.

Hell broke loose up the wadi, a very noisy hell, filled with the sound of aircraft roaring full out, guns chattering, head-on for the sangar, only to lift at seemingly the last minute, while inside the sangar two Spandaus and a Vickers deafened the men crouching under the overhang. Each plane in turn hurled spinning hot lead at them, to shatter against the rocks around the sangar, and each plane was savaged by raking fire from three machine-guns. It was terrifying—noise, dust and drifting cordite smoke, and those aircraft bodies hurtling so close above their heads. But they'd picked a good place for their sangar, and not a man had been hurt, yet . . .

LONG RUN TO TOBRUK

Gordon Landsborough

MANOR
BOOKS
INC.

A MANOR BOOK

Manor Books, Inc.
432 Park Avenue South
New York, New York 10016

ISBN CODE 0-532-15316-2

The trucks had leaguered south of the desert airfield, a good mile from the runway, tucked out of sight behind sandhills that were grey and drab and incredibly forlorn.

Three trucks – Chevs – all bearing on their door panels the insignia of Rommel's Afrika Korps, the palm-tree and sinister swastika. Earlier there had been a fourth vehicle, but one – their only 30-hundredweight – had started to overheat, and you don't ride into battle that promises to be bitter and brutal in a truck that might let you down, so it had been immobilised and abandoned. Now its ruffianly crew were dispersed among the other trucks, too crowded to be comfortable.

They waited, that awful, mounting tension upon them, their nerves silently screaming, the sweat beading their foreheads. They waited, praying for the minutes to pass quickly and let them get on with their mission of destruction, yet inwardly aghast and some of them horrified at the prospect of pain and terror that might lie ahead for them.

They were waiting for the sun to go down and already, with a long narrow stratum of low-lying cloud partly obscuring it, the light was waning and the shadows were long. In those long shadows their R.S.M. and his mopping-up parties would be crawling nearer to those dangerous gun nests, they thought. Or, more likely, would already be in position, as near as they could get without being observed ... waiting – just waiting like themselves – for the signal that would bring them to their feet, and storming into brief but murderous action.

5

A wind stirred unpleasantly, adding to the now almost unbearable moment of waiting, a thin cold wind, harbinger of the desert night to come, that bit through their KD shirts and worn pullovers, and brought them huddling close together in their open trucks.

Only one man had dismounted, Captain Alan Yeats-Urley, patrol-commander of the S.A.S., that glamorous desert guerrilla outfit, the Special Air Service. He was young, like some others in his patrol only twenty-three, a youthful age to be leading fierce fighting men bent on the killing of others of the human kind.

He was out there on the rough desert, being very casual, swiping with his heavy stick at inoffensive tufts of dessicated grass, or finding odd holes and prodding into them as if there was something of absorbing interest there. All designed to reduce the tension among his men. A good commander, Alan Yeats-Urley.

That stick was an affectation which he took on all these patrols. He liked to carry a stick, and the curious thing was that sometimes he limped slightly when using it, for Yeats-Urley had his day-dreams like other young men, and one of them was of being wounded in battle and left limping.

It wouldn't have to be a bad wound, of course, not sufficient to keep him out of hunting, or dancing at the Savoy, but just enough to give him a limp and an excuse always to use that comfortingly heavy stick. They – the limp and the stick – would be his badges of battle, to be worn like medals that would bring him distinction. Nothing like a war wound to earn a man respect from his fellows, and a limp better than most advertised nearness to death and suffering.

In his dreams Yeats-Urley saw himself on some parade ground at Aldershot – better still, at Sandhurst. He would limp slightly, just a little heavily leaning on his stick; and men would watch him and say quietly, 'That's Yeat-Urley. Stopped a packet in North Africa.' And that for Yeats-Urley and many another young man was what war was all about, winning honours and medals but above all the regard and respect of his comrades in uniform. Romantic stuff, the

6

dreams of the young male, and the thought never occurred to him that war wounds could be very painful.

Twenty-minutes before total darkness – it had all been timed and worked out far off in the desert the night before – and with the light already bad, the sun dipped out of sight, and Yeats-Urley made his move.

He looked at his men, face tense and he gave the order they were waiting for. 'Get cracking!' That was all.

Three drivers, bending over their wheels to watch him, got the order and reached for their starters. Three engines roared to life – noise no longer mattered – Yeats-Urley swung aboard the leading truck, and the gears went in and the Chevs moved and began to climb the hill.

They gave them the gun, feet hard down on accelerators, going straight up the slope and the hell with the bumps and hollows, so that in seconds they were travelling at hectic speed and the trucks were bouncing like crazy.

They came over the top, the men clinging for dear life amid the usual shambles of blankets, equipment and supplies that packed the floor of their vehicles, and that would be the signal to Sergeant-major Wallace and his two extermination squads, as Yeats-Urley called them. They'd be up at the sound, running in, arms swinging their little lethal grenades before startled German machine-guns crews knew that death had been there in the sandhills this last hour or more. Two gun-nests, strategically situated to protect the aircraft parked off the runway . . . two futile defence positions when a daring enemy came in to wipe them out.

Yeats-Urley, nearly hitting the roof of the cabin as they bounced over the rugged ground, caught a glimpse of one party going in – tiny distant figures. Then a flame erupting as if a grenade had gone off. There was the heavy stammer of Thompson sub-machine-guns, and more bangings as if from Mills bombs. He didn't look to see how the second extermination squad was going on. His eyes now were only for the targets of their destructive purpose that night – aircraft. Enemy aircraft. Mostly German but some Italian.

They knew the drill. At reckless speed three trucks raced

7

nearly parallel across the desolate scrubland, some of the men shouting crude and raucous encouragement to their drivers, others setting up a cheer that stuck in their throats as the breath was knocked from their lungs by the bouncing vehicles. At the runway they diverged, suddenly peeling away from each other like birds on the wing.

Yeats-Urley took the planes on the north side of the runway. Lieutenant Fairlop began to fire the aircraft south of the strip of levelled land. The third truck beetled off at furious pace to pick up the exterminators when they had silenced the gun nests.

In the back of each truck gunners crouched behind the mounted twin Vickers K machine-guns; the other men braced to use their sub-machine-guns; in the cab Yeats-Urley – old Eats-Early to his men – had his Very pistol out, a good weapon to start a conflagration.

They came roaring down the line of dispersed aircraft, and it was exhilarating, the light almost gone and the aircraft looming like big unintelligent monsters just waiting to be picked off. Now they were all cheering, even Yeats-Urley joining them and giving hunting cries. On them was the madness of destruction. They were young; and for youth it is good to tear down and destroy. This night it was legitimate – their superiors said so. In fact it was their duty to shoot and destroy, and the thought was wine to them and they were gleeful and their glee took expression in wild cheering and silly shouted obscenities.

Then they took on the first silent aircraft. Corporal Fullalove opened up with a swift and savage burst, and the incendiary bullets streamed into the belly of the Junkers ('Shoot low; that's where the petrol tanks are,' Yeats-Urley had instructed) and to their joy almost immediately they had the German bomber in flames. There was a second's pause after the bullets tore in, then a red glow began to develop, and then the fire became an explosion that sent flames racing the length of the fuselage, and no longer was the night growing darker.

Across the runway, Lieutenant Fairlop's truck was

savaging the Me109E and 110 German fighters. Somewhere two little battles around gun-pits were ending, all over and dead in thirty bloody seconds.

Yeats-Urley banged the side of his door and yelled a frantic tally-ho, and they were at the second aircraft, another Ju88. They went twisting and dodging among the silent, deserted aircraft, easy, sitting targets for the S.A.S. The barrels grew hot as the lead hosed into the bombers, the tanks ripping open and the petrol gushing and then the tracer flashing in, sending everything up in smoke and flames.

Plane after plane took fire, until a long line of raging, fearsome pyres edged the dirt runway, and the madness of the moment took complete hold of the S.A.S. Now a roar of delight, almost unheard with the aircraft raging furiously behind them, greeted each new act of destruction.

The heat rolled after them, unheeded in their excitement – heat so great that even a hundred yards away it scorched their hair and they could feel their eyebrows shrivelling and curling. And now the night was light again, and they knew that in the far distance, among the huddled huts, alarmed men – probably Italians as well as Germans – would be racing for their vehicles, coming out to do battle with these daring invaders of their territory, all these hundreds of miles behind the front line.

Once Yeats-Urley hung right out of his cab to look back. He wanted to know how the gun-busters had gone on, if they were all right and were being picked up by the third truck. He spotted the vehicle, clear in the bright red light of burning aircraft. It was scudding across the runway towards the second gun-nest. That meant the first extermination squad had been picked up, and soon the others would be hoisted aboard and they could all go.

The captain also saw dark shapes appearing on the end of the runway. The pursuit was on. They had mere minutes now to finish the job and get safely off into the darkness of the surrounding desert. Captain Yeats-Urley did not panic.

9

He got down to the job of depriving Field-Marshal Rommel of the bombers so vital to him in this war in Africa.

Among the Ju88s were Ju87s – the dreaded Stukas, gull-winged and with fixed undercarriages. On to these the S.A.S. turned all their viciousness, for the dive-bombers were particularly hated, and the fear was that if any were left intact the patrol might later regret it, scudding for their lives over the open wasteland.

Across the airfield, Yeats-Urley noted with approval how Fairlop was faring. Going through 'em like a dose of salts, he told himself, and indeed his lieutenant was doing a thorough job of destruction. The Me fighters were burning prettily, and so were a few Italian fighters – Macchi C-200s and Fiat G-50s.

One plane only they could not touch. That was a tiny Fieseler-Storch, the eyes of the enemy when it came to a desert manhunt. It was parked too close to the admin. area to be worth taking on. A pity.

Debris was flying around them now, hurled great distances by the exploding petrol tanks. Ammunition crackled within the burning planes as the fire got at the belts. The danger was wine to them in that glorious moment.

'Tally-ho!' roared Yeats-Urley again, and pooped off with his Very. Behind him the men caught up the cry and roared, 'Tally-ho, you bastards!' which was not quite hunting-field standards, and let off with their guns at every waiting target.

They did their work thoroughly, only one Ju88 Teutonically resisting their efforts to burn it. It took the usual scything lead; the petrol gushed because they could smell it; the incendiaries streaked in, but the damned thing refused to take fire. Yeats-Urley grew hopping mad and when they came to the last of the bombers and got it flaming, he bellowed, 'Turn her round!' He wasn't going to quit El Badim leaving Rommel with one repairable Junkers. He'd finish off that stubborn monster or die in the attempt.

It was to be talked about in messes in many parts of the world many years afterwards, how old Eats-Early, not satisfied with thirty-eight aircraft, had to turn back to polish off the thirty-ninth.

Turn back . . . but that was towards the enemy trucks scorching up the runway towards them. They weren't a mile away, lights showing, the hell with blackout restrictions with all those planes burning. They turned – for one second Yeats-Urley saw Fairlop's Chev belting off into the darkness; a second later he spotted the third truck by the second gunpit, picking up the grenadiers. They took on the Junkers, completely circling it, though two other bombers burned fiercely a mere hundred yards each side of them. This time there was no mistake – up it went with a mighty whoosh! and back on to the runway they drove again.

. . . Yeats-Urley lost his joy. Again he saw the third Chev. It was standing by the gun-nest. Standing. It should have been away by now. Were wounded holding them up? The enemy vehicles seemed almost on top of them.

Yeats-Urley felt helpless, frantic, watching the hunt close on their Chev. He kept hanging out of the cab, looking back. Behind him the men were quiet now, and almost he could feel their apprehension. They watched a drama, a race for life.

They saw the third truck pull away madly and begin the run down the dirt track after them, but pursuit was close and fire was opened upon the vehicle by the pursuing Germans. Red tracer from some mounted Schmeissers crept after the truck, seeming to move very slowly because they were almost looking down the barrels of the guns. It began to lick towards the third truck. The Chev took evasive action.

Abruptly they saw it pull across the runway, heading for the wall of fire. The tracer ended for a moment, then several sweeping lines of it started after the scurrying, clumsy truck. They were converging, almost settling on the three-tonner, when to a cheer from Yeats-Urley's men it ran between two blazing aircraft, momentarily out of sight of the pursuers.

Yeats-Urley was thinking, 'They'll come up behind the aircraft, under cover till they're on the desert.' At which moment one of the bombers blew up. It was the one they had just gone back to destroy.

It went up with a mighty roar, burning debris hurtling hundreds of feet into the air, black oily smoke rising with the orange-red flames. It blew up at the precise moment when the third truck was scudding by, less than fifty yards away. The blast hit it and they saw it go over, and then flaming wreckage showered down, and they knew no one was going to survive that holocaust.

The sight filled them with consternation. They were their comrades, those men, close to them; yet watching them die like that, from a distance, brought no shock for the moment. Instead, this curious consternation. They'd copped it. Kaput. They'd be without a third truck, only two now to go down the desert. Bloody hard lines, getting it like that. But no grief with the thought. Only when they leaguered up at a halt and had time to let the battle tension ease out of them would they remember their dead chums and feel lost and bewildered and unhappy. Except Oily Hoyle, too callous ever to feel emotion.

It was different when a comrade died in your arms, blood pouring and the panic of death in eyes that had been contemptuous of it until the moment of arrival. You'll be all right, mate, holding him and the dying hand grasping into flesh and hurting, as if trying to draw himself back from the edge of no-return. And when the grip slackened and death struck, then you walked away, and you could cry openly and no one would think the worse of you, such crying not being accounted weakness.

The men behind Yeats-Urley were shouting, banging on the cab roof to draw their commander's attention to the disaster, not knowing he had seen it all. Yeats-Urley shouted to them, very decisive. 'All right, you men, Nothing we can do about it. Just keep going.'

The captain settled back in his seat, face calm, staring across the darkening desert. He felt nothing. A truck had been lost. Some men would not return from the expedition. He would make a clear, unemotional report of the moment, file it and that, apart from some letters to wives and sweethearts, would be the last of it. Public school had been good training for such moments.

They left the inferno that was an airfield and bumped off across a desert carefully reconnoitred for escape the previous day. They saw several pursuing vehicles crawling between the twin walls of fire, and they were larger now, catching up with them. No one worried over that. The Hun couldn't even get within firing distance before they were in the dark.

The light now faded very fast. Within three minutes the world turned from a lot of light to very little light. They drove on, reducing speed but taking risks for a while. They hit rocks and bounced a lot, but that didn't hurt them. They couldn't see Lieutenant Fairlop's truck now – it had been half a mile ahead – but that didn't matter. He knew where to rendezvous.

After a time Yeats-Urley knew they need no longer take risks, and told his driver to take it easy and feel his way across the dark desert, and the speed died and the men in the back were able to sit up with greater comfort. The blazing airfield lit up the sky behind them, but now there were no silhouettes of pursuing vehicles. The pursuit had ended, for the Germans weren't silly enough to pursue the terrible S.A.S. into their own ground, the desert at night.

Slowly they crawled, easing round vague shapes of rocks and bushes, occasionally hitting rocks that sent a jar right through the vehicle and made them wonder how it kept in one piece. In another hour a bit of a moon would be up and then they could make better time until they reached The Graveyard. Some of the men even began to doze off in the back.

It was slow going, little more than two miles an hour, crawling over the dark desert, but two miles was a nice safety belt and at the end of the hour Captain Yeats-Urley's crisp voice called. 'All right. That's enough. We'll halt till moonrise.'

The truck stopped, the engine ceased to beat and turn and the silence of the North African desert took over. Behind them was a great glow, where the airfield blazed, but here was all darkness, safety for them. They all jumped down from the truck, and every man promptly unbuttoned and emptied his bladder. Never lose an opportunity, was the saying, for one never knew how long it might be before it was safe to empty one's bladder again.

Yeats-Urley's voice from the darkness. 'No one to sleep, d'you hear?' The voice very imperative, rising slightly, sharply at the end of the sentence.

A good officer. A man who would never let his men down, and they all knew it. Brave, of course, how else could he be with his background? Prep school, public school, cadet corps, Sandhurst. And of course the family influence; father, both grandfathers and every uncle except one, career soldiers ending with high rank or dying on active service. That one had joined the R.A.F. No one in the family could quite account for the aberration.

Captain Yeats-Urley – old Eats-Early – was also a thoughtful officer, considerate of his O.R.s. Firm, of course, and must be obeyed with alacrity, but kind, very kind. Kind to dumb animals and just as kind to his men. In fact Yeats-Urley did at times seem to treat his men as if they were of some lower animal order, but as this was natural to true top-drawer officer-class, men didn't mind and most even seemed to welcome it, knowing their place in society and not wanting to move from it.

Yeats-Urley said, 'Keep your ears skinned, all of you. I don't expect trouble, but Lieutenant Fairlop's party's out there somewhere and you might hear them.'

Not likely, they thought. Fairlop's trained commandos weren't going to make any sound that might betray them. They all felt safe until the moon came up, but still they weren't going to advertise their presence so close to the enemy.

So they squatted against the wheels of the vehicle, eight men listening hard for any sound from any direction. But only the cold wind came creeping in upon them, making the flesh of their faces hang in dead lumps, and their noses run so that they sat with drops upon them. Miserable hours, those times of cold darkness, and then they would sigh for the sun and warmth for their chilled bones – and when it came they'd curse and pray for the cold night.

About ten o'clock, with nothing of event happening, except that Private Hoyle began to have trouble with his bowels and squatted distantly much of the time, the moon began to rise. Within half an hour it was up high enough to give them light to move, and though it was only small, a mere waning quarter thing, as it climbed it gave more light until the desert seemed astonishingly bright.

They started up, climbed aboard and moved off. The race had begun, and all knew it, and immediately tension began to mount again. They had a thousand miles or more to go to Kufra Oasis, and the enemy would hound them all the way. At first light they'd have aircraft up from other airfields – El Adem near Tobruk, most likely. They'd comb the desert for them, and a truck couldn't hope to get beyond aircraft radius within a few hours.

Cunning – desert cunning, of which the S.A.S. had plenty – must come into it now if they were to survive. They would have to go into hiding as soon as it was daylight, and they knew only one place that could give them effective cover. The Graveyard. If they made it by dawn they would be reasonably safe. If they didn't, and they were caught in the desert, painfully open hereabouts, strafing planes would soon put an end to them. They could just make The Graveyard by daybreak if nothing happened to delay them.

They ground along in second gear, rarely more than ten miles an hour. The going wasn't bad, but there were obstacles and the light wasn't all that good, and they could not afford to take risks so early in the race. But the miles sped by, and Yeats-Urley, up front with the driver, was content. They'd make it.

Big Maurice – Private Maurice Hill, Man Mountain to his comrades because of his seventeen stone of power-packed muscle – thought he saw something north of them. He watched. Something did move, far distant, on the edge of visibility. It moved and it kept pace with them, perhaps a quarter of a mile away across the flat scrubland.

Big Maurice moved with startling suddenness. His head came round the cab door, mouth within inches of his captain's face. The engine was making a noise but Big Maurice wasn't going to add to it with any shouting.

'Sir, we're being tracked.'

Eyes widening, Yeats-Urley suddenly alert. A lift of the head, a silent query. Man Mountain's big fist came over the door, a solid thumb jerking backwards. Then the private pulled away to let his captain see beyond.

The others in the truck had got the message something was wrong. Big Maurice whispered, 'There . . . Some bastard's spotted us.' It had to be some bastard, here in Axis-occupied territory, was the first thought of men who survived because they saw death in every untoward happening.

Every eye turned. Something dark was gliding through the bushes, paralleling their course. Weapons came up immediately, but no one opened fire. No one would, not with an officer there to give orders.

They bumped steadily along for half a mile, only the driver looking ahead and not at the distant moving object. Definitely some vehicle moved out there and kept pace with them, and the hackles of their hair stood erect on their scalps and they waited for the flash of flame that would tell them they were being fired at.

Captain Yeats-Urley told his driver to stop and switch off his engine. The lumbering movement ceased. They heard the sound of a distant engine, now that theirs had died into silence. For a moment the other vehicle kept moving, then that too came to a halt, the engine quietening.

Someone said with certainty, 'That's a Chev engine.' Corporal Fullalove. And Fullalove knew his engines. But in that crazy desert war every army ran captured enemy transport, so hearing a Chev engine didn't mean much. Still, a thought was surfacing in every mind now, and Captain Yeats-Urley got it and said to his driver, 'Get ready to start

16

off if things turn out badly.' And to the men behind he called, 'One of you – you, corporal – give a shout.' If they were enemy, the sooner they knew the better. But it might be. . . .

Corporal Fullalove's voice rang out: 'Who goes there?'

And a hoarse voice told him, croaking across the desert. 'Rommel, you stupid git!'

The tension fled; every man in the truck burst out laughing. That feared thing across the desert was their second truck, Lieutenant Fairlop's.

They came together, bumping across the desert, and while the officers conferred without descending from their cabs, crude soldiers exchanged crude comments of a highly personal nature behind them, and all were happy.

'I thought you'd be in front,' Captain Yeats-Urley told his lieutenant. He'd been well ahead the last time Yeats-Urley had seen him.

The captain saw Fairlop shrug, across from him in the cab of the other Chev, the moonlight not disguising the vaguely insolent gesture. Yeats-Urley never showed it, of course, but Lieutenant Fairlop somewhat nettled him by his manner. The lieutenant wasn't – what was the word? – quite polished. That was it, thought Yeats-Urley, Fairlop lacked the right finish.

Fairlop was always correct, yet behind his manner was something calculating, a feeling of truculence kept well in check but there. He looked on his superiors with a cold eye, rarely smiling and then with the hint that he had put it on because it was expected of him. He was a man, Yeats-Urley vaguely felt, with no real thoughts for anyone but himself, a man who would, as the expression was, always look after No. 1.

A powerful man, though, a six-footer with a hard-muscled body, like a man who has worked all his life with his hands, yet Fairlop hadn't. It seemed he had just grown that way, big and strong, where others develop thin and weakly and through no fault of their own.

Public school, Yeats-Urley remembered and thought no one would know it. Fairlop hadn't got – what was that word

2

again? – polish, the veneer that makes the public schoolboy stand out. But then it had been a very minor public school, Yeats-Urley thought indulgently. Lancing, wasn't it? Not sure he even knew where the place was. And what had he been before joining the army? Selling insurance? Something very odd for a fellow to do, anyway. Altogether there was something about Fairlop that made the captain just that little bit wary, never feeling close to him or wanting to be.

'We didn't take any risks.' Fairlop's voice, rather short, a full explanation for losing a half-mile lead in five words. And then he said something, one of those undiplomatically expressed opinions that jarred and rather put a fellow's back up. 'You're a bit south of our line, aren't you?'

Yeats-Urley could have been a bit south of their intended course, because waltzing round that last reluctant bomber had meant they had to come on course at an angle instead of a straight run into the dark off the runway. But something about the statement, almost a rebuke, had to make him deny it.

'Oh, I don't think so.' Yeats-Urley looked round a moonlit desert that carried no identifiable features. He felt obstinate. Dammit, he knew best, and he'd show his lieutenant he didn't make mistakes in the desert. Not many. 'Let's move.' An order rather more curt than usual, to establish his rank above the other. Fairlop just pulled back into his cab, not hurrying, not showing if the curtness had been detected.

So the two trucks began to roll over the arid scrubland, and Fairlop, blast the man, must have been right, and they must have been projecting the error by driving at a tangent to their intended course, for suddenly they were in trouble.

Ahead of them the ground grew rougher, more stony, the Chevs bumping hard and making life a bit sore for the un-complaining men in the back. Then they came to an area littered with quite big boulders, around which they had to pick their way in a moonlight that really wasn't quite good enough for such journeying.

Then all of a sudden Yeats-Urley's driver, a diminutive and bad-tempered little man, Snowy Medman, let go with a wild shout of alarm, followed by a frantic swearing as his brakes clapped on and the truck slid in a skid under that weight.

Right under their bonnet was a wadi. They stopped within two feet of the edge, and if Snowy hadn't been alert they'd have gone over. It wasn't a big wadi, no more than eight or ten feet across, and perhaps as much as that deep, and you don't easily spot such breaks on a scrub-covered desert. If it had been wider it would probably have thrown a shadow to warn them, but this didn't.

Captain Yeats-Urley's first thought was, 'Oh, blast!' Lieutenant Fairlop had been right. They were off-course. Captain Yeats-Urley didn't so much mind being wrong, even now, as that chap Fairlop being right.

Snowy had stalled his engine. In the silence Yeats-Urley heard someone behind utter a lugubrious, 'That wasn't there yesterday.'

True. When they'd made their reccy the day before, working out their route of departure when they'd topped the aircraft, there'd been no wadi in the way. Still, they couldn't be far out.

Men were hopping down from behind. Yeats-Urley swung down from the cab. They all stood on the edge of the wadi, examining it critically.

'No way down there, sir.' Snowy Medman looking nastily into the deep ditch.

The banks were steep, too steep for a truck to descend and climb out on the other side. Expert eyes eyed the steep sides critically. And it was out of the question to think of digging a ramp down into the wadi and up the other side. Too stony. It would take hours, and they hadn't hours.

The men moved. No one gave an order, but tension, the knowledge that every minute delayed there meant a risk of being caught out on the open desert when the sun came up, far from the protection of The Graveyard, made them jump to it.

Some men went scrambling one way along the edge of the

wadi, others went the other way. Yeats-Urley, Fairlop and the drivers alone remained with the vehicles.

The sounds of men moving over earth and through bushes faded. An uncanny silence fell upon the tiny group beside their silent vehicles. The moonlight seemed to stream down upon them, like a silent white shower, cold and hard. It made them feel uneasy, with that feeling that one is exposed and there are eyes watching. Automatically they took up positions on either side of the Chevs, watching back down the desert, hands on weapons whose safety catches had been slipped. Far distant now the airfield still glowed red.

The minutes passed. No sound of returning men. The wadi must have been longer than they had realised. 'We *were* more south of our line than I thought,' Captain Yeats-Urley told himself.

He began to grow anxious and to look at his watch and then at the eastern sky, and still the minutes passed and no one came running back to say which way they should go. After a time he began to sweat, and he knew the others would be suffering too. Half an hour went by. Thirty-five minutes. Forty.

Snowy said, 'Christ, we're done for!'

Yeats-Urley said, 'We'll make it,' confident the moment a man of his began to lose heart. Yet forty minutes lost now because of this wadi would for certain catch them out of The Graveyard by sun-up, and they'd still have to hide the vehicle and themselves when they got there.

They were held up a full fifty minutes before the welcome sounds of feet stumbling through the dirt and rocks came to their ears. Instantly they were alert and ready. Corporal Fullalove came up with his men. 'The wadi loops, sir. Goes right back on its course.' Half a mile away at least, he told them, and north of where they were.

'Get the others,' Yeats-Urley snapped, no time to waste now. Snowy shot into his seat and switched on the battered headlights. It was a risk, but not a great one to take. The vehicles faced west, away from distant eyes on the still blazing airfield. The enemy would be occupied, and it was most unlikely that the Germans had any patrols out — they'd come at dawn. So would the aircraft.

Snowy kept dipping the headlights, and he kept it up for close on quarter of an hour before they heard men running hard to reach them. Engines were immediately switched on and the trucks were moving when breathless S.A.S. came racing out of the dark and clambered aboard.

They'd lost over an hour.

They lost more time later. They went hard across the scrub wasteland, trying to recapture some of the lost time, but perhaps because desperation now drove with them, they were forced into another halt. Perhaps they — the second truck, that is — should have spotted the crack in the rock, and were driving too fast to see it. Perhaps this is a little hard upon Private Tony Vecchi, the driver, for it was only a very small crack and he was after all driving in light that no more than a quarter moon could cast.

Snowy Medman, driving the captain's truck, didn't see it either, as he admitted loudly and often to console the wretched Vecchi, not even referring to him as 'Wop', this time. The lead truck just drove through, within inches of disaster. The second literally fell into the hole.

One moment Lieutenant Fairlop was hanging on to his cab door as the truck roared and lurched over the bumpy terrain. The next he was halfway through the windscreen, if they'd bothered to have windscreens on S.A.S. trucks, lying over the bonnet, the breath knocked out of him. One moment the truck was in motion. The next it was halted. It came from speed to stop just like that, all in one second.

Fairlop hauled himself back. Vecchi was painfully dragging himself off the steering wheel, sobbing with pain. 'Bloody ribs!' he kept saying. 'Soddin' bloody ribs!'

The engine had stalled. Fairlop heard his men behind cursing and one of them moaning. He swung out and down. The other truck had halted, hearing the crash even above the noise of their own straining engine. Fairlop's cold, calculating eyes looked first at the cause of the disaster, then at his men.

The cause was easy to see. The offside rear wheel had

simply dropped into a crack on a stretch of rock outcrop that seemed tailor-made to accept it. Afterwards everyone marvelled that the front wheel hadn't gone in instead. That would have been even more disastrous. Fairlop thought: 'That was a jar. Will the truck ever move again? Is it worth while wasting time finding out?'

But what was the alternative? If his truck was *kaput*, sixteen men, food, water, equipment, ammunition and so on would have to go aboard one truck. There wasn't room for them, not if it was to be a fighting vehicle, with a Vickers mounted to give defence against strafing aircraft or following land vehicles. And dawn was coming so fast now they could see the pink of it over the dismal eastern horizon.

He looked at his men. Men were necessary if they were to, literally, get out of this hole. Now he hoped they weren't all knocked up like Driver Vecchi, huddled into his corner and moaning.

'Who's hurt?' His voice came up sharply, and the cursing and moaning stopped. They were sorting themselves out from the floor where they had been thrown amid all their dunnage. A bit of talk among the men, then Sergeant Trefoil spoke.

'Don't think anyone's really hurt, sir.' A momentary protest from someone, but the sergeant's rough voice went on, 'Private Mack's hurt his back, but he'll be all right.' A lugubrious, pain-filled voice that Fairlop recognised as Mack's denied this with feeling.

'Everyone down. Let's get her out of here.' Fairlop went back to the cab to get his torch. He was relieved to see Vecchi slowly descending through the other door. At least their driver was alive. If he'd cracked a rib or two it shouldn't matter. S.A.S. didn't make much of a mere cracked rib.

'What's happened, Freddie?' Captain Yeats-Urley's voice. He had come hurrying back from the lead truck.

Fairlop said, 'Come and see.' He went round and flashed the torch on the rear wheel.

'Oh, my goodness!' Even at such a time Yeats-Urley's speech was restrained. In the light of the torch they both stared at the double-tyred wheel, nipped in the crack, down to its axle.

The captain's head lifted quickly, his anxious eyes going to the pink glow to the east, his mind calculating. They were miles from The Graveyard, the only place so close to El Badim where they could out-fox a relentless, vigilant enemy. They were going to be caught by daylight well short of their proposed hideout. So time was even more precious to them now, he thought, and sent a call back to the men on his truck. 'Everybody down. Here, at the double. Fetch hammers, crowbars . . .'

He took charge. He knew what to do. He'd spent two years in the desert learning what to do when something nasty occurred. His expert eye saw that the rock would have to be broken away where it gripped into the metal of the wheel rims. Then they would have to lift the vehicle bodily, for the crack narrowed ahead and if they tried to come out under power they would just jam again. Yes, that was the trick, he thought, lift the truck bodily, lay down a sand-track over the crack, then drive away. . . .

If, he thought, just as Fairlop had thought, the truck would ever drive again. Had the guts been torn out of her? The differential chewed to pieces? Rear axle gone? Such a lot of things that could have bent or snapped or cracked under such circumstances. They would have to find out.

He looked at the horizon. The light was distinctly brighter now. Men with hammers got to work with almost frantic haste, everyone knowing the urgency of the moment, the precious value of these seconds that ticked away while they were halted uselessly there. The crowbars drove down, too, chewing away into unyielding rock. It wasn't easy work, for the wheel itself was in the way. And when they had made progress there was a sudden movement and the truck settled lower, and they had to start again. And time was hurrying away, hurrying, hurrying, and they knew the search aircraft would be warming up on the airfields for miles around, and the patrols were probably on the move already across El Badim airfield. And they were stuck there.

They hammered and cursed, those fortunate enough to be able to work on the wheel. The others could only stand around, holding down the tightening knots of frustration that gripped their stomachs, weapons ready, watching the lightening desert, anxiety gnawing until at least one man there was nearing to panic. That was Lance-corporal Stewart M'Bain, an intelligent man who had been too long in the desert.

Only Joe Hoyle, lowering, ungracious brute, took no part in the rescue operation, and was indifferent to what might come blazing on them out of the night. His stomach was really griping, and he spent those fifteen minutes a lonely squatting figure away from the group. He too was feeling panic, a man in some fear because he had never had this experience before, this liquid running of his bowels. Hoyle, a product of Birmingham's roughest quarter, was an animal with little imagination, a crude being too often sullen and when he wasn't he still was no joy. But he was an instinctive soldier, big and hard as they came, indifferent it seemed to discomfort or danger. Now this discomfort of the guts had him in alarm. He was sure there was something terribly wrong with him – it couldn't go on, all this running. And the awful ache in his stomach, the acid burn that made him want to howl out, but he didn't. The pain of that moment, unusual in his healthy life, the demoralising effect of crouching and feeling liquid spewing where none should be, turned him childish. He was frightened.

When the edges of that narrow crack on the rock face were chipped wider, they began to lift the vehicle bodily out of the hole. They put a sand track close to the tyre, and Sergeant Trefoil and Corporal M'Bain crouched under the vehicle, ready to ram the track right under the wheel when it was raised. Then all the heavy equipment was removed from the truck, and everyone took hold, including Captain Yeats-Urley, and on the command heaved. Big Maurice Hill went under the tail on all fours and got his massive shoulders under the truck.

They heaved it out, because that was quicker than jacking,

and the brightening horizon gave their muscles strength so that they plucked up the vehicle after all with no great effort, though there was just that one first disturbing moment when it seemed completely stuck.

The track was under, the vehicle safe once more. But now came the anxious moment. Had their efforts been just so much waste of time? Was the truck so damaged as to be useless?

Driver Vecchi for all his previous moaning didn't seem too badly hurt after all. He moved gingerly, nursing his ribs, but he could climb into the cab and start the engine. Everyone stood around, anxiously watching. The day was quite bright now; any moment the sun would come into view. Vecchi gently revved the engine then slipped it into first gear. Clutch slowly released. No grating metallic sounds from the rear. The truck began to move, and rolled easily off the sand track.

'By Jove, that's a miracle!' exclaimed Yeats-Urley, his face shining with delight. The Chev had taken an appalling knock, yet seemed to have survived undamaged. One never knew, though – things could happen, bumping over that terrible desert, some weakness magnified to breaking point. The sooner they got under her and gave her a thorough inspection the better.

'Mount!' ordered Captain Yeats-Urley, a command that was a hangover from the old days of cavalry.

Everything was hurriedly heaved aboard, then the men climbed up, while Yeats-Urley and his men ran to their truck, very plain now as the rim of the orange sun came up over the east. Private Hoyle lumbered after them, and when they helped him up he sat, the sweat of pain beading his lugubrious face. He had never felt so ill in his life.

They fled – there was no other word for it – travelling at top speed over the desert, indifferent almost to any further possible disaster. They were a good hour still from The Graveyard, and when they got there they still had to hide men and trucks, and that took time. Yet the second vehicle, Fairlop's, gave them no trouble and seemed none the worse for the stoppage back there.

The sun came up with relentless speed. It helped them as they drove, but it was no friend of theirs. The aircraft *would* be taking off and scouting parties *would* be combing the desert behind them. *They had to get to The Graveyard before they were detected or that was the end for them.*

Quarter of an hour after sunrise they saw their first plane. It was north of them, low above the drab horizon, seeming to scurry along. Private Mack was the first to see it. He uttered an oath, then banged hard on the top of the cab. 'Plane!' he shouted, and Captain Yeats-Urley said instantly, 'Halt!' Moving objects caught the eye; a stationary one stood a chance on the desert – there were plenty of stationary vehicles up the Western Desert at that time.

Fairlop caught the deceleration and said, quickly, 'Stop!' So both vehicles halted with not a scrap of cover around them except scrub grass and spiky bushes no more than two feet high. To their agony the dust of their wheels rolled on before them. It was a big grey-yellow cloud, and the slight following wind blew it gently over the desert, hardly dispersing it – in fact extending it so that it was a greater object to enemy vision.

It seemed as if it would never disperse, hanging there, yet that scudding enemy aircraft never saw it, the pilot's attention perhaps caught by some dead vehicle that didn't look so dead farther north of them.

When they resumed, their flight was even more reckless than before. They were unhappily still within sixty miles of El Badim airfield, and dozens of aircraft would be combing the desert for them. It seemed impossible for them to cover all those remaining miles to The Graveyard and not be detected. It didn't take long for a few aircraft to cover a mere few hundreds of square miles. . . .

Every man knew they'd lost the race because of that damned wadi and the fissure in the rock that shouldn't have been there. Every man knew what was to come but it wasn't much good gripping weapons fiercely, because what armoury they had wasn't likely to have much effect against strafing Messerschmitts or Ju87s.

What was to come? Some had been through it before. The swift attack of fighters, if more than one, from different sides. The desert ripped up by swiftly advancing lines of machine-gun bullets or blown up by cannon shells, and maybe the terrifying Ju87s, nose-diving, fixed undercarriages like taloned claws reaching down to grasp them. And a bomb dropping as they pulled out of the dive and went screaming away. A bomb? A whole damned lot of bombs, little ones that could bounce, then explode and anything over three foot high would cop the lot.

They knew it would come, any minute now, and they rode alert, eyes hard on the horizon, ears tuned above the note of their straining Chev to pick up aircraft sound. They scuttled like crazy across that bumpy desert, mile after dusty mile going behind them, staggered at their luck in getting even so far. The sun was now fully up and beginning to be uncomfortably hot. For Private Hoyle with the guts ache and no time to stop, it was particularly agonising.

Once they had to stop. Driver Tony Vecchi couldn't continue to drive. He collapsed, his ribs, undoubtedly broken or cracked, suddenly knocking the strength out of him with their pain. Corporal Eddie Fullalove hopped down and took over, while they hauled the moaning Vecchi into the hard and uncomfortable back.

They drove on. And suddenly they began to hope, but with that hope was bewilderment. When the minutes passed and they were rapidly bearing down upon their haven, The Graveyard, and still no attack from the air, frozen blood began to stir through their veins again. They grew excited and clinging there began to say to each other, 'We might make it,' though they rarely expressed themselves as simply as that. 'Sod me if we ain't goin' to bloody do it,' was more general, the words of that Cockney, Private Leftridge, always known as Stepney after the place of his birth.

And they bloody did it, too, though it was even more agonising, those last miles, because how terrible it would

27

be to get within sight of The Graveyard and then be spotted and shot up. Bewilderingly, they never saw another enemy aircraft. None of them was ever able to understand why the Germans, the most efficient fighting men in the desert, appeared to make such little attempt to find the miscreants who had destroyed tens of millions of pounds worth of precious aircraft in one night.

The truth, that truth they were never to know, was that Captain Yeats-Urley was saved that morning by a party of German cannibals. Cannibalism was rife in the desert during those war days, though it was cannibalism of mechanical parts and not of human flesh – flesh was simply shot at and then buried.

Often more precious than human life were the stranded vehicles and guns that littered the desert between Benghazi and Hellfire Pass. They were there in their thousands, soft transport caught and put out of action by enemy fire; tanks with gaping holes where armour-piercing shells had penetrated, or were stained black with the fire that had finally consumed them; half-tracks and staff cars, guns big and small, stores, provisions and ammunition. There was wealth strewn across that vast desert, and whoever got their hands on it first could have it.

As each army in turn drove the other back, they sent out parties to examine wreckage and see what could be gained from it. Especially, of course, the technicians of each side were anxious to see the latest in enemy equipment, so that all guns and equipment, particularly electronic, in wrecked aircraft, came under the closest, most expert scrutiny. The finds were often well worth uncomfortable days of toil far out where some battle had raged in the hostile desert.

Apart from technical information, parties went out to salvage anything else of value to them. Where possible they would repair vehicles and, regardless of previous ownership, would drive them back for their own use. If they wouldn't move under their own steam they might be laboriously towed back for repair in forward depots. And if none of that was possible vehicles were stripped of tyres and wheels, and any mechanical parts likely to be valuable to an army. Ammunition, serviceable guns, food and loot generally were taken away by the scavenger ants that were soldiers for their own use.

One of the finest prizes ever to fall into German hands was a British field-bakery, south-west of Benghazi after the Battle of Knightsbridge. With it were hundreds of tons of best Canadian white flour. The Germans, hard men who lived on hard tack, lived luxuriously for weeks on fresh-baked mouth-watering British loaves, and thought this was better than winning battles. The German Staff, true, would have preferred to lay hands on the reported American tank-homer, but nevertheless saw to it that they had their share of the staff of life.

A party of Germans had been cannibalising The Grave-yard south-west of El Badim. In fact it was the same grave-yard as the one that Yeats-Urley and party were heading for, but fifty miles south of the place where the S.A.S. intended to take cover during the daylight hours.

The Germans had been working there for several days, and had managed to bring into action two big British gun-towing Matadors, valuable reinforcement for a German army that lost much of its supplies trying to ferry them across to North Africa.

The German working party had stripped other vehicles and piled any loot they fancied into the capacious interiors of the huge Matadors. That done they had turned in for the night, confident they were safe because the nearest enemy would be six hundred miles east of them at a place called El Alamein. At first crack of light they had started the drive back to their unit, two British vehicles with Allied markings, and one German truck bearing the Afrika Korps signs which weren't visible after the scouring effect of a recent bitter sandstorm.

An enemy aircraft, a Heinkel, spotted their dust, dived down upon them, saw the British markings and came to one conclusion. These were the commandos they were seeking.

The pilot radioed the news to Field-Marshal Rommel's headquarters, then in a cellar in Tobruk, and shot up the vehicles before the cannibals knew what was happening.

Swiftly back to the pilot came a message to hold the supposed plane-wreckers and not kill them all. Rommel wanted them alive, for his own satisfaction and for a questioning vital in view of the successes of the S.A.S.

The radio message brought other aircraft to where the Heinkel now circled some blazing vehicles with men beside them frantically waving white cloths. All other aircraft, however, were called off the search because fuel was particularly precious to Rommel at that time. Then a light plane – a Fieseler-Storch – landed, discovered to its consternation that this wasn't the party they were after, and radioed the message back to HQ. The search was resumed, every German more determined than ever to get the damned S.A.S. But the diversion was enough for Captain Yeats-Urley and his men. They had needed one hour to cross that daylit desert, and the cannibals had given them it.

So Yeats-Urley and party came driving the last miles to the great wreck-strewn area at reckless pace, indifferent to the bruising bumpings of their trucks on the rough desert, a tall betraying cloud of dust rising and announcing their presence for miles.

The first corpse in The Graveyard – actually a few miles before they reached the real scene of battle – was a German half-track that looked so complete and undamaged, they eyed it warily in passing, expecting it to move and open up with the gun they could see mounted in its turret. If they'd had more time Yeats-Urley would have examined that one, for it looked as if it could have rewarded a search.

But they hadn't time, and soon they began to move among obviously wrecked vehicles. Hereabouts the great battle of only months ago had left its mark upon the desert. Everywhere were wheeltracks, some of tyremarks, some the tread from tanks, an intricate pattern of trails that curved and crisscrossed in mad confusion and would stand the eroding effects of even the Sahara wind for years, so that from the a ·

at least the old battle could be refought by the evidence of tracks below.

Here, as far as the eye could see, in every direction were silent masses of metal, a tribute to the destructive power of man. Someone had named it The Graveyard, and in some way it had all the atmosphere of one. From a distance the ruined trucks, tanks and guns did look like tombstones; but above all it was the uncanny silence that held above the dead area.

They were in a hurry and barely probed into The Graveyard before stopping. In any event, Yeats-Urley's theory was that the edge of The Graveyard was the safest place in which to hide. 'People usually go deep into cover for safety, and Jerry will know that,' he'd explained several nights earlier, briefing his men about the run down the desert after they'd pooped a few aircraft. So they wouldn't go deep, he told them, and they didn't.

Yeats-Urley's problem was to hide his two vehicles and men in a place where their pursuers would expect them to hide and would search most carefully accordingly. Still, there was nowhere else where they could hide up, the barren desert hereabouts certainly offering no cover for vehicles.

The trucks were soon disguised. Both were run rather artistically up the side of a swelling sandhill. Then the wheels were removed and buried, so that it looked as if cannibals had already stripped them. All equipment was taken out, and a lot of sand thrown into the back as if the vehicles had been there a long time and had weathered several sandstorms. Then bonnets were propped open, as if working parties had been at them. Plugs and distributor heads were removed, effectively immobilising the vehicles even if someone found wheels for them.

Then Big Maurice mounted the front of one vehicle and to appreciative cheers solemnly peed on the hot engine, sending up clouds of steam and ensuring a lot of rust on an engine which normally was scrupulously maintained even in the depths of the desert. Someone peed on the other engine.

When they had finished they left two forlorn trucks seeming half-embedded in sand, gaping-bonneted and lying at drunken angles up the slope. Yet fifteen minutes work could have brought them into action again.

Captain Yeats-Urley and his lieutenant viewed the effect critically when his men had ended their swift but expert task. He was satisfied. It was impossible for anyone to say that these vehicles had recently trundled across the desert. Instead even a close examination would decide that they had been there as long as the real wrecks that littered the horizon.

They had hidden the trucks; now the men had to be hidden, and that was a more difficult task than hiding vehicles. It was no good trying to hide in the wrecked tanks and trucks; Yeats-Urley knew that soon there might be parties of vengeful enemy combing The Graveyard for them, and every wreck would be most carefully examined. They'd soon rout out his party of sixteen scruffy warriors.

If the wrecks held no promise of cover, the desert offered less. Hereabouts it was, superficially at least, dead level, a pancake of baked sandy soil occasionally sprouting withered grass or prickly camel-thorn. There wasn't a bush there that could hide a man, it was all so stunted and spindly. One look and you knew if a man was lurking there you'd spot him a mile off.

So clever Captain Yeats-Urley planned to hide his men just there in the open desert. Long ago he had thought it out, and had decided that it was the obvious that was generally overlooked, and the safest place in which to hide was where an enemy would swear no man could hole up. He had expounded his theories to his men some nights earlier, and they had even put it to the test and had come out of it enthusiastic.

Now, immediately the trucks were disguised as wrecks, the S.A.S. came staggering across the desert with their burden of guns, ammunition and supplies. They ran a brief distance – about two hundred yards from the nearest wrecks – then got out their spades and began to dig at frantic speed, sweat pouring, biting into their eyes with an acid sting, still working against time, with the race lost even now if spotted. As they worked eyes kept lifting anxiously to scan the horizon, ears pricked for the first murmurous sound of a searching aircraft, and all the time marvelling that the Good Lord they blasphemed with almost every sentence was being so kind to them. They dug – they dug four short, narrow slits into the dry grey earth, separated from each other by thirty or forty yards.

The slit trenches were as narrow as possible, for all those reasons dictated to infantry over centuries in the game of keeping alive under enemy attentions. They were deep enough to enable men to crouch down completely out of sight, yet only just long enough to accommodate four men – five in the one Yeats-Urley occupied. Men with their guns and ammunition, of course, and ration of water in bottles that never kept it cool, and biscuits and the inevitable bully.

The earth lifted out was carefully spread around them when they were satisfied it was the same colour as the top soil – nothing to betray their digging there. The edges of the trench were deliberately made ragged, for the eye is caught by straight lines in nature, and the trenching that satisfied sergeants-major in training camps wasn't practical here.

Each slit trench was located with great thought. It had to be dug in front of some of the dried scrub vegetation that somehow clung to life in all this aridness. That was so that a head could peep up to maintain watch on a possible enemy with a background of scrub to hide the cranial contour. The bush might also give some protection against a driving vehicle; for the instinct of good drivers is not to drive through scrub but to steer to one side. Anything – particularly sharp rocks – could lurk in concealment, and a burst tyre could mean capture or death at times in this desert warfare. That being said, drivers did belt through anything at times, so the S.A.S. didn't think much of their tufty protection.

Of course the trenches were so sited that they could give each other protection with crossfire if emergency arose. They didn't want emergency; for if the enemy spotted them they were likely to be in such force that any amount of firing wouldn't save them.

They worked, and within fifteen more minutes the thing was done and they all went to ground. By now the sun was well up and the heat of the desert rolled over them. It was almost unbearable, shrivelling their skin and making them frantic with thirst, but they were inured to it, stoics who could endure the almost unendurable.

Shade was needed, so each trench put up army blankets, rubbed first in desert dirt, and propped up on sticks to keep out the direct rays of sunlight. Until alarm came, the blankets were lifted clear by a foot above the lip of the trenches, so that theoretically at least air could circulate and cool them, though in practice it didn't seem all that much better. When danger warned, down would come the dirty blankets to desert level, their camouflage continuing the desert sand around them. At least from spotting aircraft their blanket covers would hide the shape of the trenches and the bods within.

The hours drifted by. Those men on the run, whose lives could be forfeit if they were detected, mostly slept to catch up on what they had missed during the night – slept noisily, but without nightmares that could have come to most men in their situation. One man in each trench stood up on watch, a solitary head faintly discerned in the shade from the suspended blanket, silent men just staring before them, between them maintaining a vigilant watch in every direction.

Only one man stirred, and he twice, sweating as the griping pain attacked again, blaspheming horribly as he ran – downwind in consideration of his comrades, even in that extremity – to drop his shorts and squat unhappily as again his bowels ran away. Private Joseph Hoyle was suffering as no other man there suffered, not even Tony Vecchi with his cracked ribs.

When Oily came back, a big dejected figure, feet dragging from the exhausting efforts of the last minutes, he was in a mean mood. As he slid awkwardly into the narrow slit trench he mumbled words that were provocative, spoiling for a nasty argument if not a fight. 'What was you talkin' about?'

Stepney Leftridge was the man on watch in his trench. His face turned for a moment from brooding across the shimmering wasteland. 'Talkin'?' He shook his head.

'You was talkin'. I 'eard you.' Gingerly Oily lowered himself into a squatting position, as if he felt the posture might suggest further activity to his aching insides.

Leftridge didn't answer. It was too hot, too mouth-drying for talk. He just shook his head irritably, denying the accusation, then jerked it significantly at the other occupants of the trench. Lance-corporal M'Bain lay huddled against one corner, mouth open in heavy slumber; Gunner Partridge was at the other end, flat out.

Oily said indignantly, working up a momentary nastiness, 'I 'eard you,' but Stepney said nothing but resumed his watch over the desert, and Oily let the subject drop.

After two hours the watch was changed, new tired and dirty faces lifting to brood under blankets that stank of old bed-sweat and were hot to the touch. Two hours, and still no enemy.

Partridge was next man on, relieving Stepney. Stepney woke him and saw him on his feet before getting down to kip himself. But as he lowered himself to the hot earth he said a curious thing. 'Someone's been mucking abaht wiv that Boche half-track.' He didn't complete his thought because no good Cockney ever does; they rely on the intelligence of their audience to do a little work for themselves.

Partridge, himself a Londoner, though Mitcham this time, understood. What Stepney was saying was that the mucking abaht had been recent. So, because his attention was drawn to it, his first glance was towards the German half-track, the nearest wreck to their hideout. For some reason, some trick of the mind, his thoughts went back to the German half-track they had passed driving in. They'd all thought it looked in good nick, no sign of damage. . . .

This one had been shot up, though, the side considerably

.mangled as if a high-explosive shell or grenade had gone off
against it, and by the way the sand had piled before the
bonnet it had been there some time. But Partridge, eyes
narrowed against the fierce intensity of sun reflecting from
the grey desert, saw what Stepney had meant. The track was
off the vehicle and lay stretched like a mat alongside it.
Someone had removed it and not too long ago, Partridge's
mind corroborated Stepney's analysis of the situation. Not
too long ago because the grease on the tracks was black, and
there were shiny parts, and if it had lain there long the sand
would have swept over it and there'd have been nothing
black or shiny.

Gunner Partridge felt a sudden moment of unease. Only a
German working party was likely to require a track from a
half-track. Why hadn't they taken it away with them?
Because something had happened to disturb them, or
because when it was removed they found it damaged and no
good after all? There were several explanations. What made
Partridge uneasy was the thought that the German working
party might return any time to pick up the track. He
decided at the first opportunity to report the matter to old
Eats-Early.

The first plane came over their position very soon after the
watch was changed. This was around nine o'clock. Private
Hoyle had made his second trip by then, which was fortunate for the occupants of his trench.

The gripes got him, attacking with ferocious suddenness,
so that he moaned and cursed and dragged himself up from
under the blanket, again ran a decent distance, then squatted
and heaved within sight of his unconcerned comrades.
Afterwards, when he had carefully kicked dirt over the
betraying evidence of man's presence, he came back crawling
like an old man.

And again he asked, 'You bin talkin'?'

Again the man on watch looked uncomprehendingly at
him. Oily looked down at M'Bain and Stepney, and both
seemed asleep. He was in a raw mood, some element of

mystery, something inexplicable driving him on to a habitual nastiness.

He said, his voice uncouth and husky, 'You was talkin'. I 'eard you. Whatjer talk about when I go aht with the squirts?'

Partridge, resolute man, said, 'What're you talkin' about, mate? No one was talkin'. An' if we talk we'll 'ave the old man arter us.'

Big unpleasant Oily wouldn't let the matter drop. The thick voice persisted belligerently, 'You was talkin'. Think I'm bloody daft? I 'eard you. Talkin'.' His voice rose in anger which could erupt too often in flailing fists or boots. A big man, and one to be wary of.

The truth was, driving Oily on was the frightened feeling within him. He had never had the squirts like this. Everything was coming out of him. In panic he was asking himself, 'Will it ever stop?' He had heard of men who contracted some Oriental diseases which simply ran all the water out of them and they died within hours. Had he got that disease? Because he was frightened, Oily wanted to take it out on someone. Oily was a fine soldier but even the few friends he had would have grown thoughtful if they had been asked to ascribe to him any great intelligence. He believed in settling problems with violence.

Now, that driving fear and the rawness of his gut drove him on. He wanted to lash out and hurt, and Partridge, a hard man himself, recognised the symptoms.

The ex-gunner eyed him warily now, two bulky men half-crouched in a narrow trench under a smelly blanket. He said. 'Bloody hell, Oily, who'd be talkin' in this bleedin' heat? Talkin' about what? You? Aw, get your 'ead down, mate, an' stop imaginin' things, see?'

'You tellin' me I'm goin' *maknoon*?' That was the army's interpretation of a native word that meant 'mad'. Oily was working himself into fighting nastiness. He reared erect, head lifting the stinking blanket. 'I'll bloody do you, you bastard, tellin' me I'm *maknoon*!'

Partridge knew the signs. Oily in an awkward mood. Oily could lash out. That was bad for the unit. Partridge was a good soldier. He kicked his sleeping corporal into wakefulness. M'Bain came out of sleep in an instant, rearing erect, hand grasping for his tommygun.

He rasped, 'They're coming?' and by coincidence at that moment far away they heard the first sound of that approaching aircraft.

Partridge said, 'No,' in disgust. 'It's Oily, Corp. The shits is makin' 'im nasty. He's bin 'earing things.'

M'Bain read the scene at a glance, Partridge holding back defensively, big Oily's lowering, threatening features. He snapped, 'What's biting you, Oily?'

The private relaxed at that. He said, 'I 'eard you talkin'. That's twice I 'eard you. Each time I've been out for a shit. Twice. But Stepney an' Party tell me I don't know what I'm talkin' about. I 'eard 'em, I tell you. Talkin'.' Voice thick with menace again.

M'Bain, listening to the gradual loudening of that aircraft, was irritable, 'Well, it wasn't me talking, I can tell you.'

Partridge was lowering the blanket, wakening Stepney in the process. 'No one was talkin', Corp. No one. You was asleep, you an' ol' Step here. An' I 'aven't got so old I talk to myself.'

'But I 'eard . . . talkin',' and Oily's persistence got through into the lance-corporal's mind, and a tiny warning bell began to sound there and wouldn't stop.

M'Bain said, 'Maybe there was talk from another trench.'

They looked out. Their slit trench was on the extremity of the position, the other three in staggered line stretching away across the dusty desert. The nearest was a good fifty yards away. M'Bain looked at the dried grass bending a little before the slight wind. It was blowing from the direction where the other trenches were.

M'Bain looked thoughtfully towards The Graveyard. 'Where did you go, Oily?'

Oily was dull. 'Go?'

'For your tom-tit.'

The big Birmingham man gestured. Downwind. Even

38

crude men like Oily can be thoughtful. Partridge was paralleling his corporal's thoughts.

'It wasn't another trench, Corp. I'd 'ave 'eard it, too, wouldn't I? I mean, I'd be nearer.'

Then the plane came too close and too noisy and they crouched down, holding the blanket just level with the top of their trench. It was abominably hot underneath, and the sweat they could ill afford to lose poured out of them. The stink of unclean blanket and close-packed, sweating humanity made even those healthy young soldiers sniff in disgust, but they held on until the plane receded before stirring and cautiously lifting the blanket again.

That plane, a Junkers 88 pressed into emergency service from El Adem airfield did them no good, unlike an earlier plane which had shot up the German working party in mistake for their own. The pilot, a Bavarian blond with the sharpest of blue eyes, soon after flying into the area saw some wheel tracks on the desert below which headed in a straight line west.

Now, there were thousands of wheel tracks all over the desert, though not many in this precise area, but for some reason the pilot, perhaps imbued with a touch of Hitler's intuition, decided these were the tracks of the fleeing S.A.S. Unfortunately he was right. They were.

He kept losing them, but picked up the trail a few times, and all the time they led undeviatingly west. Then he lost them completely but by now the damage was done. He kept flying due west and he was no more than a mile off the trail when he hit The Graveyard.

He failed, though, to spot the cunningly disguised slit trenches – the S.A.S. would have been below par if he had – and he went on to comb an area which took him farther and farther away from where the British hid.

The great damage he did, though, was in radioing back a report to Rommel's HQ that he thought he had picked up the maurauders' trail. He gave his position as he passed into The Graveyard, and that was almost exactly the position of the hiding S.A.S.

North and east of the position were several German search parties, trucks of infantry, squat scout cars and a few half-track armoured cars with each. Tobruk promptly radioed orders to the searchers to concentrate on the map position radioed by the Bavarian pilot. Within seconds vehicles were turning all over that part of the desert and beginning to concentrate on the area. Hiding below ground, none of the S.A.S. realised that from several directions German columns were closing in on their position now.

Lance-corporal M'Bain remained standing under the now raised blanket after the plane had disappeared over the shimmering horizon. He was a curious man, M'Bain, a man who shouldn't have been there. He was cracking under the strain, and perhaps the awful fear within him made him hypersensitive and intuitive in the manner of that unknown Bavarian who had just flown above them.

He stood there, just a head showing dimly in the shadow from the blanket and his nervous eyes never left the wrecked German half-track, two hundred yards away. All the time jumbled chaotic thoughts went through his mind, calculations as to how far sound travelled in the desert, noting the strength and direction of the wind, and all the time fear grew until his snapping nerves brought him to the edge of panic. That would have startled his comrades, to know that Corporal M'Bain – Old Smiler, as he had once been known in one regiment – knew fear. No one would have suspected it. No one ever does – we keep fear out of sight, like some shameful demented relative.

Stewart M'Bain – solidly English for generations in spite of the name – had been born in Derbyshire, and had lived his early life in a succession of crude cold stone houses adjacent to limestone quarries where his depressed and worrying

40

father sometimes found work. It was a bitter life, no comfort, always the anxiety of would work finish, because they ate badly in the long spells on the dole. Four children, a mother half out of her mind with strain and worry, and a father ulcerated and on a diet yet having to follow a hard and dangerous job in the quarries.

M'Bain had left school at fourteen. His teacher said he had intelligence and ability to go on even to university, but didn't speak much on the subject because he knew there was no chance. Young M'Bain was human material to be mangled and abused from the moment of birth, and for him university was as real as a trip to Heaven.

There was little work for boys in the Derbyshire Dales, and when he was sixteen M'Bain in despair one day walked out of Derbyshire to see if the world wasn't easier outside.

It wasn't. Until he was twenty-two he had one job after another, all menial, none much rewarding. He dug, he carried, he lifted, he cleaned, and never once did he get a job demanding the use of that intelligence his teacher detected in him. Often he had no work, and like other young men he tramped the streets looking for it, the despair killing him inside, hope completely gone. At such times he slept hard, in any corner or on any seat until some unfeeling policeman had him on his way because he looked rough. There were days when he didn't eat, and in all his life Stewart M'Bain hardly ever remembered a time when there was enough on his plate to satisfy him.

When war broke out M'Bain was one of the million unemployed – a million out of work even though there was an armaments boom and the prospect of war round the corner. He was sick of casual labour, defeated by the hard life he had to lead. He realised that the army was calling for men and all in one second he made up his mind and joined up.

He was a volunteer, and to his later surprise he found this was considered highly noble and patriotic. He hadn't been conscripted; he had joined the army to fight the King's enemies voluntarily. He was bemused by this talk of patriotism, for he had joined for one reason only – he was sick of the struggle to live in Civvy Street, and the army promised regular food, warmer clothes than he had ever worn in his life, and regular spending money. Above all, the King's army offered him security, and it was almost with a sigh of gratefulness that he signed away his life for the duration of the war.

M'Bain knew so little about military matters that he didn't understand the difference between artillery and infantry, and such things as REME, the REs or Signals were subtleties beyond his ken. There was the navy, the R.A.F. and the army, that's all he knew about it. It didn't occur to him even to consider the R.A.F., and the navy he dismissed instantly because he felt sure a heaving sea wouldn't agree with him.

He walked into a recruiting office in Cardiff, where his search for work had taken him, and they promptly slapped him in the infantry.

To quite an extent M'Bain took to the army. He had lived so hard and so uncomfortably all his life that infantry training he took in his stride and was a little perplexed at the moanings of city comrades.

In November 1941 his regiment was shipped round the Cape of Good Hope into the desert. They went into camp at Tahag, along the Sweet Water Canal, at a time when fierce tank battles were raging in the desert around Benghazi, and the Allied army was being hammered and destroyed and driven back. And here, at Tahag, the pattern of his life reasserted itself. He was restless, always restless – never in his life would he be anything but restless. Insecurity said he could not stay anywhere long; for what he vaguely sought was never there and must be somewhere else.

He had been given a one-stripe, and his company commander had mentioned in the mess that M'Bain had intelligence enough to go to OCTU (Officer Cadet Training Unit), but his name was never put forward because when they looked at him closely he just hadn't the manner to hold the King's commission. M'Bain never knew about this casual discussion of his possibilities. He would have been afraid to go forward for training as an officer, anyway. He had no confidence in himself or the world around him.

While the Allies were being sent reeling back along the North African coast, in Egypt they were recruiting men for the Middle East Commandos. M'Bain saw the announcement on regimental orders, and impulsively volunteered. To his surprise, he was accepted and left the regiment. Leaving proved surprisingly traumatic. When he packed his kit bag and went out to pick up the truck that would carry him and other volunteers away, he realised that he was scared of leaving his regiment. It had been real home to him, and had given him more security than he had ever known in his years before. The mob – those rough, swearing comrades – he now found were as close to him as a family – closer than his own had ever been, in fact.

About the only thing that pleased him, leaving the regiment, was that with it he dropped his soubriquet of 'Smiler'. He had never liked it. M'Bain smiled constantly because he had found that a smile kept him out of trouble, but he didn't like the name, and he wasn't always happy behind his brave smile.

The Middle East Commandos were a tough mob and the training stretched even him. Up till now he had never seen real action, and even in the commandos it evaded him because the desert army was crumpling before Rommel's *blitzkrieg*, the Allies were demoralised and on the run, and with their army retreating sometimes thirty or forty miles in a day there was no time to mount commando operations.

M'Bain wanted to see action. He didn't know what it would be like, but the restlessness that was constant within him made him want to get a closer look at war

That hot summer the Allied army finally stopped running and with incredible obstinacy gathered itself together and made a do-or-die stand by the Qattara Depression at El Alamein. From that moment commando operations could be planned and mounted.

43

Yet just when it seemed that the commandos would see action – it was a bold plan to land parties in the night outside Tobruk and wreck installations before being pulled out – M'Bain volunteered out of the unit. Perhaps his aversion to the sea prompted the decision; more likely it was just that he couldn't keep still when he had chance to make another move.

This time it was the Special Air Service, appealing for men. M'Bain *had* heard about this cloak-and-dagger outfit, how an army officer named Lieutenant Stirling had gone to HQ in Cairo and said, 'We're doing things all the wrong way. We wait until enemy aircraft take off and are in the sky and then try to destroy them, when the odds are about even that they will destroy us. No, the thing is to destroy aircraft when they can't move and haven't the use of their guns.'

He talked, a giant of a man, an aristocratic Scotsman, and they listened to his arguments. The thing to do, he said, was catch the aircraft on the ground, and there destroy them. Give him some men and bombs and he would parachute behind the enemy lines and blow up enemy aircraft on their airfields.

He got his way – aristocrats have a habit of doing that – but his first attempt with parachutes was a fiasco. So he changed his tactics, took to trucks, got himself led far behind the enemy lines by the redoubtable Long Range Desert Group, and his Special Air Service began to do terrible damage to the enemy. Stirling soon had a price on his head because of his depredations – the enemy never knew when truck loads of his men would come storming out of the desert, hundreds of miles from the theatre of war, and set airfields ablaze, shoot up soft convoys or storm isolated military posts.

Not always did they get away, however, to be picked up and brought back through the desert by the patient L.R.D.G. Some died as a result of their audacity. Others fell into enemy hands and were not always treated kindly, because the enemy felt that such tactics weren't legitimate warfare.

Soon it became apparent that the S.A.S. were destroying

far more enemy aircraft on the ground than the entire Allied air fleets were doing above the desert. Now the S.A.S. sent out a call for more bold spirits to extend their predatory activities.

Vaguely, then, M'Bain heard about the S.A.S., yet sufficiently for him to feel the glamour of the unit. So when the call came, he responded, and a trained Middle East Commando, even without actual battle experience, was exactly the kind of man that Major Stirling wanted.

Soon M'Bain was out with a unit doing up the enemy. He was on two such expeditions – both highly successful – before the El Badim foray. And from the beginning M'Bain realised that he was too much in terror to make a real S.A.S. warrior.

He built up too much tension, his imagination – that intelligence long ago perceived by a schoolmaster dead these past three months; *he* had joined the navy, and had gone down in a frigate in a skirmish off Cherbourg, his first voyage into enemy waters – M'Bain's imagination ran riot in times of action, in a way no good soldier's should. Or shouldn't it? Men in fear perform startling feats of heroism, and M'Bain, who thought himself alone with his fears, would have been surprised how many of his comrades were also in terror in the moment of action . . . yet came back for more.

He was in dread from the moment they went off on a deadly foray, yet he never showed it. In fact M'Bain overdid it. That almost incessant smile switched on and covered his terrors, and it deceived his comrades, including his officers.

'Good man, M'Bain,' Captain Yeats-Urley said approvingly in the officers' mess after the second raid. 'Comes through smiling, you know. Does everything right, too.'

M'Bain did everything right, opening fire when he had to, proving more efficient with a gun than his enemies, and tossing grenades into grounded aircraft with seeming laughing nonchalance. Even his tough comrades were respectful of him.

After the first raid, M'Bain wanted to get out of the mob, never again wishing to experience that fear when under heavy enemy fire. After the second raid he knew he couldn't go on . . . yet he did, for this third foray. For out of action, back in the barracks at Alex, he could not creep to his C.O. and tell him he hadn't the nerve to go on. And how could he face the contempt of his fellow rankers? Like many another man, M'Bain hadn't the courage to say he thought he was a coward.

But this third probe into the desert was too much for him. He was cracking and knew it, though no one else in the mob would have suspected it of M'Bain. This time the awful tension wouldn't go away. The strain was too great and he knew there would come a moment when he would snap and disintegrate as a human being and behave shamefully under enemy fire, perhaps at a time when his comrades needed him most.

M'Bain, wakened from a disturbed and nightmarish slumber, did not want to go to sleep again, for all the dreadful heavy tiredness that comes with too much heat. He stared out at the German half-track, his mind leaping from Private Hoyle and the talking he said he had heard to his own problems. When he got back to Alex, he thought, his mind fevered with too much anxiety, he would take off. He'd desert and go on the run, he told himself; he could not face the shame of asking to be posted out of the S.A.S. How long he would last as a deserter, and what awful fate would be his when they inevitably picked him up, he didn't know and at this moment wouldn't allow himself to think about it. He couldn't stand another desert operation, he thought.

It was while he was watching the wrecked half-track – a *Leichter Schutzenpanzerwagen*, if only he had known, but didn't – that they became aware of the approaching columns of land forces.

Other men had stirred into wakefulness by now, unable to sleep for long in the confines of those slit trenches. Captain Yeats-Urley gave permission for those that wanted to, to climb out and have a brew up.

He did not give any elaborate cautions to them, for he knew they were too well trained to need them. They would not move around much, for that could leave betraying foot-marks. They did not build a fire that would give off smoke, but used petrol in a can of sand. They kept close to their trenches, ready to douse the fire cans at the first sign of danger and drop down into their hidey-holes. And three men faced out and kept watch all the time.

Yeats-Urley and Lieutenant Fairlop came above ground, too, and found the heat so scorching they wondered if it wasn't better sweating it out in the shade of those stinking blankets. And Fairlop was the first to spot danger, not the sentries. Tea had been made and cans were being carefully carried to the various trenches, when Fairlop suddenly stiffened, came up with his glasses and then swore.

Yeats-Urley's binoculars immediately paralleled the lieutenant's. On the horizon was a dust cloud. Swinging his glasses, Yeats-Urley spotted a second cloud. Then a third. Almost immediately Private Mack called hoarsely, 'Dust cloud on the horizon, sir.' They knew what a dust cloud meant.

Three columns of vehicles, two to the north and east, and the third one due east of them.

No one made any hasty move. They stood there drinking their over-sweetened, desert-strong brew, seemingly casual about the moment, but all alert and watching those dust clouds and calculating. Less than five minutes later they knew the worst. The dust clouds were growing in volume and that meant the columns of vehicles were approaching. Five minutes later suspicion became certainty. Those three columns were converging on them.

When they knew that, all turned to look at their young captain. A startled Yeats-Urley was trying not to show his shock. Those converging columns would come right over their position.

His mind was racing, saying, 'That plane must have spotted us,' yet even then he didn't think so. Spotted or not, they were heading their way, and what the devil were they to do about it?

Yeats-Urley calculated the time of arrival. It would be

no more than an hour, he knew, for though a column wouldn't advance at road-speed, the ground wasn't bad and they would cover seven or eight miles within that time. The captain made his decisions and crisply gave orders.

'Clear up and get out of sight,' he was saying, when Corporal M'Bain came up to speak to him. All traces of their presence must be obliterated, and the men set to with bits of sticks to erase footmarks, retreating on their trenches as they did so. All they could do was get into hiding and hope they wouldn't be discovered. Yeats-Urley thought they had a good chance. Their position out on the open desert was a good one, and he still thought the enemy wouldn't think to look there for them. Anyway, what else could they do but lie up, and if they were discovered open fire and try to beat off the enemy? It was no good running – by the time they'd got the trucks in action they would have been spotted and under heavy enemy fire. No, their course was dictated to them. . . .

'Sir.' Captain Yeats-Urley dragged his eyes away from the advancing columns. The men had cleared up around the trenches, the fire-cans and tea dixies had been dropped into them, and the men were going to ground. He saw the lance-corporal, that smile as always upon his face, as if he found life amusing. Good man, M'Bain.

'Yes, corporal?'

'Sir, we're being watched. There's someone hiding in the German half-track.'

Yeats-Urley wanted to spin round and look at the wrecked vehicle on the edge of The Graveyard, but instantly he had control of himself. His voice was not even quickened as he asked, 'What makes you think that, corporal?'

M'Bain was very casual, too, idly kicking up the sand with his heavy boot, so that anyone watching would have thought officer and man were indulging in small talk and wouldn't take alarm. 'Twice Private Hoyle said he heard talking. We thought it was from our chaps at first.'

But something had concentrated M'Bain's attention on the *Leichter Schutzenpanzerwagen* and for one fraction of a second he had seen movement in a crack where the explosion had buckled the armour plate of the turret. That was when the dust-clouds had been spotted and many of the men had stood grouped round their officers, staring.

'I think whoever's in there wanted to know what was interesting us,' M'Bain said. 'So he got into the turret to have a peep out.'

'You're sure?'

'Pretty sure, sir. Something moved.'

'A rat?'

M'Bain hesitated, floored by the question. Doubt assailed him. It could have been the movement of a rat. For that matter, he suddenly thought, it could be a bit of ragged upholstery or cloth fluttering in the breeze. Yet there had been a breeze before, and nothing had fluttered. His mind began a logical process of elimination.

'Could have been a rat, I suppose, sir.' There were rats wherever there had been fighting and dead. 'Yes, it could have been,' and he felt foolish and wished he had thought of that explanation before. His fancy could lead to a bollocking. . . .

Captain Yeats-Urley, young man but divining what went on in the lance-corporal's mind, smiled and said, very firmly, 'Corporal, we are going to assume, because we dare not do otherwise, that there are men in that half-track. And if there are men, they are not our friends or they'd have been out drinking tea with us.'

'Yes, sir,' said M'Bain, and because he felt relieved at not being told he was a fool that warm feeling for his superior officer came over him, almost of love.

'Besides,' the captain said softly, clinching it, 'rats don't make human conversation, do they?'

M'Bain could have said, 'Oily might have imagined it,' but didn't. Oily hadn't the imagination of a louse.

Captain Yeats-Urley gave his first order to meet the situation. 'You're in the far trench?' Nearest the half-track. 'As you pass the second trench, without it being obvious to anyone watching, get word to them there may be trouble from the half-track and to be ready if anything starts. But they mustn't show any interest in it, understand?' That sharpening of the voice on the final word, the threat that if they betrayed their knowledge someone would cop it good and hard afterwards.

M'Bain nodded and walked away. He was stiff with anxiety now, feeling nakedly exposed, the only man now walking on top of the ground. If there were men – Germans – in that half-track they could have guns trained upon him. Fright almost sent him off keel, yet as always before he did the right thing.

When he came to the trench next to his own he unbuttoned and peed into the dust, to the slight indignation of Corporal Fullalove, standing watch. Fullalove said, 'You might have done it in front of your own bivvy, you dirty bugger –' But M'Bain shut him up.

He had his back to the half-track. 'Captain's orders.' Fullalove hadn't time to think if a captain would order a man to urinate close to a trench, for M'Bain said, 'Look, Eddie, we think there may be someone in that German half-track – no, don't look at it. Look straight at me. Eats-Early says do nothing to give the show away, but be ready if the balloon goes up.'

'Okay, Stew.' Fullalove bent out of sight and M'Bain, trudging on to his own trench, heard him muttering an explanation and orders to his companions, doubtless as startled as he had been when he saw that tiny movement through a ragged crack in the plating. He dropped into his own trench and alerted his men.

Captain Yeats-Urley had remained standing, binoculars to his eyes, carefully examining those three approaching columns while trying to work out a plan of action. By now he could see what type of fighting vehicles were approaching. There were scout cars, a few half-tracks of sorts – probably

50

Mittlerer Schutzenpanzerwagens, he thought, for it was the captain's duty to know what fighting vehicles the enemy had; bigger half-tracks than the wrecked one behind, carrying up to a dozen men and possibly a 2 cm. gun in its turret – but mostly there were truck-loads of infantry in those columns.

'What on earth do we do now?' Yeats-Urley asked himself over and over again. If there were enemies lurking inside that half-track (God, how intolerably hot they must be, cooped inside that sardine can, he could even think at that moment), then they had to be routed out before the columns arrived; for if they weren't they'd soon tell the advancing enemy where the S.A.S. were in hiding.

The difficulty was in deciding how to winkle them out. It had to be done quickly, before the approaching enemy came within sound of the grenades and guns that the S.A.S. undoubtedly would have to use. But – here was the problem – could they do it quickly? The enemy were in better cover than they in their trenches, sitting behind inch-thick armour-plate angled to deflect bullets. If they had any strength at all they could hold off attack for quite a time, until the enemy columns came up to their aid. But perhaps they had no guns, Yeats-Urley thought, and that was why they had kept quiet and lain hidden.

With military logic Yeats-Urley's mind made an appreciation of the situation. First, the enemy (he no longer bothered to think there might not be an enemy within the half-track; he had to assume there was) must be in inferior strength to their own. If they weren't they could have shot them down while they were occupied in hiding themselves and their trucks. But this didn't mean to say the enemy was totally helpless. Probably they would have some weapons with them, perhaps rifles or light automatics. Enough to make an attack on the armoured vehicle a deadly exercise for his small force, but insufficient to take on a larger, similarly armed force of tough desert commandos.

. . . how did they come to be there? Part of his mind grappled with this problem, for solving it could assist them to solve the problem of disposing of this enemy. They hadn't come in that wrecked half-track, that was certain. Must have walked in, Yeats-Urley correctly decided, as so many stranded soldiers walked into The Graveyard looking for food and water. Unlike Gunner Partridge, Captain Yeats-Urley's mind never travelled to that other half-track they had seen coming in, the one standing seemingly undamaged a few miles over the horizon.

Men who walked didn't carry much weight. If they had guns they wouldn't be heavy ones, and ammunition being heavy they would have only a few rounds per weapon. They wouldn't have much food or water – if any – with them, either, so if it wasn't for those wretched approaching vehicles any enemy inside that torn hull could be ignored; they'd come out in time with their hands up, without fighting.

But there *were* approaching vehicles, many of them, and all enemy. What's more, Yeats-Urley was pretty sure that fact was known to whoever lurked within the half-track. They need only lurk a little while longer, then attract attention – had they a Very pistol? – and then it was *kaput* for the British force, death, hospital or in the bag. Three singularly uninviting prospects, and young Yeats-Urley wasn't going to have any of them.

He made up his mind, suddenly. Lieutenant Fairlop was sitting on the edge of his slit trench, the one farthest away from The Graveyard. The captain risked calling to him – he wasn't going to walk over, with time so precious, leaving footmarks unobliterated. That wouldn't be good desert tactics.

'Freddie!'

Fairlop looked round, hard, solidly-boned man, that look of questioning on his face that didn't soften into pleasantness, not with men.

'Freddie, there's trouble.' Yeats-Urley spoke quite quietly, throwing his voice like an actor. Inside the half-track they would hear him talking, but he was pretty sure that from that distance – well over two hundred yards – they would not be able to distinguish his words.

'Don't get up.' Fairlop had started to rise at the words. 'We think there may be someone inside a German half-track beyond our first position. I'm going to try to winkle them out before our friends arrive. Be ready for action. We've got to get this over quickly or we're in the soup. Right?'

Fairlop nodded and dropped down into his trench to tell his men. Captain Yeats-Urley lowered himself into his own. Swiftly he explained the situation. 'I can see only one thing for it,' he ended. 'Guns aren't any good. It's got to be a Mills, dropped right inside that turret.'

Big Maurice said, 'Someone's got to get close to do that.' He was so big and so packed with muscle, yet he had a quick and intelligent mind, a man respected by his officers as well as by fellow-rankers.

The captain nodded. 'That's the problem.'

Private Hill heaved himself half erect in the narrow confines of the trench. 'It's not all that bad. I could get close to them.'

Yeats-Urley asked, 'How?' though he had his own ideas and was proposing to perform the act himself.

The big, flattened face thought for a moment. 'If I went off carrying a jerrican it might look as if I'm seeking water.' At this time, with the enemy columns coming up fast? 'I could have a Mills in my hand. They wouldn't see it.' He spread his big pad of a hand and they agree no one would see a bomb in it.

Get close under some pretext, then – wham, a bomb tossed within the hull. Then all of them out of the slit trenches and storming the half-track, knives and tommyguns silencing everyone inside. The Captain said, 'I don't see what else we can do. And we've about ten minutes left.' After that glasses would be able to penetrate the heat distortion over the desert and figures running about would be discernible.

Hill said, 'I'm off.' He was laconic about it, though they knew he might be dropped if they took alarm inside the hull. He picked up a Mills, then a rusty Jerrican, and heaved his big bulk in a rolling motion out under the blanket. They saw him stand erect, very casual in his action, even pausing to knock off some small stones that had embedded in the flesh around the knee. Then he began to walk towards The Graveyard.

In the trenches they didn't make the mistake of crowding to the edge and looking out. An enemy would have been alerted if they had seen rows of heads where only one per trench had been before. The officer or NCO watching softly relayed the scene to the men crouching below, their hands already grasping weapons which they felt sure they were going to use.

M'Bain saw Big Maurice walk steadily on a course that would bring him within throwing distance of the half-track. Without being told he knew what Man Mountain was up to. He waited, the anxiety tearing at him, the strain unbearable. God, let him get out of this and they'd never have him on a desert jaunt again. An enemy in that hull, and three columns of enemy bearing down on them. He sweated fear, yet without knowing it, still that crooked little smile twisted his lips.

Big Maurice kidded no one.

When he was fifty yards or so from the half-track, there was movement, a head appeared. It wore a familiar long-peaked cap, the cap of the Afrika Korps. A gun barrel showed.

'*Halt!*'

Big Maurice froze. He let the jerrican drop from his hand. Then he started to fall to his face, but at the first movement a spray of bullets came whipping around him, the sound of the gun seeming tremendous after the long silence of the past hours.

'Stand up. Do not move!' A harsh, heavy accent.

Big Maurice remained standing, hands above his head now. He was not going to move. At that range they could have sawn him in half.

'You will stay where you are, you and your comrades, until they come to help me.' It was not exact English, but it was pretty good. The S.A.S. knew who 'they' were and what sort of help they'd give the crouching German in the half-track.

Yeats-Urley wasn't going to stay in his slit trench. There, under those circumstances, they were helpless. He had to get out – a lot of them had to get out – somehow someone of them might be able to pick off the German with the machine-gun. But not from here. There was nothing to shoot at from this range. It was no good starting a long shooting match, either. He began to haul himself over the edge of the trench,

The captain waved, as if to demonstrate good intentions, then a spray of machine-gun bullets kicked up sand around him, followed by a wave of harsh, clattering sound, and Captain Yeats-Urley fell back into his trench, dignity departing with the urgency of holding on to life. 'He aimed to kill, that time,' he thought, and the thought was jarring even to his temperament. But why hadn't he killed Hill?

Captain Yeats-Urley again put his head above ground with great caution. No bullets came his way. He looked at the stained and crumpled half-track. No head showed now, but the barrel of a machine-gun still protruded. It pointed with cold directness at Big Maurice, a lone figure standing on that hot sand, hands above his head . . . clenched hands, one holding the grenade. Yeats-Urley thought, 'Surely they can spot it,' even in his big fist, but the German didn't.

Silence. No one moved, no one spoke. All were waiting. Yeats-Urley thought, 'They're waiting for relief to come up,' and they wouldn't have long to wait. And they – the S.A.S. – were waiting because no one knew what else to do.

Captain Yeats-Urley turned to look at his men. Sweating, dirty faces looked at him, strained and anxious. The fear of death was upon them at that moment.

'Trapped like bloody bunny rabbits,' his lance-sergeant, Vickers, growled. He was a fighting man, ex-Indian army, always wanting to get at 'em. There was some sort of light of panic in his eyes with the feeling of being trapped below ground. He jerked, 'We can't wait, sir.'

The minutes were passing by. Every minute brought those columns grinding closer. If they were to escape with their skins anything done had to be done quickly. All knew that, and all wanted to be up and storming the half-track. And then what?

Yeats-Urley held them back. 'Hold on, now.' His voice was sharp and held command. He had suddenly realised why Private Hill was standing there and being allowed to live. He was hostage to their good behaviour. Any move on their part, and big Maurice Hill would die instantly. He probably knew it, too, but showed no fear, just standing out there in the sunshine.

'Hang on a minute,' Yeats-Urley ordered, and by that they knew they would go over the top and storm the half-track any time now. 'Let me just co-ordinate a little activity.'

Over the top, the captain was thinking. A machine-gun tearing into them from the security of armour plate – no visible target to shoot at. Quite a few of them would have to die or be terribly wounded before one of them got close enough to toss in the hand grenade that would silence the enemy. Yeats-Urley was less bothered about those who would die than those who would be badly hurt and continue to live. What do you do with badly wounded comrades, men who might cry out with pain or groan and moan in agony, and an enemy all around?

What do you do when you *have* destroyed an enemy holed up in a wrecked half-track? No time to get the wheels on the trucks and scud off to safety. No use heading off across The Graveyard on foot – they'd be picked up or picked off in no time. To remain hiding in the trenches was their one chance of evading detection, and not a great one with those columns seemingly intent on rendezvousing right where they lay hidden. But hiding with wounded or dying comrades?

Yet what else was there? Still the alternative was to do nothing, and then the triumphant Germans in the half-track would direct squads of infantry to blow or burn them out of their holes. Or, ignominiously, they could clamber out with their hands up.

Yeats-Urley had little sense of humour, but he found himself shrugging ruefully and thinking, 'The alternatives aren't pleasant ones.'

He called to his lieutenant, farthest away from the half-track. 'We're going in. Put up covering fire when we move —'

The machine-gun opened up on him, and he went down out of sight again, and dirt came dropping on top of him as the bullets chewed at the edge of the trench. The message was unmistakable. No talking.

Yeats-Urley slowly, cautiously, peered above ground again. No shots were fired. Perhaps they were down to a few rounds of ammo and wouldn't waste them unnecessarily. Another few minutes and the approaching convoys would hear sounds such as machine-gun fire, so there wasn't time to waste.

Captain Yeats-Urley wasted little time. In his bones he knew he was going to his death. By now they must have spotted that he was in command and the machine-gun would turn on him immediately after cutting down their hostage . . . Hill had to go. But someone had to die in warfare. and if this was what circumstances dictated he should do, Yeats-Urley would do it.

'When we get out, disperse but keep going for the half-track. Mr Fairlop will put up covering fire.' Much good that would do them, he knew.

Those were his orders. There wasn't much else he could order.

'Good hunting, you chaps.'

He began to pull himself up. They'd be watching from the other trenches, and the moment he showed they'd all come hauling themselves out and race towards the half-track, firing as they went. A wild, mad, deadly scramble, with the bullets hitting and killing them, and all with the hope that one man could get within lobbing distance . . . and not miss. Yeats-Urley, for all his training, found his heart racing madly, fear full upon him, but he never thought to turn back.

He put the weight on his hands and even began to lift himself upwards, and his men were coming erect, when shock halted him and held him against the wall of the narrow trench as if turned into a statue. He gasped. His men looked out, and were too shaken to say anything.

They saw a man walking towards the half-track, a man seeming to come out of the desert from nowhere, coming up from behind the armoured vehicle.

Lance-corporal M'Bain knew how to get at that half-track and destroy it, but he wasn't going to do anything about it. There was the fear that it might go wrong, that his calculations weren't as exact as his training said they were, and he'd seen those bullets tear into sand and he couldn't face the thought that they might tear into him, too.

So he watched the tableau, Big Maurice halted out there before the half-track, the wind stirring the sandy earth and nothing else moving. The precious seconds ticking by, and death closing on them, his thoughts raced to tell him.

And *he* knew how to get at the German machine-gunner if no one else did. There was cover almost from behind their trench to a point well behind the half-track. At first sight, to the uninitiated, that statement that there was cover on a desert as flat apparently as a billiards table would have seemed nonsense. But to a trained infantryman it was true.

M'Bain had taken in the significances of long shadows the moment they had gone to ground when the digging had ended. While the sun was still low to the east he had done what good infantrymen instinctively do when they're dug in: he had assessed the surrounding terrain for defensive possibilities.

An infantryman looks for cover. True, in such circumstances it is cover that might afford an attacking enemy protection, but in the process taking note of what might be turned to advantage in time of need. Now was a time of need.

He had spotted, and memorised, a long curving shadow that started close behind his trench and seemed to fade away a hundred yards or so behind the half-track. He was pretty

58

sure there was three or four feet of depression below the shallow rising earth bank, and might even be much more in places. It would be no great difficulty, sliding into that depression, for he could roll out from under the blanket away from the half-track and they would never see the movement. He could crawl through the fuzz of yellow grass and thorn scrub that backed their trench and be out of sight in no time. No, there was no problem of getting into that depression and walking stooped along it to where it petered out.

It was from that point that M'Bain's courage left him. There was no cover for a hundred yards up to the half-track. If he were seen, he would be shot long before he reached it.

But could he be seen? M'Bain's soldier-training said the enemy could not see his advance. He would be approaching the half-track from the rear. The machine-gun would be pointing away from him – so would the interest of the German occupant. Occupants, he corrected himself; Oily had started it all by hearing soft conversation. He guessed that the turret was in a fixed position, unable to swing because of damage done to it.

Even without that, he thought he could approach without being detected because of the way the half-track lay bonnet down in the sand. It had ended its days coming down a bump in the desert, so that its rear stuck up oddly. The bump, too, looked as if it would give some cover right up to the last few yards.

M'Bain's training told him he could go out, and with a bit of care could walk right up to that half-track and blow the occupants to pieces, but the apprehensive man within refused to believe his training. On that last hundred yards he could be spotted – there was more than one man in that hull, and surely a second man would be looking round for danger.

The lance-jack could save the situation – the other trenches were too far away to take advantage of that depression – and yet he could not move.

He stood against the wall of the trench, dry earth sliding down inside his shirt as he pressed against it, curiously cool as it ran over his skin. He stared out through sweat-smarting eyes at the scene before him, shimmering in the refracting layers of hot rising air currents, and he thought nothing on earth would induce him to go out there alone and risk death.

Behind him, with the minutes ticking away and nothing happening after the German machine-gunner had opened fire on their captain, his companions grew anxious and alarmed.

'Fackin' caught in a fackin' trap,' Stepney kept saying, his voice rising wilder each time he said it.

Partridge, a harder man, began to growl, 'How much longer?' He was holding his tommy with his finger on the safety catch, ready to use it . . . desperately wanting to use it. 'Let's get at the Hun bastards!' his mouth biting off the words, his face a twisted mask of ferocity as he worked himself into a killing mood.

Oily had forgotten his gripes now, though he was a thicker man than the others and did not reach their state of alarm. In fact he would have just waited and done nothing until orders came to him to act.

M'Bain listened to them, and caught the determination in Partridge's voice to clamber out and start a shooting match. Hopeless, he knew. It would do none of them any good. Someone had to get them from behind. *He* wasn't going to do it. The sweat poured out of him, and he knew he was shaking, and wondered why his companions did not notice it.

Partridge, becoming insistent and angry: 'What the hell are we waitin' for, f'Chrisake! Doesn't that stupid git of a captain know we haven't time for waiting! They'll be here in no time now, and do you think they'll invite us out to have some char with 'em? Not fackin' likely! They'll have mortars, an' they'll bomb the bleedin' guts out of us, that's what they'll do. Why doesn't Eats-Early do somethin'!'

Why? But what? M'Bain knew there was nothing Captain Yeats-Urley could do. Only he knew what could be done, and he hadn't guts enough to do it. Yet it never occurred to him to invite a comrade to do what his nerve failed to let him do.

He suddenly came away from the wall. Stepney was saying in panic, 'They'll have fackin' flame-frowers! They'll scorch us aht. I'm not stoppin' 'ere for that, fack me if I am!'

Flame-throwers. The infantryman's nightmare. Bullets were bad. Bombs and shells were worse, more mangling. But death by jets of fire, that chilled the mind the way nothing else did. The nervous, jumpy imagination of M'Bain saw pictures of grey-clad men racing towards them, hosing them, and great globules of oil shooting out through a jet of roaring fire to land on them and catch light. Then they'd start dancing through the flames, limbs leaping convulsively like marionette figures, as the fire destroyed all the nerve ends of their skin, until down they went, blinded, flayed to their raw flesh, dying in an agony rarely known even to man.

That was something M'Bain just couldn't stand even in his thoughts. And they *would* have flame-throwers with them, he felt sure – those German half-tracks were often mobile flame-throwers. His hand picked up a grenade.

He found himself turning towards the back of the trench, heard himself saying, 'Time something was done. Wish me luck, pals.' He was gripped with terror but disguised it as always with the crooked little smile.

Stepney said, 'Where are you bleedin' orf?'

M'Bain found he couldn't speak any more, so he shrugged, then carefully pulled himself out of the trench under the dirty blanket. No sound from the half-track. The movement hadn't been detected.

There was grass, so dry it broke to his touch, and he crawled through it – just a yard or so, that was all, and once through he had cover behind him. But still he crawled, and he felt he was descending slightly, until he knew he was in the long depression. At this he rose and began to run.

It wasn't easy, running in a stooped position, the sandy soil too soft, so that he sank in with every stride and seemed to have to haul each foot out against resistance. He was sobbing and panting with the exertion quite soon, the heat of that powerful sun upon him, making any effort undesirable anyway.

All at once he realised he had come out of the depression, for to his left he could see the top of the half-track turret. He began to walk now, incapable of running further, and now he did not stoop but walked erect. He expected shots to come and hit him and send him writhing to the ground, but still there was no movement, only silence from the half-track.

He saw Big Maurice's startled eyes upon him as he came walking across the desert, and guessed that other watchers in the trenches would have seen him. He walked, and the thoughts went through him in chaotic confusion.

He had never killed anyone before. True, he had been in action, and had performed his share of destruction, firing grounded aircraft. He had also put up covering fire on one occasion, but if he had hit anyone that would have been rather accidental – he didn't think he had, anyway, not that time. All that was very impersonal. This wasn't. He had heard the voice of the man he was here to kill, and it made it all different.

So he trudged across the hot, yielding earth, grenade ready, going to kill his first man at twenty-three. And he kept thinking, 'This is the last time. When I get out I'm off on the run.' Even the Glasshouse would hold no terrors for him after this agony.

Big Maurice told them afterwards that the Corp just walked up to the half-track with a smile on his face, just like he was going to the Naafi for some wallop. 'Wish I had nerve like his,' he said, and shuddered to think how it was done.

M'Bain came to the bit of a mound. He thougnt he could have landed the bomb from that distance, but it was a bit far and he had to make sure – he had only the one grenade.

From the bottom all he could see was the turret, the mound obscuring the hull, but as he climbed it came into view. He could also hear talking from within, the low rumble of men in conversation who did not know they were about to be blown to oblivion. He found he didn't want to silence those voices, but he had to do it. Fate had conspired to bring him round the world to one-square yard of sand to kill men who had never done him any harm, nor he them. He moaned; it wasn't what he wanted. But on that last square yard of sand he halted, drew the pin, counted four then tossed the grenade. He was so close to the half-track that he threw it underhand to make more sure of his aim, and he saw it curve lazily in the air, spinning a little, to drop inside the turret.

He heard a startled shout, then threw himself backwards, to put himself at the bottom of the mound. The thing went off with a sharp bang, not a very loud one, which surprised him, and he felt nothing – no tremor, no blast. Just a small bang. But no one was talking in the half-track after that.

Man Mountain's voice, shouting. Private Hill went leaping towards the half-track the moment he saw the grenade fall inside the battered turret. He drew the pin of his grenade as he ran, and when he was close enough a second grenade dropped into the smoky turret. It went off with the soft bang that told the experienced Hill the explosion had been muffled as if enclosed by sandbags. Or human flesh.

From all four trenches men were leaping out and racing towards the half-track, guns cocked for action, Captain Yeats-Urley, first into action. But no action was needed. As the smoke drifted away there was no movement from within, no sound. Big Maurice, no man to stand on ceremony, grabbed a tommy from the hands of Gunner Partridge, and clambered on to the half-track.

He peered cautiously within. The sight didn't turn him, but nothing much turned the big man. He saw flesh and white bone, blood everywhere and mangled bodies. Two Huns, he noted. He could see below the gunner's seat to where the driver and his mate sat and sprayed within with the tommy, but felt sure no one was there. Just two Huns. But he had to make absolutely sure.

'Another banger, quick!' he called. Time wasn't on their side. Someone tossed him a grenade. He primed it, dropped it into the half-track beyond the two bodies, then came jumping down off the vehicle. It made more noise this time, the bare interior acting like a drum.

The men all came together round their officer. They were

panting even from that brief run, but release of pent-up fear was much more the cause of it. Just a second or so of standing, chests heaving, eyes still startled holding the events of the last few seconds. Then there was relaxation, swift reaction to recent stress. Smiles cracking strained and dirty faces, men thumping each other, men using uncouth language to show their gladness at this turn of events which could keep them alive, after all.

Young Captain Yeats-Urley also let himself relax for a second or so, accepting their congratulations as if he were responsible for the recent action. He smiled and said the right things, 'Good show, you men. We came out of that all right. Good man, Hill. Good piece of work.' Very jerky to hold back any trace of wrong emotion. 'But where's Corporal M'Bain?'

They turned, remembering him. 'Where's Mac? Where's the old bugger . . .' Affection behind their language.

And there was M'Bain coming slowly round the half-track towards them, M'Bain with another surprise for them.

For M'Bain, a man entirely unarmed, was walking between two other men, strangers, men in civvy suits, and foreigners, they knew immediately.

M'Bain rolled on to his feet the moment the grenade went off within the hull. For a moment he was doubtful – the explosion seemed too mild to have done the trick, and he quite expected to see some irate German come storming over the mound towards him, gun blazing.

But nothing happened, not like that, anyway. He heard Big Maurice's voice, and then the harsh voices of his other comrades, then a second dull explosion. At this he began to crawl up the mound, wanting to see what was going on. As he climbed higher the whole of the half-track came into view, and he could see under it.

He saw two blue-chinned faces looking at him. Two men in light-weight dark-grey suits lay under the vehicle. As his startled eyes fell upon them, he heard a machine-gun rattle and bullets bounce inside the hull. Then Big Maurice calling for another grenade, and that going off, and the half-track shuddering under the force of the explosion.

The two civvies went face down at that bang, then lifted them again to look in fear at M'Bain, kneeling there. One, sitting up in a half crouch, put his hands up. Then both came out and M'Bain was still too astonished to do anything or say anything.

It never occurred to him that he was unarmed, and when they just stood nervously there, saying nothing, he thought for a moment, then said, tiredly, 'You'd better come with me.'

They seemed to understand him, for both lowered their arms, and when he went walking round the half-track they fell in on either side of him, just a little behind, as if demonstrating some act of subservience.

So they came into view of the startled S.A.S. M'Bain, still stunned by what had just happened, saw astonished faces, and then the instinctive raising of guns to cover the civilians. Only one man spoke, Captain Yeats-Urley. His first words were, 'Good God, what have you got there, corporal?' He came walking up, and M'Bain saw him raising a Smith-Wesson revolver, and the corporal thought he was going to shoot them there and then. So did the civilians, for they stepped closer to M'Bain, as if they felt that the man who had destroyed the Germans would save them.

M'Bain spoke quickly. He didn't want any more killing. He was feeling very sick, trying not to think what was in the half-track turret. 'They were under the half-track. Civilians.' As if it might have passed unobserved. 'They didn't give any trouble.'

Lieutenant Fairlop came shoving through the group. 'We haven't time to waste.' He never had much thought for anyone except himself. 'Look!'

At that they turned and gasped. Three huge dust clouds now, but one of them so close they could see the black crawling specks that were vehicles, travelling on a route that would

5   65

bring the column precious close to them. It brought them to earth with a jolt.

The captain's eyes looked at the terrain around them. Plenty of footmarks in the sand around the half-track. That didn't matter. But those lines of footmarks radiating back to the trenches did.

'Get under cover.' His voice snapped the order. 'Wipe out all footprints as you go.' He wheeled on the civilians. 'What are you? Italians? Italiano?'

'*Si. Si, signor.*' The older of the two spoke quickly, wanting to agree with everything these terrifying British suggested.

'Where's Private Vecchi?' Yeats-Urley called, gesturing to the Italians to start moving towards the trenches. All the men were retreating on their hide-outs, obliterating footmarks as they went. 'Hurry,' as they seemed slow to respond. Someone in that nearest column might have his glasses on them. '*Presto!*' He tried his Italian.

Someone called, 'Vecchi! Captain wants you.' And someone said, 'Where's that bloody Wop?'

Vecchi had been coming slowly from his trench, hand to his side, supporting his broken ribs. He came up to his captain.

'You speak Italian.' Everyone knew Vecchi spoke Italian; Tony Vecchi was proud of his linguistic ability and let them all know it. 'Ask them what they were doing there.'

It set Vecchi back. He wasn't all that good at Italian. Now, the thing thrust upon him, his mind raced frantically for the right words, and they were slow in coming.

One of the Italians – the older one again – came to his rescue. 'We speak English. We have both been in America.' His English was American-accented.

'Good.' They were trotting now in their anxiety to get under cover, the men sweeping with frantic gestures with small bushes that made reasonable brooms. 'And what are you doing here?' Yeats-Urley was very sharp, his manner intimidating, proper to the occasion.

'We were finding spares for half-tracks and other vehicles.' Yeats-Urley thought he spoke a little quickly. They were

66

near the trench. He had to make decisions. Couldn't shoot the blighters because there was less time to hide corpses than to hide living men. He called to Fairlop. 'Take one of these Wops into your trench. I know it's a tight squeeze, but I can't get two in mine. If he makes a sound, cut his throat.' He made his voice ugly with menace, and he felt the Italians draw away, and their fear brought a thrill of pleasure to him.

'Get in.' They were at the edge of his trench. Fairlop was pushing the other Italian before him, being rough with him though the man was doing his best to hurry. The Italian slowly got into sitting position, then slid into the trench. One of the men gave him a hand, and the Italian responded with a quick smile of thanks. He was a very frightened man, trembling with nervousness, Yeats-Urley noticed for the first time.

But the captain had remembered something. Corporal M'Bain was standing by his trench, waiting his turn to get in. Yeats-Urley called to him. 'Corporal.' A tired face turned towards him.

'Sir?'

'Good show that. Proud of you. I'll mention this in my report.' Yeats-Urley expected pathetic gratefulness, the usual embarrassed pleasure, the glow that comes from a pat on the head by the master. None came.

M'Bain, who had just killed his first man, said, 'Yes, sir.' That was all. Then slowly lowered himself into his trench. For once he wasn't smiling. His comrades, though – even the crude Oily – made something of him for a moment or so.

'Cor,' said Stepney, 'you saved our fackin' bacon that time, mite! How the fackin' 'ell did you do it?'

And Partridge, only a little less Cockney in speech, said, 'You was great, Corp. You'll get another stripe for this.' As if that would be reward enough.

Oily was cruder. 'You knocked the shits out of them Boche!' His mind ran on restricted circles at that moment. Still, his voice was admiring.

Then the praise and gratefulness died down, and only minutes later they were arguing about who should have one end for squatting in, because squatting in the middle was less comfortable. M'Bain, hero of a few minutes before, lost because he'd had his turn there earlier.

The dirty grey blankets were lowered to ground level, bringing the heat and the sweat upon them again, and the intolerable thirst that couldn't be satisfied because it wasn't time for their water ration. Cautious eyes peered from under a raised part of the blankets in each trench, but at that level there was little they could see. Almost the only thing in Yeats-Urley's line of vision, in fact, was the wrecked half-track, and one of their own simulated wrecked vehicles.

After a few minutes Yeats-Urley drew away from watch and told Private Mack to take over. As he pulled back he thought he heard far-distant sounds of motor vehicles. There would be time, though, to interrogate this Eytie, and that had to be done. For Captain Yeats-Urley, shrewd man, wasn't at all satisfied with what he had been told.

He squatted opposite the Italian, their faces within inches, their knees touching. He spoke abruptly, that being the way to get best results from a captured enemy. 'Your name?'

A swift, deprecating smile. 'Antonio Bergamo.'

Bergamo. A town in north Italy. He had toured through there while at Sandhurst before the war. And another Antonio, like their own Vecchi. Were all Italians Antonios? Yeats-Urley was amused by his own thought, and it made him a little easier towards his prisoner, but condescending with it.

'What were you doing under the half-track?'

A flash of big, strong white teeth in the gloom under the blanket. 'When we saw you coming we decided to hide and hope you would pass.'

'But we didn't.' Awful moment for the enemy, seeing a larger force of wild men halt right against their vehicle and begin to lie up. 'But you were *under* the half-track. Two Germans — they were Germans, weren't they? — were inside.'

Bergamo nodded. They were Germans. And the ex-

68

planation was easy. It would have been too hot with four of them inside that armoured vehicle. The Italians said they preferred to hide beneath, leaving the Germans, efficient soldiers, to mount a machine-gun and occupy the best position for defence. Anyway, when they went to ground they did not expect to have to remain there long, Bergamo explained, but the S.A.S. patrol hadn't obligingly moved on. Must have been damned hot, Yeats-Urley thought, crouching all that time under the half-track. And scaring for civilians.

Now he knew he could hear motor vehicles, but still distant. He must hurry, though, just a couple of minutes with Bergamo.

'And you say you were finding spares?' A long way into the desert for civilians.

The Italian seemed easier under the interrogation now. His American-Italian voice drawled a confident explanation, accompanied by quick smiles and that show of white teeth.

A party had gone off – several trucks and an amoured car – on a foraging expedition through The Graveyard. All Germans, Bergamo agreed at the captain's sharp question. No other civilians? None. German military and two Italian civilians? Odd, thought Yeats-Urley, but didn't mention it and let the Italian incriminate himself a bit more.

They had got one half-track into action by dint of much cannibalising and had come out of The Graveyard ahead of their companions. So there was an enemy working-party somewhere amid the wreckage, the captain mentally noted. Two Germans non-com took turns to drive, the Italians being passengers.

The previous afternoon, when they had just cleared The Graveyard they had had trouble with a torsion bar, so they walked back to where they had noted a wrecked half-track to secure a replacement. They had removed the track from the vehicle and were working on the torsion bar when they were shocked to see a fast-moving couple of enemy trucks heading straight for them. They had gone into hiding.

It was a satisfactory explanation, yet the captain remained

unsatisfied. There was something wrong about it all. He could understand that if a vehicle seized up the occupants would go walking back to find a spare, and now he remembered the half-track they had passed coming in. That would be the one they'd temporarily abandoned. But if these were mechanics, as they claimed, why did they come out with a restored vehicle leaving a German working-party presumably still working on wrecks? Even stranger, what were two Italian civilians doing with a party of Germans? All very odd, he kept telling himself, and now he prepared, in that last moment before the enemy column was upon them, to confound the man with his own words.

'You say you are a mechanic? But you are a civilian?'

'I am from Fiat works in Turin. Many of us have been sent over.' That was reasonable. The Allies also had lots of civilians floating around the depots amid the latest equipment that required so much expert attention. Mechanics and boffins. . . .

His head came up sharply. 'Let me see your hands?'

Bergamo good-humouredly spread his palms before him. Yeats-Urley took hold of them for a moment, and turned them to examine them closely. They were big, strong hands, the hands of a man who had done much manual work with them at times, but they weren't the hands of a mechanic. Yeats-Urley's fingers stroked the base of Bergamo's fingers, those places where calloused skin forms on the hands of men constantly using tools. There were no callouses.

Captain Yeats-Urley spoke coldly. 'You're not a mechanic.' His face went intimidatingly hard. 'You have been lying to me.' The noise of the vehicles was much louder now.

'Let's see what you've got in your pockets.' There was a hesitation so slight that it was almost imperceptible, but Yeats-Urley didn't miss it. 'Your pockets. Come on – turn them out!' He was in a hurry.

From an inside pocket Bergamo pulled out a notebook and quite a wad of papers all held together by a stout rubber band. To make sure the fellow wasn't holding out on him.

Yeats-Urley went quite roughly through his pockets himself. Nothing else there. He shoved the notebook and papers inside his own shirt and rose. He could look at them later; just now his concern was for the advancing enemy vehicles.

He took Mack's place at the blanket, cautiously pushing it up a few inches and peering out. After the semi-dark of the trench the light seemed blinding for a few moments, and he winced as the hot rays glanced off the light-coloured sandy soil into his eyes.

There was nothing to see. Just a shimmering haze down there at ground level, the wrecked half-track dancing through the distorting air currents, and beyond it one of their trucks. But the sound of motor traffic was very loud now.

After a while he decided the column was passing north of them, and he reckoned it must be half a mile or so away, but didn't risk crawling out to see. He began to feel easier, thinking that the column was travelling on and had missed them, when all at once the noise of rumbling engines died away. He knew the sounds and what they meant. The column had halted. He could also guess the tactics. The infantry would be de-bussing and spreading out, beginning to search the wrecked vehicles, so thickly strewn hereabouts. Probably the other two columns they had spotted would be working more distant areas. In time, if they found nothing, everyone would climb aboard again and they would drive off to some new search position. *If* they found nothing – but what if they looked inside the half-track and found two recent corpses? Well, what if they did? Yeats-Urley asked himself sharply, and remained on watch.

Half an hour later Yeats-Urley saw his first enemy. They were Italian infantry. A few of them came into view together and for a while stood talking and smoking, and seeming in no hurry to get on with the search. Then someone shouted a command, someone out of Yeats-Urley's line of vision, and the Italians moved reluctantly towards the half-track. They still talked, still smoked, and weren't bothering about what they were supposed to do.

The S.A.S. captain saw one of the Italian soldiers clamber on to the half-track and stand with one hand on the turret, not looking within but arguing energetically with someone on the ground. For a moment Yeats-Urley thought he wasn't even going to look into the turret, and then the man turned, and even from that distance the captain could feel the horror at what the man saw inside. He came jumping off, as if the sight frightened him, and began to talk and the others crowded round him, and then someone, probably the N.C.O. in charge, clambered up and peered inside – recoiled, then began to blow frantically on a whistle. Yeats-Urley's blood chilled. This wasn't what he wanted. That damned half-track was too close to be comfortable.

He heard an engine start up, then another, and then a roaring of revving motors and sounds coming nearer until abruptly two Italian armoured cars swept into view and halted. An Italian officer got out of one of them and had a shouted conversation with the N.C.O., then clambered on to the vehicle to see for himself what had been reported to him. He was made of stouter material than the lower ranks and remained staring within for a while. Then he turned and without descending began to shout orders. Probably getting a radio signal off, Yeats-Urley guessed, because that would have been his own first act in such circumstances.

Then a reluctant working party approached and clambered up and began to drag out the corpses.

M'Bain was on watch, being the N.C.O. in charge of his trench, and he saw a bloody mangled thing heaved over the edge of the turret. He could not turn away but had to see what they had done, and he was sick and frightened, because the thought inevitably came to him, 'This could happen to me.'

The limp, torn body with the limbs dangling so grotesquely, was lowered to the ground, someone spreading an army blanket to receive the corpse. The officer came and stood over it and then a soldier, as if under orders, went down on his knees and began to go through the pockets of the body. Identification, M'Bain thought, so important in warfare to identify the dead, though they'll mostly be forgotten within a few minutes, here in the desert.

A second body was being hauled out. This presented greater difficulties and seemed more bloody and mangled than the first one. When it came up M'Bain saw it was without legs. Later some Italians somehow pulled two separate limbs out through the turret. If you were sitting and a grenade dropped in your lap your body could be torn in half. A terrible way to die, particularly if in that last fraction of a second of life your eye recognised the thing that lay there and understood what was going to happen before you had time to move.

M'Bain felt ill. Big Maurice, who had thrown that second grenade and then a third one, watched and was good-humoured about it. 'They make a mess, don't they, sir?' he said to Lieutenant Fairlop, who was still interrogating his prisoner with a little aid from Vecchi.

Private Maurice Hill was a kind man, a man of most generous instincts. Any oppo without ackers could always depend on Big Maurice for a loan, and he never bothered to ask for repayment, either. He was loyal to his comrades, to his unit including even this officer, Fairlop, whom he didn't like. Eats-Early, now, he was different. A real gentleman. Big Maurice, son of a publican, had been brought up to respect the gentry, and he still did. One day he would have his own licence and run his own pub, a big bar with plenty of noise and heavy boozing, preferably around Shepherd's Bush, and he'd bring up his own children to vote Conservative and respect their betters.

A kind and friendly man, the big Maurice, yet he killed easily, quite happily, without a conscience. If asked he might have said it was his duty; all he knew was he had been trained to do certain things, like shooting to kill, and bombing to destroy, and he followed orders and killed when circumstances required. There was no regret either, at any enemy's passing – not even the fellow whose throat he had cut that time at Agheila when they needed his silence. He held the old, comfortable philosophy, 'It's him or me.' It had always been him up to this time, and Maurice Hill intended to keep it like that. Anyway, he enjoyed it all.

So Man Mountain watched carefully from under the edge of the dirty blanket, saw the bodies of the Germans hauled out, and felt . . . nothing.

The recent killing agitated the Italians, for it confirmed that the S.A.S. had indeed passed this way and that not long before their arrival. It was a good job for Yeats-Urley that no medical man was with the Italian patrol, for sight of that uncoagulated blood in that heat would have told him the killing had been only minutes ago, and that would have restricted their radius of search.

More vehicles began to arrive – armoured cars and infantry carriers. The enemy patrol was concentrating where they knew the S.A.S. had been. What disturbed the watchers in their trenches was the fact that the trucks tended to park out in the desert between the half-track and where they lay holed up. After a while there were vehicles no more than eighty yards from the nearest trench, and everywhere Italian soldiers seemed to mill around. It brought the sweat to their faces, the fear to their hearts. Anything could give them away – an incautious movement or sound could bring unwelcome attention upon them.

The thought made the captain look down. 'Corporal –' to Corporal Fullalove –' put a knife point against the Italian's throat. If he makes any move or seems about to shout, slit his windpipe.'

'Yes, sir,' said Fullalove, hairy blond man with a ragged Viking beard. This was much to his liking, and when he put his knife against the dark-skinned Italian's flesh, he leaned on it and let it drive in, though not quite breaking the skin. His face took on a grim sadistic expression, and the Italian looked sick.

Yet Yeats-Urley's tactics in going to ground in the open desert seemed to be paying off. Several times the captain had seen Italians step clear of their vehicles and scan the desert, some of them officers. They even used glasses, and when he saw them raised Yeats-Urley lowered the blanket and kept out of sight. Yet always afterwards they turned away, as if satisfied that the blank desert didn't hold the fugitives.

A search now began of the nearest vehicles. From the trenches, breath held, because those 'wrecked' trucks of theirs meant life to them, they saw a straggling party of Italians walk up to the first of their immobilised vehicles. They moved cautiously, Yeats-Urley saw, guns at the ready. Sight of those bloodied corpses induced fear, and they weren't going to be bombed or shot down by any hiding S.A.S.

They circled the truck at a respectful distance, saw nothing to upset them, and came closer. Finally one got into the cab, and then everyone was satisfied that there was no enemy there, and they all went off out of sight, presumably to examine the next vehicle – their second truck.

Again they relaxed in the trenches. The Italians weren't suspicious; they had accepted that their truck was just another rusting wreck. Yeats-Urley congratulated himself on their successful disguise of men and vehicles.

Then an Italian came walking quite resolutely out from between the nearest infantry carriers, heading for Yeats-Urley's fox-hole. He seemed to be walking with great determination, as if he knew where he was going, rifle firmly held before him. In the trench Yeats-Urley gave warning. 'Someone coming straight for us. Be ready!'

If they were discovered they would come out shooting. Not that they would live long with that army of Eyties so close to them. Less than twenty yards from the trench, however, the Italian halted, carefully placed his rifle on a bed of dry grass, then dropped his trousers. It was evident that Private Hoyle was not the only sufferer that day. Five minutes later the Italian rose, buttoned up and walked, as if in some discomfort, back to the vehicles.

And fifteen minutes later the energetically talking, gesticulating, milling swarm of Italians sorted themselves out, climbed into their vehicles and lumbered off.

Yeats-Urley made no move to leave his trench for over an hour, not until all sounds had died slowly across the desert, though it was murderous under the blanket with the climbing sun now pouring almost straight down upon them. The captain wasn't going to fall for the old trick of revealing himself to some detachment left behind to keep watch.

When he finally made a move, Yeats-Urley slid carefully up on to the ground from under the blanket, Smith-Wesson ready in his hand, eyes trying to see everywhere at once. He rolled into the cover of some scrub and and lay there for another quarter of an hour, intently scrutinising every bush, tuft of grass or sagging ruin of a vehicle that might hold an enemy. Finally, he stood up, satisfied that the Italians had gone on, not cunning enough to leave anyone behind.

They probably imagine we're going like the clappers across The Graveyard, Yeats-Urley thought, and they'd be off searching for recent tracks, and being surprised when they didn't find them. As soon as he was satisfied that all was clear, Yeats-Urley told everyone to come out. Instantly blankets were thrown back and his men came dragging themselves into the open.

Yeats-Urley ordered two men on watch, others to tie their prisoners so that they couldn't run away and cause trouble, and others to put tea on to brew. The watchers – Sergeant Vickers and Private Mack – went trudging across to their vehicle and climbed into the cab. They were in the shade – essential in that heat – they were lifted above the ground, which gave them a wider view of the terrain, and if any enemy aircraft came over they could crouch there and not be seen.

An aircraft did come roaring up before they'd time to drink their tea, setting everyone cursing and scrambling frantically back into their sweat-pits. But it went on, probably called up by the distant searchers to help them over the horizon. The S.A.S. came up out of their holes like cautious rabbits and resumed their tea-making. The prisoners were found empty jam tins and supplied with tea. The rich, strong, sweet brew seemed as much to their liking as to the British warriors'. And when they had satisfied their thirst, however temporarily, Captain Yeats-Urley really got down to grilling them.

He and Lieutenant Fairlop first went through the note-books – Fairlop had taken one off the younger Italian, too – and papers. There was much Italian writing in them, but Yeats-Urley didn't bother for the moment to get an uncertain translation from Driver Vecchi. What interested him were the drawings. Page after page was covered with neat sketches and diagrams, much of them recognisable to the British officers.

Unmistakably some of them were of British tanks, most prominently the Crusader. Others were just as unmistakably sections of the turrets, while others were of shells showing intricate mechanism there. But most of all were electronic diagrams. Page after page of these alone, as if the Italians were trying to work out some circuit. Yeats-Urley looked at the diagrams and thought contemptuously, 'Mechanics?' Not men who could work out circuits like these.

He looked sombrely across at the two Italians, passively seated among his sprawling, dirty, hairy ruffians. They were not the men they said they were, the captain thought, and began to run through his mind all those things that had roused his supicions from the beginning.

Their English, American-accented though it was, was college English. They had been properly taught, learning grammar and sentence construction, unlike Fiat mechanics at Turin, who were much more likely to have picked up a bit of English and used a mangled form of speech. He could be wrong, of course; perhaps two Italians *had* gone to America young enough to learn colloquial American, and had then returned to become mechanics back in Italy. Leave highly-paid America for lowly-paid Turin? It didn't add up.

Besides, these Italians had an air about them. They were blue-chinned for lack of recent shaving, and their clothes looked as if they had been slept in, yet they had a manner which spoke of higher callings than simple mechanical engineering. The word returned to Yeats-Urley that had crept into his mind an hour or so before – boffins. Were these

77

boffins, scientists? Electronics engineers rather than mechanics? Perhaps they were important men, which could explain why they had been in the desert with a German patrol. Thoughts began to flow at incoherent speed through Yeats-Urley's mind. What were very important Italian scientists doing in The Graveyard, so far from the coast? And why had they come out of The Graveyard in a half-track ahead of their German companions . . . that is, if that part of their story were true?

So many questions to ask, so many answers needed. Yeats-Urley decided not to delay in putting his questions to the Italians. Anyway, what else was there he could do with his time? They had another six or seven hours before they could start to get their trucks roadworthy again, seven more hours before darkness came and they could head off into the friendly desert, during which time they did not dare stir more than a few yards from their slit trenches. . . . Yeats-Urley noted that one man was straying more than a few yards from his trench, and was being loudly urged by his fellows to go even further and make sure he was on the leeward side of them, too. Big Birmingham Oily was responding uncomfortably to the scouring effect of hot tea on his delicate insides.

Yeats-Urley had the two Italians brought over to him. 'Sit down,' he said, though he himself squatted before them. He spread the notebooks and papers on the sand before him, each action quite slow and deliberate, to make them feel jumpy. Then his eyes lifted quickly to meet theirs, and he put ice into his voice. 'You told me you were mechanics, but your hands aren't the hands of mechanics. And these papers tell me you have a great interest in electronics – military electronics.'

Both Italians sat there, stiff in posture, but that was mainly because their hands were tied behind their backs. For the moment Yeats-Urley was not ready to relieve them of this discomfort. One became gracious and kind after fear had been put into the victim; then in relief they would often say what they had refused to say under pressure.

Bluntly, voice grim, Yeats-Urley asked, 'Who are you? Come on, I want no more nonsense from you. What are you doing so far from the coast road?'

Neither man answered the question. They sat without looking at the British captain, faces stiff as if holding back emotion . . . frightened men, Yeats-Urley was sure, but hadn't they good reason to be scared? He and his unwashed, filthy, desert-stained men must have seemed a bunch of scoundrels, men who had proved they were prepared to kill and weren't likely to be gentle with enemy civilians who weren't co-operative.

Yeats-Urley made some inspired guesses to get them talking. 'Let me tell you who you are.' They both looked up startled at that. 'You are very important people, aren't you? You are scientists, electronics experts, yes?' Their eyes dropped again. He felt triumph; he *was* on the right lines. His guesses became more inspired.

'Yes, I believe you when you say you learned your English in America. I think it was in some notable college . . . and you went there not so much to learn English as to learn about electronics from the foremost electronics scientists there. Probably . . .' He took his time over this one. '. . . the Massachusetts Institute of Technology.' The greatest of its kind in the world, the one foreign scientists always tried to attend.

The younger of the pair gave the show away. His eyes came up, startled, bewilderment showing. 'How did you –' His companion spoke sharply, telling him to shut up.

But Yeats-Urley knew now he had guessed right. Not that it was at all that difficult to arrive at most of his conclusions, even M.I.T. being a fairly logical guess. These men could not suppress their university background; their notebooks betrayed their specialised scientific interests.

Yeats-Urley, face switched to severity, tapped the diagrams on the sand between his feet. 'Now, what are these all about? Tanks and electrical circuits.' Silence. 'You'd better talk, my friends. I shall make you talk – understand? *Comprendo*?' An entirely unnecessary piece of Italian to men

79

whose visible fear showed they understood too well what he was talking about.

The patrol captain's voice never departed from its normal careful public-school speech, yet somehow it conveyed unpleasant threat. The younger Italian – what was his name? Yeats-Urley looked at the notebooks: Piero Lazzi – in particular seemed apprehensive. Better to concentrate on that fellow, thought Yeats-Urley; the older fellow was tougher material.

He said, 'Now, tell me, what's it all about? Why are two Italian scientists grubbing about among wrecked tanks? Why your interest in the British Crusader? What's all this electronics stuff?' He looked again at one particular drawing. It looked like a shell on a long tube. Alongside it, as if it were an inset to the shell, was a drawing of a simple electrical circuit.

'Shells and Crusaders? And radio apparatus. What have we got that can bring scientists all the way from Italy into the heat of the desert?' Then come out of it cooped up in a blisteringly hot *schutzenpanzerwagen*. 'Why this remarkable interest suddenly in the Crusader?' He was talking because it helped to put ideas together in his mind. After all, there were dozens of Crusaders wrecked up the Blue, and for months German and Italian experts had had plenty of opportunity of studying them down to the last bolt and rivet. Why now a revived interest in the tank? And what electronics circuits were there in a Crusader that could warrant this intense interest after all this time?.

Bony-framed Lieutenant Fairlop spoke. 'What was that we heard in Cairo about the Crusader?' Yeats-Urley looked at him quickly. There was something. . . . 'A rocket carrier, wasn't it?'

His captain snapped his fingers in sudden excitement. Of course Fairlop was right. It was something desperately hush-hush and Top Secret, so everyone in Cairo knew of it and was talking about it. That was the fate of all top military secrets in a city where no secrets could be kept. The Allies, out-gunned by the heavier-armed German tanks, were experimenting with a rocket-propelled, armour-piercing missile. Yeats-Urley's eyes again strayed to the diagrams of electronic circuits . . . and he knew suddenly what it was all about.

Rocket projectiles were nothing new. All armies in the field were experimenting with them. There was even one which was controlled by wires which streamed out behind the projectile, but it was not reputed to be very successful. But the Cairo griff was that a new radio-controlled rocket projectile was being experimented with – the American tank-homer, they called it – and it had been used with some success up the desert.

Yeats-Urley rose to his feet, dusting his shorts. Now he knew what it was all about. A Crusader must have been knocked out and valuable material had been discovered by the enemy. Probably it was in a shattered mess and these Italian boffins had been flown over specially to see if they could make anything from the wreckage. By the look of it, they had.

Yeats-Urley's thoughts raced with lightning speed. He was thinking, 'We're safe now.' The search had gone past them. 'When it's dark we'll slip across The Graveyard and rendezvous with the L.R.D.G.' And their guides to the trackless desert would smuggle them over the vast wasteland without further trouble.

Yeats-Urley spoke to the nearest man. It was Private Vecchi, that Cockney-Italian, who had been hovering near as if fascinated by the Italians. 'Keep close guard on them, Vecchi.' He jerked his head to Fairlop, and the two walked away.

Yeats-Urley took off his hat and mopped his matted hair. The sun was killing. He said, 'When it's time to move, you go on to meet the L.R.D.G. wallahs. Take the Italians with you, and guard them carefully. I think they're top scientists, and our chaps in Cairo will be interested in them.' In any event, merely to deprive the enemy of their services for the duration of the war would be a contribution to the struggle.

'And you?' The sharp look from the bigger, harder man,

as if always seeking behind words for something disguised and possibly not acceptable.

'I'm going back.' A vague wave across the desert, the way they had come. 'I'll probably catch up with you by the morning.'

'Back?'

'To that half-track.' The one that had conked out in the near-by desert. There'd be no risk. By nightfall the Axis troops would have pulled back to their bases and the hunt called off. That was always the pattern with these S.A.S raids. Immediately afterwards the enemy mounted a swift and ferocious pursuit, but it rarely lasted long. They weren't at home in the desert, and were soon called in. Of course there would be shufti kites searching for them on the run home, and they were a damned nuisance and could be very dangerous, but Yeats-Urley reckoned they could give them the slip, as they had done so often before.

'The half-track?' Fairlop's face was incredulous.

Yeats-Urley was patient with his lieutenant. 'Got to, old chap. My guess is they came out with the bits and pieces of the American tank-homer, and they're in that half-track and the enemy mustn't find them.'

They began to walk back towards the Italians, prepared to interrogate them a little more. Yeats-Urley said, 'I don't anticipate trouble.'

In Field-Marshal Rommel's headquarters in Tobruk nothing of event was occurring. Merely the routine of getting on with a war, of working out plans to destroy an enemy when he broke out from behind his lines of defence, as they knew he would. That day Rommel was a little gloomy. Vital supplies, being ferried across via Italy and Sicily, just weren't coming through in quantity – the Royal Air Force and British Navy were seeing to that. Only forty per cent of recent convoys had got through even on that short journey, and already Rommel had a sickening feeling that he'd lost the war in Africa. His lines of communication were too long. He could run rings round his opposing generals, and his equipment generally was far superior to the Allies'. He would also back his officers and men against any army in the world. But if he had insufficient men and equipment even he couldn't fight on.

Still, Rommel showed nothing of his thoughts to his staff, but worked hard in that arid heat, and made plans for every eventuality when the battle was joined at Alamein.

Of course the S.A.S. raid that night on El Badim did not please him. At this moment he could ill afford to lose so many aircraft to a daring enemy who so unsportingly shot at sitting birds. Neither could he afford to divert large forces of troops to mount guard on every airfield and supply dump in the battle area. The S.A.S. were annoying, and Rommel expressed his annoyance with vigour, then forgot about the manhunt, leaving it to his colonels to watch over that part of their affairs.

It was to a Colonel Stedmann, then, that reports began to flow, and for a time his general was untroubled by the results of the S.A.S. foray. Then pieces began to fit together, and all at once the colonel knew he had no alternative but to put the matter to Field-Marshal Rommel. Suddenly a very serious aspect had revealed itself. . . .

It began with a flow of reports about the dawn search for the ruffianly S.A.S. All were negative until an aircraft pilot reported sight of the S.A.S. and said he was going in to strafe them. Minutes later another radio message reported that the S.A.S. had surrendered and were waving white flags.

Half an hour later came the first shock. The 'S.A.S.' turned out to be a German reconstruction party returning to base with some booty. One man had been killed by their own air-gunners, and two others wounded, one critically. The search for the S.A.S. was immediately resumed.

Next report was from a pilot with the flat accent of Bavaria, quite sure he had spotted twin trails heading west which were those of the night raiders. The hunt was concentrated on that part of The Graveyard to which the tracks appeared to lead.

A long silence now. Then, nearly two hours later, another signal. Evidence had been found of the S.A.S.'s murderous activities. Two recently killed German non-coms had been found in a wrecked half-track. . . .

About this time a member of his staff, a major, came up with a thought. 'Herr Colonel, didn't those Italian scientists go out to examine a wrecked tank yesterday? And shouldn't they be with this party we unfortunately . . . peppered?'

'Yes.' The *Oberstleutnant* swung round in his chair, not knowing where the questions were leading.

'Then what's happened to them?' demanded the major keenly. 'No report has spoken about them.'

'Better find out,' said the colonel abruptly, and returned to his work. So the major sent out a series of radio signals, and the result was startling to them.

His first signal, to the *leutnant* in charge of the working party, elicited a brief response. The two Italian scientists had gone ahead the night before in the cool of the late afternoon. He had sent them off in a half-track which they had managed to salvage, in company with two German N.C.O.s. He had remained with his reconstruction party, anxious to put into working order two excellent British towing vehicles, invaluable to the Afrika Korps in view of their shortage of transport, and the Italians had been equally anxious to get out of the desert. They had taken away with them some valuable electronic equipment, the report ended.

The major carefully read the report, and something clicked in his brain. A half-track and two German N.C.O.s. A second signal to the *leutnant* asked for the names of the N.C.O.s. They came. They were the same as those reported killed inside a half-track by the S.A.S. But the Italian search party had made no report of finding, dead or alive, two compatriots, the scientists.

A quick signal to the Italian search commander produced a negative report. No, there were only the two dead Germans. No, there had been no signs of two civilians.

The major assembled his information and then precisely detailed the situation to the colonel. 'And what do you think happened to the Italians?' The colonel was already rising, knowing he must report the matter to his general.

'I think the S.A.S. took them prisoner and are trying to get them back to their lines.' He was a very shrewd major.

Field-Marshal Rommel agreed with the analysis. He also said that the S.A.S. must not be allowed to get away with their captives. 'Find them,' he snapped, and when he snapped, this general, so well liked by the opposing British because of his humane treatment of enemy wounded and prisoners, revealed the real ruthlessness in his character, that streak of self-interest which must be there if a man has to rise to the top in any efficient army.

'The hunt must not be called off until those commandos are found.' That meant the search parties would have to stay on in the desert, thought the colonel. They wouldn't like that. 'Those Italians must be rescued, and the search goes on until they are.'

He gave orders establishing priorities. It meant that more aircraft would be placed at Stedmann's disposal than had ever been used in a desert manhunt before, more men and vehicles would join the search, and he even offered his paratroopers, fresh from Crete, if required to cut off the absconding S.A.S.

Those Italian scientists were too important to be allowed to fall into enemy hands. The balance of war can be swayed by invention at a critical moment. The moment was critical. The Allies were experimenting with rockets, crude things but getting more deadly with this radio-controlled device. Those Italians experts might have knowledge which could make the Allied rocket-missiles less crude. Rommel had no illusions about prisoners not talking in time of war. Every army knew how to make men talk, and these were civilians and Italians, probably as reluctant as most of their country-men to be engaged in dictators' wars. They'd talk. Well, they must be brought back, out of enemy hands. Or silenced.

Anyway, thought the field-marshal, put out by the troublesome S.A.S., it was time the marauders were given such a lesson that they would drop this idea of sneaking in the back way to fire his planes. Yes, this time the S.A.S. must not be allowed to get away. At all costs, Field-Marshal Rommel told his colonel, the S.A.S. must be captured or destroyed, and the way he said it, his colonel knew that *his* head was on the block if the S.A.S. made good their escape.

He went back to his office and gave out a string of instructions. The radio crackled and his signals ordered all search parties in the field to stay there until they had found the desert raiders.

Unaware of the attention brought upon them, particularly by their capture of the Italian scientists, Captain Yeats-Urley quite happily set off that evening for the wrecked half-track out in the desert.

He took only a small party with him, a good officer not wishing to put unnecessary numbers to additional desert rigours. His driver, Snowy Medman, went, of course. And of course big Maurice Hill went with him. Maurice always went with his captain; it would have been unthinkable for him not to have accompanied Yeats-Urley on even a minor expedition – that was the relationship between the massive publican's son and the slim officer from Sandhurst.

Corporal M'Bain went with them, too. He didn't want to go; he wanted to get out of this blasted desert with its dangers as quickly as possible. But Captain Yeats-Urley looked kindly at him and said, 'You come, too, M'Bain,' as if the choice bestowed some sort of accolade upon the lance-jack. M'Bain had proved he was a man who could rise to the occasion, and that was the kind of man Yeats-Urley chose to have around him when he went off with a small and select party. Just four men, then, quite enough to skip back to the half-track before rejoining Fairlop at the L.R.D.G. rendezvous.

They took some risks, creeping out of their fox-holes a

couple of hours before sunset, and quietly getting to work on their vehicles. In quick time they were ready to move out, but it was still too early, twice searching-aircraft being spotted so that they had to go to ground again. Then they had a brew-up and some tasty mush made of corned beef and soaked biscuit. There was a lot of satisfied belching, and then, half an hour before dark, Yeats-Urley told his lieutenant to get on his way. The 3-tonner went lurching off, overflowing with men and supplies. Then Yeats-Urley climbed into his cab and his truck set off back the way they had come.

Within an hour, while there was still a suspicion of light from the western horizon, they saw the dim outline of the abandoned half-track standing alone in the desert. It looked, as someone had remarked earlier, in very good nick, and they found themselves approaching it cautiously, weapons in hand, but of course it was not occupied when they got to it.

Yeats-Urley went inside, using his torch. His search was of short duration. There were two ammo boxes on the floor of the half-track, and it needed no expert to recognise that the contents were electronic, and there was a couple of shells among them. Yeats-Urley did explore around for a moment, to make absolutely sure. Obviously he was looking at some electronic wreckage, as if some radio set had been severely mangled. That would be the radio control, he thought, the important part of the invention. The Italians must have had a job, though, sorting this out into something comprehensible, but by their notebooks they had made something of it. Well, neither Italians nor Germans were going to get their hands on this valuable equipment, battered though it was, again.

He clambered out, and started to instruct Hill and M'Bain to haul the ammo boxes out of the half-track, but then lapsed into shocked silence. His men, gloomy spectres in the darkness, were standing away from the vehicle, backs to him, looking away across the desert in the direction from which they had just come.

Captain Yeats-Urley swung round to follow their gaze.

Far distant he saw white light, flares hanging over the desert. 'What's that mean?' was his instant, apprehensive thought. Fairlop and party must be in that area by now. Had they run into trouble?

M'Bain spoke out of the darkness. 'Something's going on, sir.'

'Something is,' agreed his captain grimly.

'We think we heard sounds of gunfire,' M'Bain added.

Gunfire. Then there was trouble. It could hardly be the L.R.D.G. – the rendezvous was much farther west than The Graveyard. Therefore it was certain now that Fairlop had copped a packet.

'Let's get cracking,' the patrol officer said briskly. No need to let anyone do any unnecessary thinking and get morbid about what might be happening out there. 'Two ammo boxes inside. I want them. *Jildi!*'

Hill and M'Bain clambered on to the half-track. There was a lot of grunting because the boxes were awkward to get out of the turret, but finally they were dragged out and heaved on to the 3-tonner. They all resumed their positions; Snowy started up and off they went, turning back towards The Graveyard and the distant flares, though the fireworks were soon over and the desert became dark again.

They travelled cautiously, nerves keyed to the highest pitch, eyes straining for first sight of hostile presence, hands gripping weapons in the lurching vehicle. No one spoke, and the sound of the engine, even driven with tender care by Snowy, appeared to make an appalling noise in the night's silence, something to betray them for miles.

Beside the driver, Captain Yeats-Urley was saying, 'They shouldn't be there.' The game wasn't being conducted according to the old rules. In the S.A.S. you reckoned that if you survived the first day's search, you were fairly safe thereafter from enemy land forces. Not quite cricket, the captain decided, and was concerned about the safety of Fairlop.

They drove by circuitous course to the L.R.D.G. rendezvous, making a wide detour round the area that told of trouble. All the time tney expected trouble to fall upon them, too, but nothing happened and hour after hour went by with no sign of hostilities.

Eventually they came to the big escarpment where they were to meet their desert guides. It was a struggle getting to the top, the sand soft and giving no purchase to their tyres, so that several times all had to get their shoulders to the straining vehicle and shove it out of drifts, Yeats-Urley pushing as hard as his two comrades. Then easy going over the escarpment, two steady hours leaving the enemy far behind and daylight hinting in the east, and a feeling of peace and safety descending on them. The one worrying thing was; had Fairlop survived? Or any others of his party? And their radio set?

Finally they came to the far edge of the escarpment and halted, waiting there for the good light of day to show them their way down. When there was enough light to see, the truck shoved its nose into a steep descending gully and with much noise from the engine in low gear they lurched and slithered their way to the bottom. Once on the flatland again they were no more than half an hour in finding the wadi that was their rendezvous.

They came to it, tyre marks from recent days telling them that this was the place and no mistake – tyre marks from this vehicle, among others, which had impressed into the sand on their way north to raid El Badim. They turned into the steep-sided rocky chasm that wound back into the escarpment, alert for danger, as always . . . and found the wadi deserted.

They came to a halt, and a wave of disappointment swept over them. The L.R.D.G. should have been here, laconic navigators of the vast wastelands, ready to lead the raiders far across the desert to Kufra Oasis and safety. But they weren't here.

Yeats-Urley didn't waste time in worrying about the L.R.D.G. They were well able to take care of themselves, and their failure to be here on time had little significance. At the parting, five days ago, when the three truck loads of S.A.S. had turned north towards El Badim, the L.R.D.G.

had raced off to relieve their road-watchers east of Tobruk – impudent men who lay day after day in the scrub, glasses fixed on the one road that led to Alamein and a forthcoming battle, faithfully radioing exact information about enemy troop movements. An awful, soul-destroying job, Yeats-Urley had thought when they left the L.R.D.G., but one of tremendous value to the Allies' cause. The Allies had their eyes right behind the Axis lines, and the enemy never even suspected it. Good old L.R.D.G.

Anything could have happened to delay them, and Lieutenant Jamie Patterson, L.R.D.G., patrol commander, had warned them not to panic if they weren't there on time. If there was a lot of enemy activity in the vicinity, for instance, they would have to go to ground and not move until the danger had receded. Well, there had been a lot of recent enemy activity, Yeats-Urley knew, so he would forget the L.R.D.G. for the moment.

The worrying thing was that Fairlop and his party weren't there, either.

Fairlop had a good two hours start of them. By rights he should have been here with a brew-up waiting for them. So he *had* run into trouble. That *was* Fairlop catching it in the neck in the night on The Graveyard. But how much trouble? All killed? Or in the bag?

They clambered down from the over-heated vehicle, stiff and tired from the long ride amid the dunnage that filled the back of the truck. The weariness was upon all of them, that awful draining tiredness that comes when the elation of success no longer sustains; when the ashes of pessimism rise and fill the soul and make men question whether any of it was worthwhile. Gone was the exhilaration that accompanied their swift and deadly raid upon the enemy, the fierce thrill as millions of pounds worth of aircraft were destroyed by their hands. Gone the glow that had held them in the later hours, and the keyed-up nervous tension that in some way maintained their morale all during those racking hours of pursuit and manhunt.

Now the strength seemed to run out through their feet

and their hands. They were tired, so terribly, terribly tired. They wanted to drop and sleep and not think about anything, certainly not give a thought to Fairlop and their other comrades.

Yeats-Urley felt as depressed and exhausted as his men, but he was a first-class officer. There was no sign of his dismay and apprehension when they were all down and grouped round the cab of their precious 3-tonner. He forced himself into briskness, his tone sharp and commanding. He knew how to keep men going when they no longer wanted to go.

'Well, it looks as if we've got the place to ourselves. Let's get the old tea can brewing and some breakfast. Then we'll get our heads down until someone turns up. Right? Go to it!'

And they went to it. The firecan in seconds flaming against a tall rock, precious water poured from a jerrican into the blackened butter tin that was their kettle and teapot. They had canned beans as a treat, along with the inevitable bully. Yeats-Urley almost ordered them to break into the American canned food they had knocked off on a night raid while down at Alex recently, but decided to hold it for a celebration meal when the others turned up. When. He was sure now few or none of the others would come out of that desert alive to join them.

Breakfast. Then kip. Glorious sleep. Tired minds and tired men stretching in the shadow of the wadi and instantly going off into exhausted slumber. Only one man stayed awake, on watch. That was their captain. He sat above them, no less tired than they, eyes always alert and watchful, taking the first watch because that was the hardest, giving his men the rest they needed. And sometimes his eyes strayed to the forms that twitched in sleep, and sometimes – from M'Bain – moaned as if things troubled him in dreams. And Yeats-Urley felt affection for the unshaven, sweat-smelly, muscular men who put their trust in him. Good chaps, he even managed to think, with a flicker of enthusiasm. Jolly good chaps.

He took two hours as his turn on watch, which was an

hour longer than he expected his men to do, then woke M'Bain and passed out himself. He did not twitch because he did not dream. Yeats-Urley was sure in his assured world, even when that world was a hostile desert.

M'Bain had been on watch for about half an hour, crouching against an overhang to keep as far in the shade as possible, when he heard sounds up the wadi. For one second he froze, heart beating madly. In that moment he again heard the sounds of someone approaching, someone who appeared to be coming stealthily but kept slipping on the rocky wadi floor.

M'Bain rolled out into the sunshine like mad, then came on to his feet, rifle ready with one up the spout. He shot down the slope to where his comrades slept, shook each in turn, and they were awake instantly, even Captain Yeats-Urley, who had had so little sleep. They came up off the ground, hands on weapons, and M'Bain was signalling frantically for silence, then pointing up the wadi. They all grouped around the truck and waited.

Another sound, much louder to M'Bain now. It sounded, after all, like one person approaching. And walking.

A moment later a man came into view. It was Lieutenant Fairlop.

They lowered their weapons and moved out to greet him. He looked exhausted, and there was a lot of dried blood down one side of his shirt. He halted when he saw them, swaying a little, no sign of gladness on the hard face at sight of his comrades. He had a rifle in one hand and a haversack and water-bottle on his back.

'Where's the rest? What's happened to your men?' Yeats-Urley's first words to his lieutenant.

The bigger officer just spread his arms a little, then shrugged. Their hearts dropped with dismay at the gesture. Did this mean *all* their comrades had gone under?

Fairlop simply walked past them, climbed into the shadowed cab of their last remaining truck, and began to drink from his bottle. They waited patiently until he had drunk. He was very, very tired, and when he spoke his story came out slowly.

When they parted, just on dusk, at first the going was good for Lieutenant Fairlop and party. He was in front alongside Sergeant Vickers, who drove in place of the injured Driver Vecchi. Vecchi was in the back sitting with their two Italian prisoners, talking to them whenever he could to practise his Italian, and seeming to get on well with them. He was not a happy man, though, because his ribs gave him pain, and there was no comfort perched upon the piles of kit and supplies in the back of the truck. Besides, it was uncomfortably crowded, the Vickers on its mounting occupying valuable space, and thirteen men having to find room around it. The other men didn't worry over the discomfort, of course, but then they didn't have cracked ribs, as Vecchi more than once plaintively remarked.

After dark set in, their pace slowed but they kept going by compass and continued to make good ground. There was no moon, yet a dim sort of light that covered even a moonless desert, perhaps from the myriad stars that spangled the cloudless night sky, helped them on their way.

It was eerie going, though, for after all they were traversing The Graveyard. Time after time shapes loomed up, sometimes right in their path so that they had to be quick to avoid them. Disabled field guns, burnt-out trucks, wrecked tanks, armoured cars, Bren carriers – all were there. The thing was, in that light they didn't look wrecks but the real thing, and it seemed as if they were travelling through the lines of a sleeping army, and any moment they expected to run into men, enemy soldiers who would open fire upon them.

Which is exactly what happened. They found themselves travelling amid vehicles which seemed more thickly clustered together. It took Fairlop, in front, a few seconds to grasp the situation. Then he realised these were no wrecks; these were armoured cars and trucks leagured up for the night. They had run slap-bang into the camp of a sleeping force – enemy he was sure, so far from the British lines – probably the night camp of their Italian searchers.

All those thoughts raced through Fairlop's mind, immediately he sensed that these were no wrecks – too close together. too many of them in a group, some even drawn neatly into line. Before alarm completely gripped him he had time to think, 'No sentry? Sleeping on duty?' Thinking they were safe here in the vast desert. Couldn't be Germans.

And then a sentry proved he *was* alert, for quite close to them a cry rang out. They saw a man moving towards them, something glistening in his hands.

Fairlop reacted instantly. 'Step on it!' he shouted, and Vickers' foot went down on the pedal instantly. The Chev roared and got into lurching speed. The men behind were startled, and he heard their oaths and cries. He also thought he heard shouted Italian, as if one of their prisoners had called out to the sentry.

Then the sentry was level with the cab and only yards away. He fired, and Fairlop felt blood smack into his face. Not his blood. Vickers had stopped the bullet in his head. He felt Vickers fall against him, warm wet liquid soaking through Fairlop's shirt, a crumpling figure that told of death. The engine revs died as a dead man's foot fell off the accelerator, and the truck began to weave with no one to control the wheel, narrowly missing some massive vehicle, probably an armoured troop-carrier.

Fairlop acted promptly. He leaned across the sprawling Vickers, pulled the catch and swung open the driver's door. Then he tumbled the dead sergeant out, and hauled himself behind the wheel. The truck steadied under his touch; the engine roared again as he stamped hard on the accelerator. He risked switching on the headlights – anything to help them get out of the enemy midst quickly, and they couldn't afford to run into anything. He drove as fast as possible, the men behind having a hell of a time of it amid the bouncing equipment as the truck lurched and bumped at crazy speed, the driver's door banging, refusing to fasten itself and the lieutenant needing both hands for the wheel and unable to fasten it.

They got through the enemy lines, but Fairlop knew men

were roused and up on their feet. Flames spotted the darkness. White lights streaked past his cab at tremendous pace. Tracer.. Someone had opened up with a machine-gun. His men were firing back.

Fairlop heard cries from the men behind. Afterwards he learned that Italians with rifles had also opened up, and a regular fusilade of bullets buzzed around the S.A.S. in the back. Almost immediately Sergeant Trefoil stopped one – this night was being particularly rough on N.C.O.s – it got him in the throat and he tried to get to his feet, struggling for air, but was thrown overboard by the bouncing of the vehicle before anyone could get a hand to him. Then Stepney Leftridge was hit and badly hurt, and moaned for a time but quickly died. Miraculously, no one else was even hit – just two bullets out of all that barrage hit two men, but they killed them both.

They drove out of range of the Italian camp, their pace never slackening. After a time Eddie Fullalove got his head round the cab door. He seemed surprised when he saw his officer driving. He shouted that an armoured car was pursuing them; what's more it was keeping up with them.

So began a deadly chase through the night. Those Italians were relentless pursuers, apparently without any thought of giving up the chase. However hard Fairlop drove, he could not shake them off. Twice when they lost speed due to particularly rough ground, the armoured car came within range and opened fire on them. But the armoured vehicle was bumping too much, too, and the tracer sped away to their right and above them. When he could, Fullalove belted back at them with the Vickers.

When Fairlop realised he could not elude his pursuer, he resorted to cunning. He switched off his headlights, so that they were more difficult to see from behind, and immediately pulled at right angles to his course and tried to give them the slip. But the Italian commander was a cunning man, too.

He too doused his lights. Perhaps he suspected a trap, that the S.A.S. had halted in the dark and were lying in ambush for him, and he had no wish to find grenades being suddenly lobbed at him out of the night. He switched off his engine and listened, and of course in the quiet of the vast desert the Chev 3-tonner was kicking up an appalling row, and the Italian car commander had no difficulty in tracking its new course.

For the next few hours they indulged in a hair-raising cat-and-mouse game. From that time on, neither vehicle used lights. Fairlop did everything he knew to lose his pursuer, but the one thing he could not do was to get away without making engine noise. Whichever way he twisted and turned, his enemy could follow him by simply switching off his own engine and listening for the roar of the 3-tonner.

Fairlop himself tried switching off and sitting quietly, hoping the enemy would blunder away and leave them alone, but the Italian also very smartly switched off and sat there waiting, ready to move when Fairlop gave away his position by starting up.

The lieutenant *had* to keep moving. The moon was rising now, and once it was well up it was no use sitting in a stationary vehicle, for the superior-armed Italian car would nose them out and soon shoot the daylights out of them.

The odds were all on the side of the Italians. They had a vehicle as fast as their own, but *they* sat behind one-inch armour plate, whereas the Chev had none. The armoured car would have twin machine-guns mounted in its turret, giving greater firepower than their one heavy Vickers. No, the S.A.S. had to give the Eyties the slip if they were to survive. Just let the Italians come within effective range and their number was up, and this and other similar sentiments were whispered by the men in the back, during their times of halting, eyes and senses alert for sign of the enemy riding in from the darkness.

When moonlight came, Fairlop finally abandoned silence as a tactic and again concentrated on driving hard and trying to lose his pursuer. He never succeeded. In fact the Italian seemed to be creeping closer to them, and constantly now ripped off a few experimental shots to see if they could halt the clumsy lorry. Luck held for the S.A.S., for a while, at least.

It ran out for them when they reached the foot of the escarpment. This meant a long haul up a sloping bank, and as always there was soft sand in the way. To their horror, quite soon they got into a wheel-spin, and for one wild moment they thought the Chev was going to stop. Then Fairlop eased off the accelerator and slowed the flying wheels and then they gripped and the Chev continued to climb.

But a second time the sand was too soft, and they did stop, and immediately men hurled themselves over the side to lift their vehicle out. Even Private Vecchi of the sore ribs would have crawled down to do his bit, but Eddie Fullalove shoved him back and snapped, 'Man that gun!' A man with cracked ribs wasn't much good shoving at a stuck truck, but he could provide cover with the machine-gun. Presumably, too, he could keep watch over the Italian prisoners, but that didn't seem necessary. They just lay huddled there, making no move under any circumstances.

They got the truck moving within minutes, scrabbling frantically at the sand, now curiously cold to the touch, two sand tracks shoved under the rear wheels, then everyone pushing, the sweat pouring again after the cool night ride. And they moved and got away, every man running and catching the tailboard and hauling himself back on to their uncomfortable perches before the Italians came close enough to realise their enemy had been sand-stuck.

They almost reached the top of the escarpment, in the open now and in the moonlight in full view of their pursuer – and they too could see the armoured car, could see it too plainly – when they got into another wheel-spin. Frantically they went overboard again. Frantically they strove to get the Chev moving. But all knew this time they were going to lose the race. The armoured car was coming up too fast. If it just bothered to halt and open steady fire they were dead ducks.

Yet they got the Chev inching through the sand, and then gripping firmer ground and getting into speed again. At which moment the Italian opened vicious fire upon them.

Fairlop said, 'I saw the tracer and heard screams. The men didn't stand much chance.'

7

But he thought they scattered, the instinct of their training not to be caught grouped; and he was sure some of them opened fire in return, though it wouldn't do much damage to the armoured vehicle.

'I drove on. I kept driving because I couldn't stop – there was wheel slip all the time.' His audience nodded. They understood. You can't stop if there's soft sand under your tyres. 'We pulled on top of the escarpment, and by now *we* were the target.' The machine-guns were concentrating on the truck, raking it with fire. 'They got us, too. Must have hit the petrol tank,' said Fairlop tiredly. 'All at once we stopped, fuel run out.'

Yeats-Urley said sharply, 'There were just the four of you? Fairlop, Vecchi and the two Italian prisoners. You mean not one of the men was able to climb back aboard?' He was appalled. So were the others, listening. Fairlop nodded. 'I don't think they even tried to. I think when they came under fire they just scattered and after that they couldn't have caught up with us.'

'No.' Yeats-Urley nodded. It was tragic, but he knew how it must have happened. All gone. 'What did you do, then?' He was thinking of their precious radio set. Without it they were without communication with their own kind. They could not radio for help, and equally would not know what was happening to the war effort east of them. Had the big push from Alamein started, for instance? That could be important to them.

'I left Vecchi with the prisoners.'

'Left them?' Vecchi with his cracked ribs wouldn't be much good on his own with prisoners. 'Why didn't you bring Vecchi with you?' Hill, M'Bain and Medman were watching the lieutenant closely. Vecchi was a comrade. Men always wanted to know how a comrade was treated.

'Vecchi was in a bad way. His ribs had taken a hammering during the night.' Vecchi had got down when they halted, aided by the two Italians, but though he could walk a little he said it was no good, he'd never make it to the wadi.

'The armoured car was coming up the escarpment,'

Fairlop told them. 'I could hear it. There was some firing, too.' So not all his men had been killed, Yeats-Urley thought hopefully. Probably they were trying to hold back the armoured car so as to give the Chev chance to escape. Good chaps, he thought approvingly.

'It was no good standing there. It wasn't far from daylight, and once it was light that armoured car wouldn't have difficulty in picking us off.' No, that was true, they silently agreed. 'So I told Vecchi to get food and water, ditch the prisoners, and try to hide. With a bit of luck we might be able to pick him up when the hunt died down.'

'And you came on?' To the R.V. Leaving Vecchi alone to manage his own survival.

'I couldn't do anything, just hanging about. I thought it best to keep walking and report to you.'

Yeats-Urley said, graciously, 'You did right,' and yet he asked himself. 'Would I have done that in similar circumstances?' He thought no. His immediate thought was that he would have stayed with an injured comrade and helped him to hide, and even then remained with him to give him all aid and protection possible. That's what he thought he would have done. But would he, if he'd really been faced with having to make the decision, and little time to make it, too? He wasn't sure. On paper, anyway, Fairlop had done the right thing. At least they knew now what had happened to the truck and his men – and where their radio was.

Yeats-Urley said, 'We must try to help Vecchi.' They couldn't go on without attempting to rescue the poor chap. They must also try to recover their radio. He said so.

Fairlop drank again, the sweat rolling from under his chin and down the cleft of his dirty, blood-caked shirt. He shook his head. 'No good, Alan, They'll be up the escarpment by now, and they'll have the truck. They'll have Vecchi, too. Because those damn prisoners would be able to tell the Eyties where he was hiding.'

It sounded hopeless. Yet Yeats-Urley thought, all the same, he would go back and see. Must satisfy himself they weren't leaving Vecchi alone in the desert. And the armoured car mightn't have climbed to the top of the escarpment. Armoured cars had more weight than Chevs and were notoriously difficult in soft sand. It was possible it had never made the climb. Besides, by the sound of it some of his men had survived, and if they kept up their fire it meant that no Italian would be able to get out from behind the protective armour to shove sand-tracks under the wheels.

They went and sat on the shady side of the truck, Yeats-Urley thinking things out and building up hopes. Then everyone except M'Bain, who had already resumed his post on the hill, just fell asleep without realising they were going off.

Yeats-Urley hadn't intended to drop off. He had to work out plans for their survival, and he must include in them some search for Vecchi and any other survivors of his patrol. It was also imperative that he should try to get hold of the radio, if it wasn't in enemy hands. He fell asleep because the heat was too great, even in the shadow of their truck, and because he was exhausted from a wakefulness that had lasted most of thirty-six hours.

He woke to painful discomfort. The world had moved round and now he was almost completely exposed to rays that came from a midday sun. He came to slowly, racked with thirst, his mouth and throat so dry he could hear the rasp as his tongue moved in search of moisture, his nose bunged with desert dust so that he was having to breathe through his mouth. The skin on his exposed face and limbs burned with pain, and seemed to have shrunk upon him, tight and dry, while the hair on his arms and head seemed to be curling under the dehydrating heat.

He dragged himself to his feet, his head swimming as it always did when waking in the heat of the day. He leaned into the driver's cab and got his water-bottle. Fairlop was there, stretched out and fast asleep. A drink – not too much; water was precious – revived him. The world stopped swimming round, and he found he could focus again. Memory returned and he knew now what he had to do and what he should have done before sleeping. He snapped into action.

Medman was crouched up there on a slight rise, a shadow

from a rock overhang keeping him from frizzling like bacon. So Yeats-Urley had slept at least an hour, the watch changing, M'Bain going off to sleep and Medman taking over. Slowly he climbed the bare slope to join Medman, who greeted him without enthusiasm. Medman never thought he should do anything except drive, and didn't take kindly to sentry-go, certainly not in this awful heat.

'Seen anything?'

Medman shook his head. M'Bain had told him there'd been some aerial activity during his watch. A couple of planes had been very interested in something far across the escarpment, and M'Bain had said they'd dived a few times, as if bombing, and he'd seen some smoke rise one time.

Their second truck, the captain thought tiredly. It had been spotted and destroyed. No hope for their radio now.

The planes had then quartered the area systematically, searching for S.A.S. on foot, no doubt, but by good luck their search had gradually taken them farther east across the escarpment, so that at no time had the men been in danger. Medman himself had seen distant aircraft a few times, but they were distant, systematically searching the desert for their position. He had seen no human activity, however, not on the ground. No sign of any survivors from Fairlop's truck, Yeats-Urley thought, but did not allow the information to depress him.

He decided to go back to his men and waken them – they'd all had more sleep than he, except Fairlop, so they should be able to move now and start a search across the escarpment. They came reluctantly out of sleep at his sharp call, and began the usual task of brewing up. Some canned beans and meat were opened, but while everyone drank as much as was put before them, the heat was too great and only Maurice Hill ate of the food.

It was while Yeats-Urley was telling them their programme – 'We've got to go back and see if any of our chaps are still out of enemy hands.' They might be lying up, even wounded, and certainly there was a possibility that the injured Vecchi might be in the vicinity. 'And if we find things get too hot for us here, we may have to move out after dark.' There was a second rendezvous with the L.R.D.G. in case of emergency, another wadi hide-out forty miles south of them, and deeper into the Sahara Desert, it was while they were drinking the last drops of tea that Medman called from above.

'Can you bring your glasses, sir.'

Medman had spotted movement far across the escarpment. Every man grabbed his weapon and went racing up the slope. Medman pointed. 'I think I saw something, sir. A long way off.' But he wasn't sure. In that heat, with vision at ground level distorted by rising air currents, no one could be certain of what they thought they saw. Yet as they looked someone else called out that he could see movement, men out there across the arid, scrub-covered escarpment.

Captain Yeats-Urley turned his glasses on the spot. For a moment the distortion settled and he saw men – three of them, then the picture jazzed and broke up and wouldn't resolve again for some time. They were three or four miles away.

Yeats-Urley rose. 'I think our old friend Vecchi's trying to find the wadi,' he said. He couldn't be sure, but it did look a bit like him, he and the Italian scientists. Poor bastards, he thought, it must be a nightmare for the civilians, unaccustomed to the terrible desert conditions. He wondered why two able-bodied men didn't turn the tables on their injured captor and walk the other way, back to the searching Italians.

He made a decision. They couldn't use the truck – too dangerous to bring it into the open, away from the cover of the deep wadi– so someone would have to walk out and help Vecchi in with his prisoners. He would go and take two men, leaving the rest to guard their precious vehicle.

'Hill . . . M'Bain.' They would go with him.

They set off. It was the wrong time of the day for moving about the desert, but it was all part of being in the S.A.S., and after a moan from big Maurice, silently shared by M'Bain, they went clambering out of the wadi and away towards the distant figures.

It took them over an hour of very hard walking to reach them, and long before they came together, Yeats-Urley's glasses assured him they were Vecchi and the Italians. What shook him was to see that both Italians supported Vecchi as he walked and one of them was carrying a rifle. So they approached the trio with some caution, their own weapons ready, just in case the Italian opened fire on them.

It wasn't necessary. The Italians had had enough of the desert. They were in desperate condition. But Vecchi was much worse off. Without their aid he could no longer stand. When they saw the approaching patrol captain and his companions, the trio stopped trying to walk and collapsed slowly to the ground.

'You poor old bastards,' said Private Hill, when they came and stood over the almost unconscious trio, but his tone was kind. They each supported a man and poured water into him, and once again Yeats-Urley was astonished at the way dehydrated men recovered when life-giving water was poured into their mouths. They did not linger – about ten minutes rest, Yeats-Urley gave them; he didn't want to be caught so far from their truck by any roving enemy patrol, or spotted by the aircraft he could faintly hear now, droning to the north of them. In that time Vecchi gave some explanation of recent events, but he was so tired it was difficult to keep him coherent. They'd started off with water, but it had all gone hours ago. It had been terrible, terrible.

'What happened to you after Lieutenant Fairlop left you?' Yeats-Urley had to repeat the question several times before he could get Vecchi to answer.

'We just stood around for a time, wondering what to do. I told the Eyties they could go back to try to join their oppos –' Oh, you did, did you? thought Yeats-Urley. They were valuable prisoners, and Fairlop had ordered Vecchi to keep guard over them.

Vecchi, even in his tiredness, seemed to divine what went through his captain's mind. 'But they wouldn't go. They wouldn't leave me alone. Bloody good blokes, these two.' Yeats-Urley was sure there was affection in Private Vecchi's tired voice. 'Anyway, they were afraid they might run into some of our mob, and they were pretty sure they would be shot if they did.' You're dead right, thought Hill, listening. I'd have shot 'em if I'd seen 'em. Couldn't have enemy – even enemy civilians – walking about the desert at such times.

Vecchi said they'd heard sounds of firing beyond the escarpment. It was distant – probably three or four miles – but they could hear it, and it went on almost until dawn. 'Some of our lads, pinnin' down that armoured car, so that it couldn't climb the escarpment.' Vecchi's interpretation paralleled his own, Yeats-Urley noticed.

But by this time, he and the Italians were on the move. Vecchi found it was as painful to sit or stand around as it was to walk, so he had decided he might as well start off for the wadi hide-out and his chums as stay by the useless truck. He knew, anyway, that to linger beside the vehicle was dangerous, for with daylight the planes would find it and bomb it to bits.

He had put the proposition fairly to the Italians. They could come with him to the wadi – there would be food and drink for them there, and some sort of safety from the desert. Or they could try to make their way back to find their own patrols.

Both Italians conferred, then said they would keep with Vecchi. Perhaps they thought there was some safety in a British soldier's presence, with so many ruffianly S.A.S. clearly active between them and their own patrols. They had set out to walk, Vecchi confident he could find the wadi. Their troubles and sufferings had really begun with daylight. After a time Vecchi could hardly keep going, and then the Italians had taken hold of him and helped him along. 'Good blokes,' Vecchi kept saying. 'Could have cut my throat or just walked away an' left me, but they didn't. Looked after me like a brother. Good blokes. . . . We must look after them now.' Some thought made him struggle up in the arms of Yeats-Urley, his eyes widening as if in suspicion of his captain's intentions towards the prisoners.

Yeats-Urley said, 'All right, all right, Vecchi. The way they looked after you will be remembered. They won't be harmed, either.'

He rose. His eyes went round the horizon. They fastened on a distant speck. That blasted plane was doing another search across the desert. Soon, inevitably, one would begin to comb this part of the escarpment. They must be under cover when that happened. 'Let's go,' he ordered. 'Come on, old chap. On your feet.'

They helped them to their feet, then each supporting a man they began the laborious walk back to the wadi. After a time, Piero Lazzi, the younger Italian, seemed to recover and said he didn't need M'Bain's supporting arm, and he walked on carrying Vecchi's rifle and no one was bothered by it. Vecchi, suffering from his cracked ribs, gradually grew weaker, however, and the last mile or so ended with him being carried cradled in the arms of M'Bain and Hill.

At last they brought them down the slope to where their truck stood in the hot sunshine. Medman was still at his post. Fairlop had got the tea can on the boil, ready for when they returned. Exhausted, they came into the wadi, and dropped their burden in the lengthening shadow of a rock face. Then they lay panting, relaxing, grateful for the shade and for the fact that no further physical exertion was required of them.

Fairlop came over with battered enamel mugs, brimming with steaming tea. One each to the Italians, a mug for Vecchi. The others could wait a minute or so.

Vecchi opened his eyes reluctantly when he felt the hot mug pushed against his hand. Opened and slowly focused, and Lieutenant Fairlop was in his field of vision. Some were watching him, and saw a curious reaction. He seemed to struggle into a half-sitting posture, though the pain of his ribs made him moan, and he looked at the lieutenant and they heard him say, accusingly, 'You wouldn't stop. You drove on. You left the poor bastards.'

There was a moment of shocked silence – a moment when

they found it hard to believe that an ordinary private was accusing an officer of deserting his men under fire. Captain Yeats-Urley heard the words and was too startled to say anything for a second. He glanced at Lieutenant Fairlop. Fairlop was standing there, still holding Vecchi's mug of tea in his hand. He looked startled, too, but Yeats-Urley noticed that he didn't look upset or angered as most men would have been in the circumstances. Just . . . what was it? – wary. He seemed to be looking at Vecchi as if calculatingly. But then that was typically Fairlop; always he seemed to be considering how things affected him personally, rarely reacting openly to situations as most men did.

Vecchi said again, that accusation in his voice, 'You scarpered. You didn't give 'em a chance.'

Yeats-Urley snapped out of his astonishment. 'Cut that out, Vecchi. None of that talk or you'll be in trouble.' Must maintain discipline. Couldn't have privates shouting their heads off like that against officers. If it were true? For the moment Yeats-Urley shrugged away the possibility. The thing was, officers must always stand together, that was the Army code.

Vecchi rambled on, a weak and exhausted man, but anger kept him talking, dangerous to himself. 'You could have waited, top of the escarpment. Some would have made it –'

Yeats-Urley had had enough. 'One more word, Vecchi, and you'll be on a charge.'

Even then Vecchi seemed inclined to open his mouth, but Maurice Hill shut him up. Maurice, only a private himself, could do that. 'Don't be a bloody fool, Vecchi. Get your head down and sleep on it.' Sound advice, and the big private seemed to interpose his bulk between officers and driver, and the knot broke up and Vecchi seemed to collapse and go to sleep immediately, anyway.

But later – just about the time they had another visitor – Hill came to where Vecchi lay, more hot tea in his hand for the injured driver, and said, 'Here's some char, mate. Get it down you.' He squatted beside the man, huge and bulking,

106

a wild figure with his long matted hair and several days' growth of fair beard on his massive chin. His manner was kind, but his tone was firm. 'And tell me what really happened back there.' His head jerked towards the escarpment where their second truck might still be.

Hill wanted to know. He would never have doubted Captain Yeats-Urley's conduct, and it wasn't so much loyalty as certain knowledge that this patrol commander could never let his men down. But Fairlop. Something about Fairlop never quite gelled with the men, He seemed admirable in every way as a commando-type, as hard as they came, unflinching under fire. But there was something about the fellow that made men somehow wary of him. He never seemed quite to relax with them; there was always something withdrawn about him, as if his thoughts were private, to be kept close to himself. Yeats-Urley himself always felt that in the end the man had no thoughts really for anyone but himself, but he never said as much to anyone; he just wondered how the sagacious Major Stirling had come to select him for S.A.S. work when there were so many damned good chaps about, men from his own school, for instance.

Vecchi wanted to get it off his chest and he talked. He'd been badly knocked up by the rough ride in the night, and he was in acute discomfort, and big Maurice thought there was a touch of delirium about him. Certainly his tale rambled, but over all it made sense.

He told how the men had been working frantically to get the Chev into movement again, he sitting in the truck, the Vickers trained back down the slope. In the moonlight he saw the Italian armoured car. It wasn't as much as a hundred yards away, coming rather cautiously across the wasteland. It had paused – they had been seen, struggling up the escarpment in the moonlight. Then the car had opened fire, and now Hill learned that Vecchi had opened fire with the Vickers, too.

Vecchi was troubled by memory of that moment. 'They couldn't miss at that range, Maurice. Christ knows why they weren't all wiped out at once.' But in war that was always the miracle, how many survived the hazards of bullet and shells and bombs.

Some went down at once, some crying out as they were hit. Partridge was one of them, he thought, one of his particular oppos in the mob. The others scattered immediately, but the truck was gripping and beginning to move just at that precise moment.

'We went up the hill, getting a fair turn of speed on,' Vecchi said, and still remembered his surprise at the way all at once the truck got into motion. The armoured car didn't approach closer, but after searching with its machine-guns for the scattered S.A.S., it tried to rake the departing truck.

'We stopped a lot of lead,' Vecchi told his fellow private. 'But none of us got touched.' They were all lying down amid the baggage. 'But they must have holed the petrol tank.'

'What about the men?'

'They'd spread out and got under cover and a few of them began to fire back at the Eytie. That's why he didn't come on right away, I reckon.' Then the anger returned to him. 'When we were on top, out of sight of the Eytie, I expected Fairlop to stop. I reckoned our blokes would work their way up top and we'd be there to pick them up. But the bastard kept going. Never halted until we ran out of petrol.' And he used hard and bitter language about the officer.

'Fairlop says he kept going because the armoured car was after him.'

Vecchi exploded. 'The bloody car would never have made it up that hill. If a Chev gets stuck, what chance has five tons of armoured car?' Hill nodded. That thought had been in his mind. 'It didn't try to follow –'

'How do you know? You couldn't have seen.'

Vecchi shrugged, looking mutinous, not wanting to have his story destroyed by doubts. But he admitted he didn't know for certain. He'd heard the men firing, though, so some were still alive and Fairlop's first thought should have been for them. He rambled on.

Hill went away to talk to Medman. Snowy was notoriously

hard on officers who didn't come up to scratch like Yeats-Urley. Both agreed that Fairlop's conduct — at least according to Vecchi — had been curious. The one thing men cannot tolerate is an officer who runs off and leaves his O.R.s to fend for themselves. But had Fairlop run off? They only had Vecchi's version of events to go by, and Fairlop's original story had seemed reasonable at the time.

Yeats-Urley was troubled, too. He was a shrewd man, and what Vecchi had blurted out appeared to reveal inconsistencies in Fairlop's story. For instance, Fairlop had given the impression that almost immediately after gaining the top of the escarpment, the truck had petered out. But by Vecchi's account, they hadn't conked out immediately; he'd spoken of firing three or four miles behind them. That was rather a long way. You didn't go three or four miles in the night and expect hard-pressed comrades to find you. No, you stopped as near to them as was safe.

'How far do you think you were from the slope when you ran out of petrol?' Difficult raising with a fellow officer the niggling thought that his story had suddenly become a little unconvincing. But Yeats-Urley had to know the truth.

He didn't fool the big lieutenant. They were both drinking tea, Yeats-Urley sitting half out of the passenger seat of their Chev, Fairlop sitting with his back to the front wheel, the shade from the truck upon him. Yeats-Urley saw how the bigger man looked up at him over the top of his chipped enamel tea mug. And still there was no anger or resentment at such a question; only that wary look, though the face had hardened and was not inviting.

Fairlop shrugged. 'I don't know; it was dark.'

'How long in time?' Yeats-Urley persisted.

'God knows. Quite soon.'

Yeats-Urley, afraid of no man, said quite deliberately, 'Vecchi says you didn't stop until you had to, and that was three or four miles from the beginning of the escarpment.'

Fairlop said, coldly, 'Do you believe a driver?'

'No. Not necessarily. He's hurt and might be imagining things in his pain. But he spoke up before the men, and you know how men feel about each other. Protective, you know. If they thought an officer had left their comrades in the lurch –'

'I didn't. Fairlop got to his feet. 'Go back and see where the truck is. That'll answer your question.'

He walked away. It wasn't a thing a lieutenant should have done in the presence of his superior officer, but Yeats-Urley said nothing. Fairlop's reply seemed pretty convincing, the only snag was – they hadn't time to check even on such an important matter.

Anyway, Private Hoyle came walking down the wadi only minutes afterwards. He was nobody's favourite, but they were all glad to see him. He looked unusually dishevelled and filthy, but didn't seem too bad considering the exhausting time he must have had in the past twelve or fourteen hours.

All except the sentry crowded round him as he ate and drank, and sighed with satisfaction because he could lie in the shade on soft sand and relax. They wanted his story. The trouble with Oily was that he hadn't much sense of story-telling, and anyway didn't appear to feel he had anything to tell. Most of it came out, in fact, by questioning from the patrol commander.

'When you're ready, Hoyle, tell us what happened last night.'

Hoyle, wolfing beans from a can, some of the liquid immediately staining his scrub beard – a dirty feeder, thought Yeats-Urley, watching the performance; a dirty man, Hoyle – looked vaguely in surprise at the question.

'You mean when they opened up on us?' An uncouth voice. Only big tolerant Maurice Hill had any liking for the fellow, but then he got on with everyone. He shrugged. 'We scarpered.' Then he shoved more beans into his maw.

Yeats-Urley continued to be patient. 'Yes, you scarpered. That is, you dispersed and presumably took to cover. And then what?'

'We fired back at the bloody Eytie.'

Christ, he was heavy going, thought the captain. But a good soldier, as he'd just proved by surviving and finding his way to this wadi across the escarpment. They got little out of Hoyle. He had lost touch with his comrades. They'd put up a steady fire on the armoured car to deter it from trying to rush the hill, and Hoyle had gradually worked his way up the slope until he was on top of the escarpment. The firing had stopped by now. Hoyle did express one. original opinion, he thought that the armoured car had belted off with so much machine-gun ammunition that it had probably run out of it.

'You don't think it tried to climb the hill?' Yeats-Urley was getting on to delicate ground. Lieutenant Fairlop was standing there, listening.

Oily belched ungracefully and said he didn't know, but he didn't think so. In his own words he thought it had just fucked off at daylight. Later they learned that Oily had found the truck. Private Leftridge's body was in it. He'd got food and water and then set off to find the wadi. He was thick, old Oily, but things like finding his way across a desert escarpment appeared to come naturally to him.

Yeats-Urley waited until he could ask one certain question in privacy. The others finally drifted away, leaving captain and private alone. Yeats-Urley got in his question, though he tried to put it in such a way that it neither led Hoyle to an answer nor roused any suspicion in the big private's mind. If he had one.

'You said you got to the truck and picked up food and water?'

Oily sucked a bit of bean from between yellow, wolfish teeth. 'Yes, sir. There was plenty there.'

'Did you have to go far? I mean, to find the truck?'

Hoyle looked dumb, then shook his head. His answer was very vague. 'No, sir. It was just there.'

'Near the escarpment top?'

Again Hoyle looked vague, and answered accordingly. 'Well . . . yes. Not far.'

Yeats-Urley sighed and rose. It was some sort of answer, and in some way was satisfying. Plainly Hoyle didn't share Vecchi's opinion that they had been deserted. He certainly had showed no animosity towards the lieutenant. Yeats-Urley thought they would never know the truth. Well, he would just go on believing a brother officer; after all, Vecchi was only a private, he thought.

'Did you see the truck bombed?' Yeats-Urley was pretty sure that had happened.

Hoyle nodded. The planes had found the truck when he'd left it by about an hour. That was why he had taken so long to walking; he'd had to seek cover while they came buzzing around. 'They got it, all right.' Hoyle grinned, as if the destruction had given him a kick, even though it was their own truck going up in flames. 'Made quite a fire, sir.'

So all was gone.

'Did you see anything of the other chaps?'

And Oily surprised him. He thought he *had* seen movement far back on the truck when he'd left it. It was only instinct, but he felt pretty sure they were some of their own men.

'Why didn't you go back to them? Or wait?'

Oily said, because the bombers had got them. He was unmoved by the thought. The planes had come over just at the time when he had spotted the distant figures. They'd come in with guns blazing and bombs dropping, and they seemed to hit the truck right away. Perhaps the figures around the vehicle had attracted attention and invited attack: a deserted vehicle was usually left alone for their own recovery parties to bring in.

Oily had simply come straight on to the wadi when it was safe to move. Either he hadn't thought to return to see if they were his comrades and in need of help, or he genuinely thought they'd got a pasting and were past it. Yeats-Urley sighed and turned. A good soldier, Oily, but trying. Lieutenant Fairlop was watching him from beside the truck. The shadows were getting very long now. Soon it would be dark. And then what?

Yeats-Urley had to make decisions. Should they sneak out under cover of darkness and find the second rendezvous, or stay on, dangerous though this area was, in the hope that more men might struggle through?

Part of his dilemma was solved a little time later. Maurice Hill was on watch. He called that again there was movement far across the scrub. His voice was reassuring. Not enemy, he thought; more of their own men.

They came in, moving quite fast, as if with urgency, four of them. Frankie Mack, Tommy Shiner with the short powerful legs so that he almost looked a dwarf, Corporal Fullalove and Gunner Partridge. Vecchi was startled when he saw his old oppo, Partridge, walking with the party.

'Thought you'd got topped, you ol' bastard,' he said affectionately.

Partridge showed his arm laconically. It was broken and bloody and held in a crude sling. 'Got it in the fin, that's all,' he said, as if it didn't matter. In spite of his wound he had remained with his comrades while they held back the armoured car, and had kept up with them all the way across the desert. Fortunately they too had been able to get water and food from the truck before the aircraft found it and started to shoot them up – only just in time.

But Fullalove had disturbing tidings. When they had been given the inevitable tea, put on to brew the moment they were identified in the distance, Fullalove told his captain, 'Sir, we'd better get moving.'

'Oh? Why? They're after us?'

Fullalove nodded. They'd spotted dust trails far behind them at one time, telling of vehicles moving around the escarpment. Fullalove thought they'd been radioed up to examine the bombed truck. 'They'll be across here in no time,' he ended pessimistically, but didn't seem deterred by the thought.'

Yeats-Urley said, 'Perhaps,' and sent another man up to join Hill on watch. Half an hour later the sentries called down that trucks were on the move over the escarpment coming nearer. There was also a plane beginning to quarter the terrain. Yeats-Urley looked at the sun. It was still too high in the sky for them to make a break from cover.

Yeats-Urley made quite a series of decisions then. Principally, it was that as soon as it was safe to do so, they would move from the wadi and find the second RV with the L.R.D.G. There was no sense in staying here any longer. The enemy knew there were S.A.S. on foot in the area because they had bombed the truck and no doubt had seen men running for cover. The escarpment would come in for a pretty systematic combing, and they must be away before the teeth of the comb reached into this wadi and dug them out. Fullalove, anyway, had said it wasn't much good hoping that any other men would come through, like they'd done. By his account the first burst of fire from the armoured car had done for several of his comrades, and later he knew of two more who had got caught while retiring up the slope.

The problem wasn't one of making a decision whether to stay or move out – it was deciding *when* it would be safe to go. Almost immediately Yeats-Urley came to the opinion that there never would be a time when it was safe for them to move; not this day, anyway. There were still four hours to go to darkness; with that shufti kite spotting around they couldn't take to the desert while daylight lasted because their dust trail would be picked up within minutes. And if they remained in hiding, the patrol captain was growing increasingly certain that the hunters would come upon their wadi long before darkness reached them.

Yeats-Urley lost none of his composure with the thought. If you joined the S.A.S. you had to expect some sticky times. He got on with other activities while waiting to see how things developed across the escarpment.

There was that stuff in the ammo boxes which they'd picked up from the disabled half-track. After all their efforts it musn't finally end up with the enemy. That would have made it all purposeless. Must bury the damn stuff, Yeats-Urley thought. Bury it so that if they were killed or captured it didn't fall into enemy hands. After all, it mightn't have any value to his own people if they did cart it down to Cairo for them. Probably not. Probably they'd take one look at it and say, 'Thanks, old man, but why did you bother? We've got plenty more circuits' – or whatever they were – 'here as it is.' What was more important than carrying the stuff back was ensuring that the enemy learned nothing from it.

He told Medman to get a spade and haul the ammo boxes out of the truck. Fairlop heard the order and went off to assist the driver. But Yeats-Urley did not immediately order a hole to be dug to receive the ammo boxes. Instead he walked round the truck to see where the Italian scientists were. They mustn't know where the stuff was buried in case one of them came out of the next fracas alive.

But both Italians were up the slope a little, lying stretched full out in some shade against the rock face of the wadi. They were with Driver Vecchi, and Yeats-Urley could hear the murmur of their voices. Vecchi, recovering a bit from his ordeal, no doubt was using his Italian on them. They seemed very friendly, all three of them, thought the captain, and wondered if it wasn't dangerous for a man to get too friendly with captives. After all, Vecchi did go on about being Italian. . . .

Vecchi was one-eighth Italian only. A great-grandfather had come over from Naples, a poor young man, while Victoria graced the British throne, and was far from her last years at that. He had made a two-wheeled barrow with a little roof over the top, painted it with the gay abandon of his kind, and had shoved it through the streets of Islington, selling ice cream in summer and hot potatoes in winter. He had married an English girl, and so had his eldest son, and so had his son, Tony Vecchi's father, so there wasn't much Italian in the patrol driver now.

But Vecchi was like many another man – Hitler, for instance – loving some other country more than his own. To him Italy and all things Italian were wonderful and glamorous. He had never been there, but had fully intended to go – in fact, would have gone if the damned war hadn't broken out that September. He looked Italian, with the heavy thighs and rounded blue chin of those people, and he was proud of it. If anyone mistook him for an Italian, it made his day, which was known to his comrades who treated the foible with good humour and some badinage. They often referred to him as 'the Wop', and Vecchi was so in love with Italy that he didn't object at all to the title, derogatory though it was. Now, in spite of his cracked ribs and soreness, he was in his element. He had two real live Italians to talk to.

Satisfied that the scientists would not see what was happening, Yeats-Urley walked back to the truck and told Medman to dig a hole beyond it, out of sight of anyone else. The stuff buried, and the sand smoothed down, Yeats-Urley then got everything packed aboard the truck, ready for instant move-out.

While they were stashing away their cooking cans and kit, for the first time they had a call from a shufti kite. The aircraft, systematically quartering the escarpment, finally made a run almost directly across the wadi. Yeats-Urley wasn't worried. The shadows were quite long now, and most of the truck was in shade. They had put their camouflage net pegged out to eliminate the Chev's own shadow. It was most unlikely that the plane would identify the Chev. The enemy never could, when the S.A.S. had time to hide their vehicles.

The plane went droning away north of them. When it was safely out of sight, Yeats-Urley trudged up the hill to where his spotters lay. It was still mercilessly hot, perhaps hotter than at any time of the day because it was mid-afternoon and the land had taken its usual roasting and was radiating heat in addition to the efforts of the sun. Yeats-Urley was glad to flop down beside his men, the sweat biting into his eyes, his lungs heaving with the exertion.

Big Maurice Hill gave a grin when his captain flopped beside him. 'You're out of condition, sir,' he told him. 'Time you got some exercise.' Hill could get away with any sort of speech with his commanding officer. But then Yeats-Urley knew the big private would never go too far, would never presume on familiarity.

'We'll get it soon,' observed the captain laconically, raising his glasses. Too soon, he thought, and his pulse did quicken at what he saw. Though the air over the desert still shimmered and produced distorting effects, Yeats-Urley could now make out vehicles moving. That showed they were much nearer.

He reckoned they must have been no more than a couple of miles away. That meant, at this rate of progress, they'd reach the wadi long before sunset. He raised his glasses again. A light plane was slowly circling the area of search, rather like a predator bird watching for prey. Yeats-Urley guessed that the area was being thoroughly combed, probably by a line of infantry, certain the S.A.S. on foot couldn't have got far away. The plane was to spot any movement if the British bolted for cover.

Not much chance of getting away from that intensive search operation, Yeats-Urley thought, and for the first time he consciously thought, 'They're really doing the job thoroughly.' Putting a lot of effort into this search. That wasn't quite usual. Why was it so important to the enemy to devote so much time to finding the S.A.S? It didn't occur to the officer that that unusual element in their patrol, two captured Italian scientists, might also have stung the enemy into unusual activity.

For a long time they lay there, up against a rock and hidden by the shadow it cast, so that aircraft patrolling the escarpment came over twice again but never spotted them. All the time the widespread cordon of enemy infantry and vehicles came slowly nearer. Very slow, but Yeats-Urley knew how painful it must have been, tramping over the desert in that blinding heat. Only vigorous prompting from a chain of command stretching right back to Tobruk and Field-Marshal Rommel could have kept them at it, and this somewhat dawned on Yeats-Urley too.

Maurice Hill spoke for his mates when he said, 'The poor, poor bastards, having to sweat it out on a day like this just for us. We're not worth it.'

'Too damn right you're not,' agreed his captain, and that was the nearest he ever got to humour. Privately he was thinking, 'A bit nearer and *we'll* begin to sweat.'

Three hours to the safety of darkness, and now the enemy little more than a mile away. They could even hear motor engines starting up, as they moved to catch up with the infantry. Soon they'd be hearing men's voices, and then it would be time for them to make a run for it, daylight or not, shufti kite or no shufti kite.

It began to look as if their number was well and truly up. The advance was slow but relentless. When the distorting air currents ceased their play for a second, the infantry could now be seen with the naked eye. On they came, steadily, remorselessly. At the rate they were advancing, they'd be on top of the wadi within an hour.

No good holing up in the wadi and trying to hold them off till darkness, thought the captain. They'd soon ring them round and seal off the entrance, and for certain they'd have some mortars with them, which would soon make a mess of anyone trying to hide in the dried-up watercourse. No good running for the open desert, either. With two hours of daylight to keep them a target for the bomber droning overhead at that moment? And other bombers within radio call to add to the attack. Too flat and without cover, that desert, for men seeking to elude aircraft on the attack; yet in the end they would have to take to it, for there was no hope if they stayed in the wadi.

Yeats-Urley thoughtfully rubbed the sand off his forearms. Sand was always getting into the hairs on a man's limbs; it didn't irritate, but you found yourself tidily dusting it off. In an hour the balloon would go up. They didn't have a chance. Hill and M'Bain knew it, too, and Hill seemed very cheerful about it and made the usual remarks about dying for his country and no bastard back home would know he was going under and shed a tear for him. M'Bain gave that curious lop-sided grin but said nothing. Good chaps, Yeats-Urley thought mechanically. Oh, damned good fellows, these O.R.s.

But he was watching the sun, his watch, and the rate of progress across the desert towards them; he was calculating, and his calculations seemed to indicate that by four-fifteen at the latest they'd have to move . . . and by four-thirty that shufti kite would surely have them. Pity about that desert; a bit of cover and they could have driven that pilot mad.

About three in the afternoon, still a mile away, unexpectedly the search came to a halt. Suddenly very alert, Yeats-Urley, through his glasses, saw men gather together in groups, always around some vehicle. Then they disappeared from sight, and the captain guessed that they had sunk to the ground in tiredness.

'I think,' he told his companions, trying to keep the exultation out of his voice, 'they've stopped for a brew-up and smoke.' Though if they were Italians they'd have been smoking all the time, he corrected himself.

'Then that gives us a break, sir,' said M'Bain quickly. He could work out the inferences of declining sun and advancing infantry, too.

'It does.' Yeats-Urley couldn't take his glasses off those vehicles now. Every minute that the hunt was suspended improved their chances of survival. 'Let's hope they get down to sleep afterwards.'

It was too much to hope, but it cost nothing to put something into wishful thinking. The minutes passed. The aircraft – the big fellow, a Savoia, making the long runs, and the smaller aircraft still patrolling the line of search – didn't pause for tea, however, but maintained their watch. Still, time was passing and the sun was slowly – awfully, awfully slowly – descending. Shadows lengthened, but still weren't long enough, and they even imagined that some of the heat was going out of the day.

The minutes became half an hour. Then an hour, and still no move to re-start the search. By now the trio were joyful, optimism riding high again. Perhaps the Eyties had had enough for the day and had called off the search. Even if they dossed down for another hour, the S.A.S. stood a chance of getting away. Two hours to go to dark, and the enemy only a mile or so away and kipping down beside their vehicles.

'Sod the bloody shufti kites,' said big Maurice, rolling on his back to watch the bomber cruise by. But for them they could sneak off across the desert while the enemy slept. He noticed how the bomber flew in an elongated figure eight, patrolling something like ten miles each way north and south of them along the edge of the escarpment, as if recognising now that the fugitives were holed up somewhere there and at any moment would be forced to bolt from out of cover.

Captain Yeats-Urley had long ago noted that pattern of flying and knew how to make the most of it when the time came for them to move out. . . .

He cried out with annoyance. 'Oh, blast!' Everywhere men were rising from the ground. They'd been given one hour of rest and now were being driven back to the search again. Yeats-Urley guessed they'd *have* to be driven, to resume their search in such uncomfortable circumstances, and he felt rather flattered.

'We seem to be very important people,' he even said aloud, and his own words made him thoughtful, and he built upon previous speculation in this matter. Did the S.A.S. warrant such a search? Must be a whole regiment on the move out there, at a time when Rommel had need of every possible soldier near the Alamein front. 'We really must have stung the blighters with that raid,' he thought, and he was delighted, in spite of their peril, that they had so upset their enemy.

All the same, it took the infantry a long time to take up their positions preparatory to resuming their search. Almost Yeats-Urley, watching through his glasses, could feel the reluctance of the Italian soldiers to begin the hunt again. With a slowness that must have been exasperating to their own officers, they moved away from their vehicles. Quite twenty minutes passed before someone in charge was satisfied that the line was intact and the sweep forward could begin. Then a whistle sounded, and other whistles took up the order, they heard engines start up, and the line began its slow crawl forward again.

The S.A.S. had been given a break, Yeats-Urley thought, but it hadn't been quite long enough. Still an hour and a

Pardon this interruption, but...
if you smoke
and
you're interested
in tar levels

you may find the
information on the back
of this page worthwhile.

A comparison of 57 popular cigarette brands with Kent Golden Lights.

FILTER BRANDS (KING SIZE)

REGULAR	MG TAR	MG NIC	MENTHOL	MG TAR	MG NIC
Kent Golden Lights	8	0.6	Kent Golden Lights		
Parliament	10	0.6	Menthol	8	0.7
Vantage	11	0.7	Kool Super Lights	9	0.8°
Marlboro Lights	12	0.7	Multifilter Menthol	11	0.7
Doral	12	0.8	Vantage Menthol	11	0.8
Multifilter	12	0.8	Salem Lights	11	0.8
Winston Lights	12	0.9	Doral Menthol	11	0.8
Raleigh Lights	14	1.0	Belair	13	1.0°
Viceroy Extra Milds	14	1.0	Marlboro Menthol	14	0.8
Viceroy	16	1.0	Alpine	14	0.8
Raleigh	16	1.1	Kool Milds	14	0.9
Marlboro	17	1.0	Kool	17	1.3
Tareyton	17	1.2	Salem	18	1.2
Lark	18	1.1			
Pall Mall Filters	18	1.2			
Camel Filters	18	1.2			
L & M	18	1.1			
Winston	19	1.2			

°FTC Method

FILTER BRANDS (100's)

REGULAR	MG TAR	MG NIC	MENTHOL	MG TAR	MG NIC
Kent Golden Lights			Kent Golden Lights		
100's	10	0.9°	100's Menthol	10	0.9°
Benson & Hedges			Benson & Hedges		
100's Lights	11	0.8°	100's Lights		
Vantage 100's	11	0.9°	Menthol	11	0.8°
Merit 100's	12	0.9°	Merit 100's Menthol	12	0.9°
Parliament 100's	12	0.7	Virginia Slims		
Eve 100's	16	1.0	100's Menthol	16	0.9
Virginia Slims 100's	16	0.9	Pall Mall 100's		
Tareyton 100's	16	1.2	Menthol	16	1.2
Marlboro 100's	17	1.0	Eve 100's Menthol	16	1.0
Silva Thins	17	1.3	Silva Thins Menthol	16	1.3
Benson & Hedges			Benson & Hedges		
100's	17	1.0	100's Menthol	17	1.0
L & M 100's	17	1.1	L & M 100's Menthol	18	1.1
Raleigh 100's	17	1.2	Kool 100's	18	1.3
Viceroy 100's	18	1.3	Belair 100's	18	1.3
Lark 100's	18	1.1	Winston 100's		
Pall Mall 100's	19	1.4	Menthol	18	1.2
Winston 100's	19	1.3	Salem 100's	18	1.3

°FTC Method

Kings only 8 mg tar

100's only 10 mg tar

Simply put, they're as low as you can go and still get good taste.

Of All Brands Sold: Lowest tar: 0.5 mg. "tar," 0.05 mg. nicotine;
Kent Golden Lights: Kings Regular 8 mg. "tar," 0.6 mg. nicotine.
Kings Menthol 8 mg. "tar," 0.7 mg. nicotine av. per cigarette,
FTC Report August 1977. **100's Regular and Menthol**—10 mg. "tar,"
0.9 mg. nicotine av. per cigarette by FTC Method.

© Lorillard, U.S.A., 1977

half at least until dark, and the line of enemy soldiery once again advancing relentlessly upon the wadi.

When the Italians were a mere quarter of a mile away, Yeats-Urley looked at his watch. Still an hour to go to darkness, though the sun was closing down towards the horizon now, big and red with the dust in the air. Too much daylight left. They still couldn't make the break for it yet.

He gave an order to his men. 'Down to the truck, you two. When you see me running, start her up and throw off the camouflage net – don't bother to try to save that – and move the moment I touch the tailboard.'

He gave even more precise instructions. 'Tell Mr Fairlop to see that Vecchi is comfortably bedded down, *and tell him to have a man ready to slit the throats of those damned Eyties if they look like shouting again.*' He was remembering what Fairlop had told him, how he thought the Italian civilians had called a warning when Fairlop's truck had run into the enemy leaguer. It mustn't happen again.

'Yes, sir.'

'Tell Mr Fairlop to sit up front with the driver – I'm travelling in the back.' So that he could see what was happening during the inevitable chase; sitting inside the cab was hopeless. 'And Medman must start the engine quietly, and he mustn't hurry out of the wadi, understand?'

They would all understand. Everything the captain ordered seemed part of the instincts of the S.A.S. Don't panic, don't go rushing away because you'll only attract attention. A truck, probably too far really to be distinguished as British, casually wandering off into the desert mightn't attract much interest. They'd be puzzled, but might for a moment think it was one of their own, gone on ahead and doing a reccy by itself. The penny would drop when the Chev continued to beeline across the desert, but the S.A.S. could perhaps gain a minute or two by their restraint, and this represented as much as half a mile and out of machine-gun range in other terms.

'I'll bang hard on the cab roof when I want speed,'

Yeats-Urley ended. 'And when I bang, he's really got to stamp on it. Okay?'

'Okay, sir.'

'Watch out for the shufti kite.'

They waited until it was safely on its way, then both ran down to pass on the instructions, leaving their captain on watch alone. He, for his part, played it cool, holding his position almost until it was too late.

He saw the Italian infantry, tired from their day in the field, move through the scrub and rocks and get nearer and nearer, armoured cars and infantry carriers with them. A nasty little scout car, too, Yeats-Urley now noticed for the first time. A fast little whippet, with a mounted machine-gun behind that could traverse three-sixty degrees.

He waited, watching the sun touching the horizon, listening to the two aircraft on patrol. . . . The planes must have been relieved, he thought, but he hadn't noticed the change-over. Aircraft couldn't sail around all that time without refuelling. We *must* be important to Rommel, he thought once again, and again it was accompanied by a satisfied feeling.

When the infantry was no more than a hundred yards from the edge of the wadi, Yeats-Urley knew he had bought as much time as he dared. Leave it too late and there'd be disaster. One more glance aloft – safe, the planes well away. Then down the slope, slipping and slithering, the dust rising, but not enough to give the show away. Five minutes at most before the aircraft was back, unless someone from the ground called it in.

Running towards the truck and hearing it start, and seeing the camouflage net go dropping off the side. The enemy were welcome to it, and their tent pegs, too. The truck just beginning to move. He grabbed the tailboard, and strong hands hauled him aboard. One pair of hands belonged to the lumbering Private Hoyle.

'Bowels all right?' Yeats-Urley asked, as if nothing untoward was happening. Hoyle looked dim, as if he'd already forgotten the anguish of the day before. 'Better be.' The other chaps grinned, and it reduced the tension, and that was why Yeats-Urley had said it. A very wise officer for twenty-three.

He clambered over the dunnage towards the cab, ducking under the Vickers. All the men were well down except Eddie Fullalove, who loved the Vickers and now stood behind it, ready for action. Yeats-Urley saw Vecchi, well-bedded in blankets, and the two Italians, looking very lugubrious with their blue chins. Depressed men, and why shouldn't they be? he thought.

Turning, his back against the cabin, he called, 'All right you know what to do.'

The Chev picked up speed. They bumped down the uneven floor of the wadi, every eye looking up at the rim of the cliff, expecting to see enemy movement before they were clear. Yeats-Urley was particularly tense, wondering if he had left it too late . . . yet even seconds might be valuable in the end. The sun was going down in the west, the lower edge now obscured by ragged hills.

No sign of the enemy. The truck took a turn and came out on to the level desert that wasn't level at all. In fact it was hellishly bumpy, and for a long way out from the escarpment it was just a floor of uneven rocks, so that Snowy Medman ground along at no more than ten to fifteen miles an hour, and they lurched and bumped distressingly. Yeats-Urley – and not just him, either – prayed that the tyres would stand the strain, and wondered how they had managed not to have a puncture in the past forty-eight hours.

A minute passed. They were drawing away from the escarpment now, out in the open. No sign of the aircraft. Probably at the end of the figure eight, but turning. The escarpment was a long rugged cliff extending for miles in either direction, the top level but eroded, presenting difficulties in descent.

The ground began to get easier, the farther they pulled away from the wadi. Soon they would be on sand and among dunes, though Yeats-Urley wasn't sure that was necessarily in their favour. At least on hard rock they didn't get bogged down in a wheelspin.

Another minute . . . quarter of a mile out now. Yeats-Urley had his glasses up, doing his best to keep them on the receding escarpment, but having a difficult time with all that heaving and swaying.

He stiffened, seeing movement. At last the searchers had come to the edge of the wadi. He saw uniforms, Italians. A group of soldiers. He got them steady in his glasses, and they looked quite big at that range. A lot of them came together, as if baulked by the slope. Yeats-Urley saw them milling around. Then he was sure he saw one man look directly at them across the desert. The Italian stood, staring, then turned away.

Yeats-Urley let his breath exhale slowly, a moment's relief upon him. Another hundred yards . . .

The group of men had turned. He saw an array of pink faces in the last light of the reddened sun, all turned out towards the desert. 'We're seen,' he groaned. This time the heads didn't turn away. More Italians came to join the first audience. Then Yeats-Urley saw a vehicle come close to the edge of the escarpment. A man got out, an officer. The going was smoother now on the sandier desert, and Yeats-Urley could hold the picture without difficulty. But he still didn't give the order to Medman to step on it. Nothing must give the enemy premature alarm.

Another hundred yards sped by.

The Italian officer had his glasses up, and Yeats-Urley thought, 'He'll see me with my glasses up just as plainly as I can see him.' Someone staring at the Italians through field-glasses, in the back of a truck uncomfortably packed with men.

Yeats-Urley waved. Why not? he thought. Couldn't do them any harm, and might kid the Eytie for another few seconds that, unaccountable though it was, that receding truck was friendly.

But the Italian wasn't to be deceived. Yeats-Urley saw him drop his glasses and turn. The next thing an aerial was going up on the vehicle – the scout car with a machine-gun, Yeats-Urley now realised. It was an aerial with a little cross on the top, and Yeats-Urley knew what was being transmitted through it.

We've found them, would be the glad cry. The blasted S.A.S. have been driven into the open. They're here, making a run for it across the desert. And all ground forces would immediately begin to concentrate and descend to the desert and set off in pursuit.

But it was the aircraft, for the moment, that concerned Yeats-Urley most. That same radio would be calling the pilots into the attack. He saw the car get into motion and disappear, and all the Italian infantry began to climb down the escarpment. He banged hard on the cab roof. Snowy really put his boot down.

Still, they'd made a few more hundred yards. The sun was half-way to setting and they'd have a lead of several miles over any enemy vehicle by the time it reached the desert floor. Probably the Chev could hold its own against most of the Italian vehicles, anyway – except that nippy-looking scout car. Once it got on to this more even going it would have the heels of them, and Yeats-Urley knew it. Still, by the time it caught up with them it could be dark, and once all light had gone, the S.A.S. could laugh at their pursuers.

But not at Savoia bombers.

It was coming over the escarpment at speed, on a wrong course that would carry it far to the east, but the pilot must have seen the fleeing truck, a big cloud of dust going up now with speed, for instantly it banked and headed towards them.

It sailed over them, to the east of their course, as if the pilot and aircrew were making sure of their identity, then it began to climb and turn and Yeats-Urley knew what that meant.

He shouted round the edge of the cab to Driver Medman, 'It's coming in to attack from behind. You know the signals.' Medman would know.

Yeats-Urley heard some of the men calling and when he looked the second aircraft had come over the escarpment. The next minutes were going to be hot. But the sun was reducing in size, every minute bringing them closer to darkness. Already, here amid the dunes, the light was failing. Quarter of an hour and they would be safe.

The Savoia came in diving. Eddie Fullalove shouted, 'Heads down, look in!' the old cry, the old joke, but nobody laughed. He got the Vickers up. It wouldn't be much good at that speed, but at least machine-gun fire from the fleeing truck would be noticed and would have a deterring effect upon the Savoia pilot.

The bomber came down and down, faster with every second, down to within a hundred feet of the deck, and then the machine-guns began their strafing. Yeats-Urley timed it well. When instinct told him the guns were going to open up he gave one hard bang on the cab roof. Medman promptly took evasive action.

Without reducing speed, he hauled round on the wheel, throwing the Chev into a skid that almost halted them and almost stalled the engine. Then the Chev got into its stride again and carried them out of danger.

Italian machine-gun bullets sent up fountains of dust in a long line following their tyre marks, but the gunner was too slow and didn't swing to bring his aim upon the truck when it pulled out of line. Missed. A deafening roar as the aircraft flew over them, engines straining as it sought to climb out of range of their gun. A big shadow flitting over them; they were as close as that to the Savoia's line of flight. Then it was away, pulling round south of them.

Fullalove had got in a burst from the Vickers. Only a few rounds, then Medman's evasive action had thrown his aim. He had done no damage, but it did them all good to smell the cordite after he'd ripped off at the enemy.

Medman didn't need telling. The moment the plane was past, he swept round and got on to his old course again. Always go straight when there's ground pursuit, was the

S.A.S. motto. If you didn't they could cut across the arc of your flight and soon catch up with you.

And the scout car was already within sight.

Yeats-Urley was shocked to see how close it had come. It couldn't have been much more than a mile to their rear, and by the dust cloud was going like hell. They could only hope it wouldn't do so well on the soft patches, its tyres, narrower than the Chev's, tending to dig deeper in sand.

Medman needed no urging. The Chev went off again at top speed. The Savoia was circling, preparing for another run, but it takes minutes for a heavy bomber to make its circuit and get on course again, and minutes were what the S.A.S. were fighting for.

Still too painfully light, though. Still plenty of time for a few bomber runs. And now the other aircraft was well in sight, winging low on the eastern horizon.

The Savoia dived down to about two hundred feet, then came roaring in on a level course. Yeats-Urley got the significance of that and shouted round to Medman, 'It's bombs this time!'

The Savoia seemed to be on them before they realised what was happening. Yeats-Urley had just time to give two quick frantic bangs on the cabin roof. Medman knew the drill and dropped his anchor. The brakes bit hard. The soft sand helped them. From thirty miles an hour the truck came to a dead stop. Everyone was thrown on top of each other. Yeats-Urley felt all the breath knocked out of his body as he crashed against the back of the cab.

But Medman's swift reaction did the trick. The bomber let go with two small bombs – even in such a moment Yeats-Urley noted that only four bombs were slung under the Savoia's wings. They saw them detach and gather speed towards them. For an awful moment they were all sure both would strike the Chev. Then they whistled by overhead, and dug themselves into the soft sand fifty yards forward, and though the Chev rocked to the force of the blasts, the explosions did no harm.

The Savoia went off, climbing, circling again. Far away

from it the other plane flitted near to the ground. Then it too began to turn towards the truck. They'd be talking to each other by radio, the patrol commander knew, the pilots of those aircraft. They'd be planning a concerted attack now, he guessed, and wondered what manner of activity it would take.

The Chev *had* stalled that time, halting so abruptly, but Medman instantly re-started the engine and got them into motion. The scout car was within half a mile of them. Someone was saying there was a curious noise from the transmission, but Yeats-Urley's attention was only for the scout car. He knew they couldn't dodge two planes and the scout car in the next manoeuvre.

He looked at the sun. There was still enough of it for what he wanted. Strange that, when all their efforts were to keep alive until the sun had gone and with it all light, now he wanted the sun to hang above the horizon just a little longer. He needed that bit of sunshine, but they would have to hurry.

Yeats-Urley leaned round the driver's cab. 'We've got to do for that scout car behind us.' It was the first those in front knew they had a car on their heels. He gave swift instructions, then pulled himself back and looked round.

The Savoia and that other plane were scooting fast low over the desert, a hundred and eighty degrees out from each other. Both simultaneously banked, as if on some radio command. Both started to manoeuvre to make their approach run.

But Medman was doing his stuff nicely. The Chev had scurried between rolling sand dunes and had followed the curve of one of them westwards, at right angles to the way they had been going. The dune now intervened between them and the fast-approaching scout car, so that for the moment they were hidden.

Driver Medman carefully drove up the slight slope directly towards the last remnant of sun – the sun, all fire and glow in the dust-laden atmosphere in the minutes before final extinction. The brakes went on and the Chev halted. It had to be quickly over; those planes were steadying for the run in now. Bombs and machine-guns this time, thought Yeats-Urley.

'Right, corporal,' he said. 'It's up to you. All yours now.'

Fullalove crouched behind the Vickers, teeth bared in a big grin. Almost everyone else jumped out. Tommy Shiner stayed with Fullalove to handle the belt; Vecchi didn't move – he was past it. The Italians stayed aboard, too, because no one had said they could alight. Even the one-armed Gunner Partridge got down with his tommy.

They dispersed, running swiftly, then going to ground, rifles and tommies pointing towards the end of the dune. All waited. They could hear the straining engine of the scout car. It was really batting along.

It came round the corner not so much like a whippet as an incautious terrier scudding into a dog fight. The scout car came swerving, following their tyre marks. The Italians never saw them because they looked straight into the sun and momentarily were blinded. Before they knew what was happening, Fullalove got going with the Vickers. It could fire 250 rounds a minute, rapid fire. Fullalove's burst lasted ten seconds. The other men opened fire, too. Several hundred bullets smacked into that car or into the four men inside it in a matter of ten–fifteen seconds. Probably all died instantly.

The car went out of control, swerved, then started to roll over and over, shedding bodies as it did so. The Italian scout car would not menace them any further. And the sun expired completely at that moment. The men hauled themselves aboard. Yeats-Urley banged on the roof to get them going. The Chev seemed reluctant to get into speed now, and this time Yeats-Urley did notice a curious noise from the transmission. But the aircraft were upon them.

The bomber made another run from behind, plainly intent on shedding his last two bombs. The machine-gunner in the nose of the aircraft sprayed at them the whole of the time. The other plane came diving in from the west, at right angles to the Savoia's course. Between them they were going to nullify any manoeuvres by the villainous S.A.S.

Yeats-Urley heard some fathead in the truck pick that moment to identify the second plane. A Breda 83a, he said, as if that were important. Probably Private Shiner who was mad on aircraft identification.

. . . a Breda? All the same the information automatically recorded in Yeats-Urley's brain. Then it would have four machine guns mounted forward. . . .

He shouted round the cab at Medman as the planes came crashing down towards them. Ony one manoeuvre possible in those circumstances if they were to have the slightest chance of staying alive . . . no good telling the men to bail out and disperse. The truck must be saved. All or nothing. . . .

Yeats-Urley gave the cab top an almighty clout and set up a yell that no one heard because of the Vickers belting off and the aircraft noise beating their eardrums in. Medman swung on the wheel again, this time towards the Breda tearing in from their right. Too fierce a swing. They made half a turn, then stopped dead again, engine stalled.

The stall saved them. The first time in his life he had ever been grateful for soft sand, Yeats-Urley told his survivors afterwards. The Breda got the top of the cab, metal holing and splinters flying, so that Yeats-Urley spun away like a scalded cat. But the lead only cut the corner, whereas if the truck had completed their manoeuvre and made the complete turn the captain was sure they'd have taken a whole line of bullets down the centre of their vehicle.

The Savoia missed with his guns and shed his bombs again too late and they exploded well ahead. Eddie Fullalove swore it was because of his fire. 'Got 'em nervy,' he boasted, and he was probably right. Perhaps the Savoia machine-gunner didn't like the sight of those tracers coming up from the Vickers, only Perspex between him and death, and he aimed hurriedly and badly.

So again they got away with it, and now, darkness closing in upon them, Yeats-Urley reckoned they were going to survive. Well, last the night out, at least. He wasn't sure about the following day.

He was less sure when he heard the Chev get into gear. There was a most disturbing whine from the transmission. Those sudden halts had bent something, he decided, and bent things didn't last long under the strain of desert travel. They were in a mess.

Vecchi and Partridge were in a bit of a mess too. Both had suffered during those abrupt halts. Someone large had landed on Partridge's broken arm, and he looked very white and ill now, propped against the side of the Chev. Vecchi was being attended to by the Italian civilians, and he was moaning. Yeats-Urley thought, 'We must get them to a doctor quickly.'

The Chev moved laboriously now, but Medman didn't risk getting it out of second gear, for the moment. It seemed to everyone aboard that any second there would be a harsh jangle of breaking metal and that would be the end of their truck. No truck, no escape out of the desert. It was a grim prospect.

But at least they were moving. The aircraft were sweeping round for another attack. Yeats-Urley sought a shadow and gave the order to halt. Running did them no good now. If they were to escape it would only be because the fading light offered protection, so they might just as well sit still and hope they wouldn't be spotted.

The planes came over. There was no gunfire. The S.A.S. had won. The light was too bad for them to be seen. They heard the aircraft drone off, and when the sounds finally died away, Yeats-Urley said, 'Move. One hour and then we brew up.'

They found a hollow and lit their firecans, knowing that the flames would not be seen. Yeats-Urley gave them an hour's rest, during which time Corporal Fullalove and Private Shiner got under the truck with a torch, but they found nothing and came out all oil and muttering transmission, which didn't advance anyone's knowledge.

In that halt the two Italians came to Captain Yeats-Urley. They were shaken and desperate men. Desert warfare was new to them, and their nerves couldn't stand any more.

'Go on and leave us,' pleaded Antonio Bergamo.

'In the desert?' Yeats-Urley thought they were mad. 'You'd die in no time.' Civvies would never find their way out of this vast desert.

'We'll take our chances,' said Bergamo; his American accent sounded harsh. 'We just don't want to go through anything like that again.'

'And you think it will be the same tomorrow?' He was interested to know their thoughts.

Bergamo nodded, though Yeats-Urley could hardly see the movement in the starlight. 'They'll never give up. They've got to find you.'

Yeats-Urley's head came up quickly. 'Why?' Why had they to be found? Something in Bergamo's tone told him it was more than the obvious.

Antonio Bergamo, distinguished product of America's M.I.T., was a shattered man and told him his thoughts, though that is never wise with an enemy. 'I guess it's us they're after.'

'You?'

'That's what we've figured out, Piero and I. They're bound to know that we're in your hands.' Everything had started with that realisation, and the Italians had quickly worked the rest out. They were known to be in the desert; their bodies hadn't been found, though those of their German comrades had. Not much effort would be required to know where two Italian civilians might have gone, with the piratical S.A.S. in the vicinity.

'They won't want us to fall into the hands of the British,' Piero had said. No, they had knowledge too valuable to the enemy. And later he had said, 'Antonio, I think our people will want to kill us rather than have us alive with the British.' It was a chilling, awful thought, but that strafing and bombing had confirmed the theory in their minds.

Now Antonio, made reckless by his terrible fear, said,

'They want to kill us – our own people.' He spread his hands in despair that the world should ever have arrived at such a state. 'You must let us go. It might make things safer for you.' A cunning bribe, but Yeats-Urley was unmoved.

'Can't do that.' Very vigorous. You didn't release valuable prisoners just because it might ease off the hunt for them. Anyway, the captain didn't see how it could. His tone became a little kind. He knew how the civilians were suffering. 'It's out of the question. You'd simply die within a few hours, before anyone had time to find you. So make the best of it.' And that was the end of that conversation, though Yeats-Urley did find time to say to his lieutenant, 'Freddie, the Wops think they're the target, they are to be killed rather than go on with us.'

Fairlop, carefully draining the last of his tea, spoke through the darkness. 'Sounds reasonable. They *are* crowding us a bit harder than usual.'

'That's what I've been thinking.' Then Fullalove came to report that nothing could be done to the truck, and after a time they all crawled wearily aboard, and the night ride began.

They had run south-east away from the pursuit, and now had to strike back north-west to get to the second rendezvous with the L.R.D.G. Still about sixty miles to do, nothing on a good road, but a long night's journey over trackless desert even if your vehicle was in good nick, and theirs wasn't.

The noise from the transmission made them wince, and it grew more agonising with every passing hour, yet to their astonishment the old Chev kept chugging along, though rarely in the night, even when the moon came up, did they get so much as into third. Slow going, and the petrol burning away, but that wasn't of much concern to Yeats-Urley now. If the truck went, as it would inevitably do, they'd be stranded deep in the Sahara desert, with limited food and water supplies, their only hope the L.R.D.G. turning up.

In the darkness Yeats-Urley sighed. Somehow they had to make the hills and try to hide up there until the L.R.D.G. came along. They might even doctor their limping vehicle, he thought, yet guessed the job was beyond their first-aid.

Hour followed hour, a time of bitter cold, for quite a strong wind kept coming up, chilling them to the bone, so that it was impossible for them even to doze and so reduce their feeling of discomfort.

M'Bain particularly hated the night. He'd had enough, truly enough. Never, never, never, he vowed to himself, would he get into such a situation again. What the devil was he doing with the S.A.S., anyway? Why had he volunteered? Because he didn't know what he was letting himself in for, he told himself. It had all seemed so glamorous, getting away from bullshit and parades, but this was the reality. Deadly peril and a life of discomfort that no man ought to have to endure. He just could not understand his comrades who seemed, in spite of their moans, to accept it all and even somehow enjoy it.

When daylight broke – a dismal dawn – they were still some miles from the RV. That meant they'd have to keep running along for at least two hours before being able to find cover. What worried Yeats-Urley was that they were leaving tracks in the sand, and aircraft could follow tyremarks easily. Normally he would have taken to the rocky parts, to avoid leaving tread marks, but with the Chev in such a bad way it had to be nursed over softer going and that was going to betray them. Still, all they could do was to keep going.

As daylight strengthened, so did the wind. Snake-like wraiths of sand were twisting and turning all over the surface of the desert, making a sibilant hissing sound that strengthened as the wind blew stronger. Yeats-Urley remembered the red haze around the sun the previous evening, always a sign of a distant dust-storm. Well, here it was, coming swiftly upon them. That wouldn't make the men feel any happier.

Half an hour after daylight, the first plane picked them up. It was the Italian two-seater observer plane, the Breda. They heard the roar above the moan of the rising wind and turned stiffly to face the new peril. It came straight at them, passing almost directly overhead, but it did not open fire and for a moment they thought they hadn't been detected.

But immediately the Breda pulled up and away in a tight turn, and they knew they had been spotted.

They weren't easy to see that morning. Any dust they made with their tyres was lost amid the swirling sand turned up by the wind. From above their truck would look like a lone vehicle partly submerged in the waves of the sea, difficult to detect. The Breda must have seen them too late in passing, but it had seen them, and was now turning to come into the attack.

Yeats-Urley thought, 'This is probably the end.' Caught in the open. All he could do this time, with a truck beyond any fierce manoeuvring, was to get his men off it and dispersed. That meant the Breda would finish off the truck, and then turn to finish them off. He had to lower his head to give the order, and when he looked again he found that he could not see the Breda, though he could still hear it.

He straightened suddenly. If they couldn't see the plane, it was unlikely the plane could see them. He looked with interest at the dust-storm. It wasn't fully upon them yet, but the wind that preceded it was stirring up the desert to quite a height now. By Jove, he told himself, we might be saved yet.

They lost the Breda in that brief forerunner of the dust-storm proper, and they had cover for twenty minutes or so before it died down, as so often it does die down for a while in such circumstances. Then came the lull, and they rode out into a clear atmosphere again. South of them another plane was patrolling. They rode on, eyeing it anxiously, but it didn't turn towards them, and a short while later the dust-storm really hit them and after that they knew they were at least safe from enemy aircraft.

They travelled as well as they could by compass, but there were times when the fury of the storm brought them to a complete halt, the driver unable to face the stinging sand particles that came hurtling through the glassless windscreen. They made some miles, though, for there were times when the storm abated briefly and they could make progress. Early in the afternoon, in fact, Yeats-Urley decided they couldn't be far off the L.R.D.G. rendezvous. Sure enough, some time later they began to run into rocks, and in lulls saw they were driving parallel to a low chain of hills, stark eroded things that looked particularly hostile, that bleak and bitter day. Still, the hills could represent safety, if only the L.R.D.G. were there.

Unexpectedly the storm blew out. Within fifteen minutes there wasn't a grain of sand stirring, and the sky was its usual flawless blue. Eyes searched the horizon anxiously. Not a plane in sight. They guessed the air hunt had been called off while the sand-storm raged.

'Crack in now,' Yeats-Urley called to the driver, and they did crack in, anxious to make as many miles towards safety as possible before the aerial hunt was resumed.

They found the RV without much difficulty. In its way it was a pleasant place. The broken face of yet another escarpment formed a rugged wall to the north, and there was a break in it, not a wadi this time, more a sandy inlet. They drove in cautiously, never trusting what might be round the corner. Below them was firm sand; on either side towering black walls of rock. The crack in the cliff face curved, putting them nicely out of sight of the open desert, then, after fifty yards, it ended. The rock walls closed together, and that was all there was to it. But there was a nice deep, cool cave part way up the rock face at the end of the cleft.

The L.R.D.G. were not there.

Their hearts sank. Their miserable journey that day had been buoyed with the thought that at least they would find their guides across the desert, and within hours would be trekking out to the pleasures of Alex or Cairo. And the L.R.D.G. weren't there.

'Too much activity in the area,' Yeats-Urley said to his lieutenant, when they climbed stiffly off the truck. The L.R.D.G. could hardly go swanning around the desert with such an intensive manhunt on. The squadron captain thought again how they missed their radio. If only they could communicate with the L.R.D.G. For all they knew they might be just around the corner.

The men knew the drill. Some went back along their tracks doing a sweeping job. Mustn't let their tyre-marks into their hide-out give away their presence. Tracks that ended abruptly, mystifyingly, in the desert would perplex an enemy perhaps sufficiently long to give the S.A.S. time to slip away. . . .

Slip away? On that old truck? Corporal Fullalove crawled out from under the Chev after only a few minutes. 'Nothing we can do, sir. Not here,' he told his captain. It was the transmission, he repeated, a depot job, probably unrepairable, anyway.

'Thank you, corporal,' said Yeats-Urley, and he even smiled when he said it, so as not to let the man know how blue he felt inside. Not that he hadn't expected the news, but as always under such circumstances confirmation of one's fears was depressing.

The men were busy disguising the shape of the truck. Because they no longer had their camouflage net, they were having to drag up bushes and pile them over the vehicle. While some men got on with that work, Hill and M'Bain were boiling water preparatory to brewing up, and opening cans of food. Yeats-Urley saw the two Italian civilians helping Driver Vecchi up the rocky path that led to the cave. Gunner Partridge was following slowly behind. His head was bent and he walked as if in pain. Got to get a doctor to them quickly, thought the captain yet again. But how?

He conferred for a moment with Lieutenant Fairlop, not going into the cool shade of the big cave while any of his men had duties in the hot sunshine. 'We're really stuck now, Freddie,' he said, and sounded quite cheerful about it. 'It's no good trusting to the old Chev any more.'

Fairlop shook his head in agreement. It had brought them so far, and they had been lucky it hadn't cracked up hours ago, but they knew it wouldn't last many more miles.

No, they couldn't look to the Chev to get them out of the desert.

'Our only hope's the L.R.D.G., Alan.'

'Our only hope,' nodded Yeats-Urley. Here they must stay until their guides were able to get them, then everything would be all right. It might mean waiting for days, until the enemy activity in the area abated, but after the rigours of travel through the desert, a few days lying up in a cool cave wouldn't come amiss. The only trouble was, Partridge and Vecchi couldn't really wait that long for a doctor, Partridge especially with his mangled arm.

Not much more than an hour after they had settled in, the air hunt was on again. M'Bain, on watch on a ledge above the cave, called down, 'There's a plane, sir, coming straight for us.'

It did come straight for them. They heard its roar steadily deepening, and then it flashed by about quarter of a mile away over the desert. Watching from their hide-out, they saw it was their old friend, the two-seater Breda. After flying a few miles parallel to the escarpment, the Breda banked and turned, then made another run back the way it had come. Minutes later it was turning again, and retracing its path. It began to look as if they had an aerial sentry patrolling the entrance to their hide-out.

Lying together at the entrance to their cave, well screened by the deep shadow, Yeats-Urley and Fairlop watched the noisy performance, and both knew what it signified.

'They followed our tracks.' – Yeats-Urley. 'Picked them up from the scout car we shot up yesterday.' Hereabouts there wouldn't be many tracks in the desert, and with the abating of the sand-storm the Breda would have been able to follow them quite easily. The sand-storm wouldn't have made much difference. At ground level the wheel-marks mightn't be detectable, but from the air they were always apparent, even though driftings had partly covered them.

Now, if their Chev hadn't been in such an unhealthy state they would have sought out hard going, a stony surface where tracks didn't show, and that would have thrown any possible pursuers.

The captain said, 'They'll be radioing for more aircraft and ground forces.' Just like yesterday. He cheered up. It would take many hours for troops to reach them in vehicles, and snugly hidden in this rocky cleft they had little fear of aircraft. Darkness wouldn't be long coming, and they'd be able to slip away. . . .

Yeats-Urley halted his thoughts and lost his cheerfulness. What was he thinking about, slipping away? They couldn't slip away, not in the old Chev. Lack of transport held them prisoners here, and it was only a matter of time before the enemy tumbled to their whereabouts and dug them out.

The patrol captain came up on to his knees. 'Freddie,' he said thoughtfully, 'I think our position's a bit dicey.'

They looked at each other, neither now minimising the gravity of their situation. Yeats-Urley spelled it out. 'We haven't a chance of walking out from here alive.' Vecchi and Partridge in particular couldn't face a desert journey on foot. Anyway, they hadn't enough water for a long trek on foot through the desert, so they could dismiss that one immediately.

'And they won't be long in finding us, if the infantry are brought in to search.'

The enemy would begin their hunt where the tyre marks mysteriously ended, and that was a mere few hundred yards from where they had turned into the rocky cleft. No, it wouldn't be long before they were routed out.

Fairlop also sat back on his haunches. He wasn't a man Yeats-Urley quite took to, but at this moment he faced their plight very calmly, no getting worked up and showing panic, and Yeats-Urley approved of him for that. 'Our only hope is to hang on here until the way's clear for the L.D.R.G. to find us. That means we have to throw them off the scent.' Both men had accepted that even at this moment land forces would be streaming across the desert to seek for them.

'Yes. But how?' Yeats-Urley's eyes fell broodingly on the

Chev. Damned thing, letting them down like this. But they couldn't trust to it . . .

'Freddie.' Fairlop looked quickly round, something in Yeats-Urley's voice demanding attention. 'I think I know how it can be done – giving them the slip, you know.'

He rose to his feet, still keeping to the shadow.

'The old Chev might still have a bit of use in her.' He told his lieutenant what was in his mind, and when he had finished Fairlop considered and then said, 'I think it might work. Anyway, what else can we do?'

So they called the men together in the cave and told them what was in their minds, and immediately there were volunteers for the disagreeable job when the opportunity arose. Yeats-Urley settled it by saying that Fullalove would accompany Driver Medman, and then they all got down to wait.

About an hour later, the Breda stopped beating about the desert, disturbing them with their noise, and winged away north towards the coast. Its fuel must have been about ended, they guessed, but they didn't spend much time in speculation. Immediately they were sure that this time it had gone, Corporal Fullalove and Driver Medman went sliding down the rocky path to the truck. It took only a few seconds to pull away most of the brushwood that had been camouflaging it. Then they climbed into the cab, started up, and went groaning and complaining at slow speed into the desert.

Yeats-Urley and the rest of the men except one sentry followed them out into the open, brushing away the tyre marks as they did so. The truck went limping off along the face of the escarpment, the S.A.S. following, energetically wiping out the tyre marks. Yeats-Urley told them to keep it up for as long as possible, because the greater the gap before the tyre-marks resumed, the safer presumably their hide-out. When they'd gone about half a mile, however, he decided that was enough, and they all hurried back to their shelter. No good taking too many risks, thought Yeats-Urley, for he didn't want to be caught in the open by any aircraft in this vicinity. That would give the show away.

It was many hours later – after dark – before Corporal Fullalove and Driver Medman came slipping into the cave again, two very weary men. They reported to their captain that the Chev had held together for about seven miles – seven nice miles of false trail along the foot of the escarpment. Then it had given up the ghost with a horrid jangle of tearing metal.

'Reckon her guts came out of her that time,' said Fullalove, knocking back the old brew that came quickly to him from the kitchen at the back of the cave.

But that was after the Ju 52s had landed, and he and Medman had seen them – how could they have failed to see them? – and they had been hours sneaking back under cover of the harsh eroded escarpment top so as not to be spotted.

Late in the afternoon, with no sign of resumption of aerial observation, Yeats-Urley had begun to hope that the L.R.D.G. might seek this moment of inactivity to come driving in from the desert. He was not alone in that hope, and most eyes watched the entrance to the sandy cleft all that afternoon for first sight of the cheerful Arab head-dressed L.R.D.G. They were disappointed.

About four that mercilessly hot afternoon, Private Hoyle, watching from the shelter of the ledge above them, called hoarsely down, 'Plane!'

Everyone stopped doing what they were doing at that moment, which amounted to very little, and listened for the sounds of approaching aircraft. They began to hear it, which meant it was coming their way. Their hearts sank. Not that bloody Breda again, kicking up its din while keeping watch until the land forces arrived!

'Sod the thing,' said Hill to Frankie Mack, who contributed a thought that the plane could perform a sexual act upon itself. The language in the cave was vigorous and colourful. It grew even more so when Oily called down again. 'Two more planes coming up, sir.'

Three aircraft? Yeats-Urley looked quickly across at Fairlop, who just shrugged, as much as to say, 'I don't know what they're up to.'

They kept to the shadow but watched out. They were hoping the aircraft would carry on, bound on some mission which did not concern them. But the aircraft – three Ju 52s – did not carry on. Instead, they landed.

They saw the leading plane sweep low over the desert, circling as if the pilot was scrutinising the ground carefully. The other planes came up but stacked well out of the way of the reconnoitring aircraft. After two or three circuits, with the S.A.S. not knowing what they were up to, the aircraft came in, almost at stalling speed, to land. They gasped when they realised what it was doing. Planes landing in their vicinity held an ominous significance. Especially Ju 52s. For among their other roles was that of troop-carrying.

It came down and made a bumpy landing, wheels throwing up immense streamers of dust, the three propellers revving madly at the last, striving to cushion the impact with the uneven ground, and blowing up a miniature dust-storm that drifted for miles. But it made a safe landing, and taxied to a halt about five miles south-west of their position.

A second plane was making a cautious circuit of the area, obviously preparatory to landing, but Yeats-Urley had his glasses on the first aircraft. The big loading doors had been swiftly opened. A ramp came down. Grey figures appeared – so these were Germans – dropping to the desert and seeming to haul on something in unison. Then a small vehicle was manhandled into view and down the ramp.

Yeats-Urley got it clearly in his glasses. It was a light car that the Germans used for scouting – probably an Opel. Rommel himself sometimes rode in one in the midst of a tank battle, standing up and holding on to the guard-rail above the windscreen. They carried three men, and the one in the back was the machine-gunner. Yeats-Urley remembered the Italian scout car of the previous day and did not like what he saw. These Opels were ideal for desert travel, very fast, and light enough to be lifted out of trouble such as loose sand or awkward holes. With the mounted machine-gun – a Spandau – they also packed quite a punch. The captain's heart sank. It sank even lower when a second scout car was hauled down the ramp.

By this time the second Junkers had landed, and the third was scanning the terrain from a low height. Yeats-Urley saw the second plane taxi close to the first, and then the procedure was the same. Two more scout cars appeared from the capacious interior of the Junkers. There appeared to be about a dozen German soldiers with each aircraft, more than the complement required to man the scout cars. The Germans were doing the thing in style.

The third plane came in to land. Because of the hanging cloud of dust where the first two aircraft had landed, this one came down much closer to the escarpment. Yeats-Urley lowered his glasses to watch the operation. It was little more than a mile out into the open desert.

They all watched. They saw the Junkers land, and the dust spurt up in twin jets from the wheels, then it appeared to bounce into the air, as if the wheels had encountered a bump. And that proved fatal for the Ju 52.

They heard the roar of the engines, as the pilot tried to pick up speed, but the laden aircraft hit the deck with another bounce that made the wings shake to their roots, and it seemed to continue to bounce, as if some uncontrollable rhythm had been established, the bounces getting shorter and harder, as if the ground wasn't as level as it might have seemed.

Yeats-Urley had a feeling of a pilot desperately trying to smooth out the landing or take off again, and succeeding in neither. Then the landing gear began to disintegrate under the strain, and the plane came round, so that it was heading straight for the escarpment. A wing dipped, striking the ground, and began to tear to pieces. Still the propellers turned, the engines roaring, as if the pilot still tried to maintain control of the disintegrating aircraft, but it was no use.

Horrified – some, anyway; not Hill and Fullalove, who cheered ecstatically – they saw the landing gear collapse utterly and the aircraft land on her nose. The tail shot high into the air, then came down with a bang, and the aircraft lay flat on her belly in a cloud of dust. The engine noise died instantly, but the dying flailings of the propellers stirred up a cloud of yellow dust that hung above the stricken plane and almost obscured it.

Private Hill said with satisfaction, 'That must have shaken 'em up a bit, sir.'

Yeats-Urley nodded. There'd be some dead and injured among that lot, he thought, and waited to see the plane go up in flames, but it didn't. He had a fleeting thought that they ought to go out and help the injured, humanitarian instincts which were immediately subdued. His glasses swung to where the other aircraft were standing. They must have witnessed the disaster, for the Opel scout cars began to stream across the desert at a fast pace towards the wrecked Junkers.

They had a grandstand seat, squatting in the shadowy interior of their cave on the hillside, just able to see through the rocky cleft on to the desert beyond. The crumpled aircraft was no more than a mile away, growing more visible each minute as the dust-cloud settled.

They saw the German scout cars come tearing up and skid to a halt about fifty yards from the stricken Junkers. Yeats-Urley approved of the discipline which made them halt beyond the destructive radius of a possible petrol explosion. He saw German soldiers pile out and begin to run towards the wreckage.

By this time there was movement from within the aircraft. As the dust settled the S.A.S. saw that the side of the Junkers had been partly torn away, leaving a gap through which crawled a man. He fell to the ground as if he had hurt himself, and when he tried to stand he got no higher than all-fours, and in this position, head drooping, he waited while help came to him.

Yeats-Urley put his glasses on to the scene. He saw that this plane, too, carried scout cars. One car, in fact, was hanging out through the hole, as if the crash had sent it hurtling against the loading doors, smashing them and the surrounding panels open. The officer's glasses picked out movement in the interior. So others had survived the crash.

The rescuers went clambering into the wreckage and began to bring out survivors. A few walked out, with a little assistance, but other forms were inert, and the S.A.S. guessed there were some dead.

Until near nightfall the Germans worked hard upon the injured, attending to them, and bandaging them, then loading them on to their scout cars and with great care taking them across to their aircraft. Watching the distant scene through his invaluable glasses, Yeats-Urley saw that the wounded were being carried into one of the aircraft, the dead into the other. He also noticed that the surplus personnel who had arrived with the Junkers had established a camp. A couple of tents had gone up. No doubt someone was cooking a meal for everyone, the usual routine of desert camping regardless of fatalities to comrades.

Just on darkness the two Junkers finally took off in turn, their three engines filling the world with tremendous sound, and seeming to shatter in deafening waves upon the rocky escarpment. It was some relief to the S.A.S. to see them go. But the Germans were still in camp less than five miles away.

Yeats-Urley and his men saw a final load being taken from the wrecked plane after the dead and injured had gone. These were the survivors who had somehow come through the ordeal with little injury and just a violent shaking up. They watched the last Opel speed off towards the German camp, a cloud of dust hanging in the air for a long time afterwards, marking their passage across the desert.

'But they haven't completely gone,' thought Yeats-Urley. Not right out of the area. Five miles meant nothing in that desert. The enemy would find the abandoned truck – had probably seen it, in fact, from their aircraft before landing – and would know the S.A.S. were now without transport and in the vicinity. With their scout cars they could virtually set up a cordon around the area, while systematically searching every square yard within miles. That was one thing that could be said about the Germans. They were a very systematic people.

'While they're camped on our doorstep, the L.R.D.G. won't be able to get through to us,' Fairlop said to his captain.

'That's for certain.' And without the L.R.D.G. they couldn't get out of the desert.

As always, Yeats-Urley's mind went over the situation, evaluating it in terms of possible survival. The result was depressing. The Germans wouldn't leave the area until they had searched it intensively and were satisfied the S.A.S. weren't there – or had found them. While the Germans were there, the L.R.D.G. were incapable of helping them. If they took to the hills on foot they'd be hunted by aircraft, and how long could they survive?

'We really are up agen it,' the young captain decided, then he became briskly efficient.

The Germans were safely out of the way now, and there was still quite a lot of light left. He ordered all fit men to go down to where the truck had been and obliterate every vestige of their presence there. The supplies and equipment which had been off-loaded when the Chev went out were to be brought into the cave, Yeats-Urley ordered.

Vecchi and the ex-artillery-man, Partridge, did not go to help their comrades. They were lying at the back of the cave, where it was coolest, the two Italians quietly sitting by them, intently watching the proceedings at the entrance to the cavern. Seeing them, Yeats-Urley frowned. What with wounded and two Eytie prisoners, they had too much on their hands. It affected their plans – the only plans Yeats-Urley could make at that moment. He wasn't going to surrender or stay and be caught.

The men kept staggering up the rocky path bearing boxes of ammunition, cases containing food, spare equipment, jerricans of petrol and water. . . . Another worry. Not enough water, the captain thought. Losing the second truck had thrown too many thirsty men on to the meagre supplies of their one surviving vehicle, now no more. And the prisoners were a strain upon their water rationing, too. Blast the prisoners. He wondered now if he oughn't to have done something about them before this. What, he didn't care to think in that moment.

He went down to where Fairlop was standing, a few yards down the slope, giving a hand up to the struggling men. He said, 'Freddie, we must keep a very close eye on our Eytie friends. They mustn't be able to betray our position, right?'

Fairlop nodded, his face setting very hard. The Italians had once betrayed him to the enemy and he had never forgotten it.

'They must be watched, night and day from now on. We can't take risks with the Boche just down the road from us.'

Fairlop said, picking his words carefully, 'No matter what we do, they'll always be a risk. What do we do if the Germans start searching around this place? Gag 'em?' He looked away from his captain, staring hard into the fading light where the wrecked Junkers lay. 'I think we ought to dispose of them, Alan. They're too big a risk.'

Yeats-Urley didn't ask what he meant by disposing of them. Instead he switched the conversation. 'Freddie, we're in a jam and you know it. It's no good stopping on here. If we stay they'll find us, sooner or later. But they're not going to find me.' His voice was grim. He wasn't going into the bag without an attempt at escape.

'What are you going to do?'

'I'm going to break out – tonight,' said the captain firmly. 'As soon as it's dark. I'm going to have a bash at walking out of the desert.'

'To Siwa?' That was the nearest oasis. 'But that's about a couple of hundred miles, and could you find it without the L.R.D.G?' He thought for a moment, then said, decisively, 'It's in enemy hands, anyway.'

'It mightn't be. Not now. Remember when we set off

on this jaunt the Free French were mounting an expedition against Jalo. Before they take Jalo they'll have to capture Siwa.' Jalo and Siwa were just about the most southerly positions of strategic value in the desert war, hundreds of miles from the coast where most of the fighting was.

'Could be.' Fairlop nodded. They were both climbing up to the cave mouth, all the men down below now, doing a sweeping operation. 'Anyway, count me in.'

'Good man,' said Yeats-Urley approvingly. 'We'll put it to the chaps when they come up. Anyone who wants to stay and give himself up can do so.' He didn't think any of the fit commandos would listen to that idea. 'It means we'll have to leave the injured.'

'Yes.' That was inevitable. Probably Partridge especially would be better off being treated as a prisoner by an enemy doctor, for otherwise he might lose his arm and possibly his life. Gangrene soon set in under such circumstances. 'But what about the prisoners, Alan? We can't take them with us, and we can't leave 'em, either. We want all the time possible for a getaway. Leave them and they'll soon have the Boche after us.'

They halted for a moment, staring at each other, their minds going over all possible permutations of survival. The hardfaced Fairlop, that man who had been brought up to think only of Fairlop, spoke again. 'There's only one thing with them, Alan. Just one thing.'

Yeats-Urley drew in his breath for a moment, then said, simply, 'Is there?'

He turned and took two last climbing steps that brought his eyes above the level of the cave floor. Private Vecchi was standing just within, leaning against the rocky wall of the mouth of the cavern. He looked ill, his face feverish.

As they halted he came out, slowly, holding on to the rock. He walked a little distance then, head pressed to the rock as if he were dizzy, Vecchi urinated. 'Watch yourself.' Yeats-Urley called warningly to the driver, then gave him a hand back into the cave. But later he said softly to Fairlop,

'I think that bugger heard us.' And Vecchi had cause enough – or thought he had – to hate the lieutenant.

All the cynical Fairlop said was, 'And he's too damned friendly with the Eyties. We'd better watch Driver Vecchi, I think.' Fairlop went and sat in the last of the sunlight, looking down at the working party below, then finally at the wrecked Junkers. Suddenly, after only a few minutes, he rose and walked back to where Yeats-Urley was trying to knock a nail down in his shoe.

'Alan, I don't think there's any need for us to do any walking, after all.' He gestured towards the wrecked Junkers. 'I can see a perfectly good car there – probably there's a pair inside this one, too. Why don't we knock 'em off in the night, and ride off in style?'

Yeats-Urley said, 'Good lord, I never thought of that!' But the big, raw-boned lieutenant, with his strong instincts for looking after his own good, most certainly had.

Both put their glasses on the wreckage. Yeats-Urley was tingling suddenly with excitement. Riding off in style appealed to him. So did the impudence of stealing enemy vehicles. As they stared through their glasses they conversed in short jerky sentences. The light was fading, but they could see well enough, and anyway previous vision, under better conditions, was strongly imprinted on their memory, helping them now.

'You're right, it does look possible.' That Opel was hanging half out of the plane.

'The door's practically ripped off. Get Hill and Hoyle on the job and they'll soon do the rest.' – Fairlop, talking quickly.

'There'll be noise. . . .

'They're five miles away.'

'Sound travels. . . .'

'We'll just have to work quietly.' There was a touch of desperation in the lieutenant's voice. Or was it ruthlessness? Almost brutally – 'It's got to be done. We don't stand a chance without vehicles.' And in that moment he spoke the truth about their previous plan to try to walk to Siwa

Oasis on foot. They would never have survived, and in their hearts they had really known it.

' Yeats-Urley lowered his glasses. 'Quite right, Freddie. We've got to get those scout cars.' They conferred, making plans. They would have to wait until the moon was up, because they would need light by which to work, and they could hardly go around flashing torches. That might attract attention, even five miles away. 'A pity,' added the captain. 'There won't be much of the night left by the time we get on the move.'

Fairlop said, 'They might mount a guard on the plane.'

Yeats-Urley didn't think so, but if they did they would have to dispose of it quietly before getting on with the work. He called down to the men to desist with their operations. If they were leaving it didn't matter if they left the stuff below.

The men came toiling up the rocky path to the cave, and obedient to their patrol commander's order, grouped around him. With a nice sense of drama he told them – 'I've just had an interesting conversation with Mr Fairlop. He thinks it's time we left this place, and he thinks we ought to borrow a couple of cars from Jerry.' They sat up at that, their eyes sparkling with the thought. 'So that's what we're going to do. They're there, in the Junkers, waiting for us to pick them up. When the moon's out, we're going to do a quiet job of winkling those scout cars from the wreckage. So, gentlemen, my advice to you is to get your heads down now and catch as much sleep as possible.'

The men were delighted, relief at this chance to escape from their parlous position evident in their quick laughter, the excited talk among themselves before settling down to sleep.

At two in the morning, with the chill of night upon them, and the moon beginning to show, the men were roused. There was still time to have a drink and a meal before the moon attained a useful height, and anyway there was a job of reconnaissance to do before tackling the aircraft. Lieutenant Fairlop undertook it alone, on his insistence. He was a man of steady nerves in a crisis, a man of some contradictions,

Yeats-Urley thought, watching him go silently down the rocky path, then disappeared into the darkness. He wondered yet again if there was anything in Vecchi's story, about leaving his men to fend for themselves.

Fairlop came back within half an hour. There was no guard on the plane, he said. What worried him was that there was no light to say if the German camp was still there, and he thought they ought be able to see one from out on the desert. Yeats-Urley argued that they were unlikely to have a light on all night, which was true, but that wasn't the point of Fairlop's unease.

'Suppose they shifted camp after dark? Suppose they're not far away?' Both thought these were unwarrantable suppositions, but they had to be entertained because men survived in the desert by anticipating the unusual.

'We'll have a patrol out while we work,' Yeats-Urley decided, though that wouldn't leave many men for the heavy labour involved. They could lie up in the dark, half a mile away, and if the enemy made a surprise attack, *they* would be surprised instead. He gave orders. Mack, Shiner and Medman, their lightest weights, would go off and lie up in the dark. They were sound men and would know their job without officers or N.C.O.s. The rest would go out to the plane.

Fairlop stopped him at that, and asked if he could have a word with him. Surprised, Yeats-Urley stepped outside the cave. Fairlop spoke softly. 'What about the prisoners? This would be their chance to make a dash for the German camp.'

It was a possibility, though the Italians, intelligent men, gave no impression of wanting to indulge in heroics. 'We'll have to put Partridge on guard over them.' That was all they could do. They needed every able-bodied man for the night's work. 'Let's ask if he feels fit enough.'

Partridge was awake and listening from his blanket against the cave wall. Yeats-Urley shone his torch on him. The man was wasting with suffering and looked half his normal size.

Yeats-Urley spoke kindly. 'Can you do one job for us, Partridge?'

'If I can, sir.'

'Are you well enough to keep guard on the prisoners while we're out there?'

He looked tired, very tired and in pain, but his answer was prompt. 'I am, sir. I'll do it.'

'They mustn't get out of this cave, you understand?'

Partridge understood. They brought his blanket to the mouth of the cavern and left him there with his tommy-gun. Driver Vecchi did not seem to understand the manoeuvre, for it was done very quietly. Then Yeats-Urley led the way to the plane.

It was not altogether a pleasant feeling when finally they walked out of their rocky cleft on to the open desert. M'Bain said it felt like a hermit crab being deprived of its shell, and Yeats-Urley heard the remark and thought it revealed more of the man than he had expected. But he told him to stop talking.

The moon silvered the landscape, picking out the shiny surfaces of rocks on the long wall of an escarpment. It wasn't a good light, but it was good enough to see their way across to the crumpled Junkers. The tiny patrol, consisting of Shiner, Medman and Mack, left them there, moving off into the silent landscape to hide up and provide protection. The rest got quickly on with their work.

The moon was inadequate for much of what they had to do, and after a time Yeats-Urley took risks and used his torch. Then things moved more briskly.

It all took time, however, much longer than they expected, and all the while they were tensed and alert, expecting every moment attack to come from the darkness. The trouble was, they had to drag the smashed door clear away in order to get the two vehicles out, and it was held by torn and twisted metal which was the devil of a job to break off. They made noise, too, and the sounds seemed appallingly loud, and they were sure they must have alerted the distant Germans, but later their patrol, a mere quarter of a mile away, said they heard sounds, but it didn't amount to much.

A couple of hours passed before finally they were able to drag the first vehicle out of the wreckage. The second one came easily, in a matter of minutes. But by now they were feeling frantic, for dawn couldn't be far off – much less than two hours away – and they had a lot to do, and anyway they must be well out of this neighbourhood when the hunt resumed with daylight. To make matters worse, there was a very heavy dew, quite usual after a dust-storm, and when they weren't hard at work they shivered uncomfortably, their thin clothing clammy against their bodies.

They pushed the vehicles to their hide-out, though that took time, for they felt that to start up the engines would be a sure way of drawing attention upon themselves. Still, the going was pretty firm, and the men big and husky, and they took the scout cars across at a run. Even so they felt relieved when finally they came to the security of their hide-out. Now they could make noise and even work by the headlights of the two purloined vehicles. The fighting patrol was brought in, then sent out to sweep away all traces of tyre marks leading from the Junkers to their hide-out. In time the Germans would rumble things, but the longer they were perplexed the better.

Then the tanks were filled up with petrol – Lieutenant Fairlop reported that with two vehicles their reserve of fuel wouldn't go far. Yeats-Urley's retort was they'd think about that when it ran out. Just now all he wanted was to get out of this unhealthy neighbourhood. He was just as worried by their shortage of water.

Their kit, food, water, ammunition and supplies were distributed between the two vehicles, while Fullalove, their mechanical expert, checked each car and started the engines. They ran perfectly. Their hopes rose at the sound, and they even managed to forget the shivering cold and dampness of their surroundings. Then some of the men went up to bring down the prisoners and their injured comrades. Gunner Partridge reported that there had been no trouble with his prisoners, and then asked for morphia, because he was feeling very bad.

During this time the lieutenant sought out his patrol captain and told him what was in his mind. It was Fairlop whose wits seemed sharpened by their danger, and who was doing the thinking now.

'You're still planning to run to Siwa?'

Yeats-Urley was surprised. 'Where else?' It was the only place on the map so far into the desert.

'We'll never make it.' Fairlop was abrupt, a man with a limited amount of tact. He gave his reasons shortly, and it was evident that he had done some hard thinking all during the night.

They hadn't the L.R.D.G. with them, he pointed out, those superb navigators of the desert. Their own ability to navigate successfully across the vast expanses of featureless desert was, to say the least of it, limited. He pointed out that they had to find a tiny spot – the oasis – in the Sahara, and to do so they would have to drive close to the Great Sand Sea. This treacherous area of soft sand, the size of Ireland, was a formidable obstacle on their route. If once they strayed into it, their vehicles would sink and be lost to them.

Yeats-Urley said, with surprising good humour, 'Yet you were prepared to walk to Siwa. Why?'

Fairlop gave a simple answer. 'Because you said you were going,' and at that Yeats-Urley laughed aloud.

'All right, Freddie, you're putting across a sales talk.' He checked himself. Fairlop had been a salesman of some sort, hadn't he? Mightn't like reminding of it. 'What's in your mind?'

What Fairlop had in mind was audacious. 'Let's double right back on our tracks and head for the coast road. It's the last place they'll think of looking for us – at first, anyway. When they find we've nabbed their Opels they'll be sure we're continuing our run into the desert. In fact, they'll suspect Siwa as being our destination. They'll concentrate their search that way, and while they're doing so it gives us chance to make tracks north. I tell you, Alan, it's the safest thing to do – we won't get away with it, heading south.'

Running right back on to the enemy lines? It sounded crazy at first, but there was logic in Fairlop's argument, and Yeats-Urley was a good enough commander to give every suggestion his careful thought. What impressed him about the idea was that for a time, anyway, the tactic would throw the enemy and have them on a wild goose chase. How long that would be, he didn't know. All he knew, as quite a veteran of the S.A.S., was that even a few hours' grace could mean life or death – or going into the bag – for them.

He looked at the sky. He thought it was beginning to pale. If they set off now, by dawn they could hardly be ten miles away, possibly with no cover. Besides, their way to Siwa lay past the German camp, which meant time being wasted in ravelling round it. He made his decision.

'I think you're on to something, Freddie. Any more thoughts?' His voice was respectful. This awkward lieutenant was proving a man of resource.

Fairlop said, 'We've got to keep them foxed as much as possible, as long as possible. When we drive out of here we must obliterate our tread marks. Then we must drive back along our old tyre marks. They mightn't tumble to it for quite some time.'

Captain Yeats-Urley spoke with vigour. 'Right! We'll do just what you say, Freddie. Jolly good idea. I just wish the Lord was kind and didn't come up with daylight so fast.'

In fact the Lord was very kind. True, he came up with daylight at the appointed time, but he brought a thick ground mist with it that hung over the desert for a good couple of hours. The heavy dew that had chilled them during the night was now turning to their advantage.

That again cheered them as they set off. Apart from the cover it gave them, holding up any search, they knew it would muffle the sounds of their departure, and that too was a big advantage.

So they drove out of the cleft, boldly using their headlights. All they needed, thought Yeats-Urley, was a captured radio so that they could talk to their friends, the L.R.D.G. The

Germans had failed them in that respect. Out on the desert they swung east until abruptly the tyre marks of their old Chev appeared in the sand. Both vehicles ran on to them, though their tracks were narrower than the 3-tonner's, then halted while men came up from behind, obliterating all marks leading from the cleft that had been their home so briefly. Then the scout cars, far too heavily loaded for comfort, each with six or seven occupants, were started up again and off they went.

They had three hours' run before the mist began quite quickly to disperse, but in anticipation of that moment they had already begun to take evasive action. It was no good sticking to their old trail too long, Yeats-Urley explained, because once the German land force spotted the ruse – 'Bound to, the moment someone takes it in his head to examine those tyre marks,' he said, German treads being so distinctive – they'd radio the Luftwaffe, and a plane would be along their tracks in no time.

So with daylight they kept a look out, limited though it was by ground mist, for hard ground, and when they saw some they pulled on to it, and thereafter sought hard going as much as possible. That would fox the enemy even further, they told each other with satisfaction.

Even so they did not continue to run once the cover of the mist had gone. Not long, anyway. They found a promising *ghot* – a depression rather profusely covered with camel thorn and other scrub – and went to ground there. They reversed the vehicles into the thickest part of the scrub and added more torn-up bushes until both were undetectable from a range of more than a few yards. Then they tucked themselves away to rest up until darkness provided safe cover again.

The day passed slowly, the men dozing as much as they could, but all the while everyone subconsciously alert and listening for the approach of danger. Yeats-Urley had two sentries on watch all the time, strategically placed, taking no risks of surprise.

The heat was suffocating in that bit of a hollow, the

sandhills that ringed it seeming to reflect the sun's rays directly into the centre as if like some converging lens. The flies found them, too, as always, crawling for the moisture of their eyes and into the corners of their mouths. They came in black droves from nowhere, making Yeats-Urley suspect they were near to some Arab village or camp.

It was an exhausting day, but for the two injured men the torment was greatest. Some time after noon, with the heat at its greatest, M'Bain heard Partridge start moaning. He was a bit of a pal of the Mitcham gunner, and he went over to where Partridge lay under some bushes and asked if he could do anything to help him. Vecchi, for all his own discomfort, hauled himself off his blanket and came to where Partridge lay, very concerned. Like most of the men, Vecchi was a good-hearted chap, thought M'Bain. Just Oily, he didn't like; and he never quite took to the lieutenant, either, his thoughts added.

Partridge didn't want to make a fuss, but his arm was now so inflamed it was making him half-delirious. He had a raging thirst, too, and he asked if one of them could get him some water. M'Bain went off and roused the captain. 'He's in a very bad way, sir,' he pleaded. They were on a strict water ration, a mug of tea three times a day, and that was all the liquid they got. In that dehydrating heat, three gallons wouldn't have been too much. 'We'd all do with a little less if he could have some.'

'Nice of you to make that offer,' said the captain. 'Get him a pint. And if Vecchi wants some, let him have some, too.' They'd run out of petrol before their water cans were all dry, he thought. Still, for the rest the ration must be maintained.

So M'Bain took the mug of water back to Partridge, who drank greedily, finished the lot in his awful thirst, then lay back exhausted. Vecchi, who seemed a little brighter than previously, perhaps because for most of the past twenty-four hours they'd lain up resting, muttered, 'Seen his arm?'

M'Bain said, 'Let's have a look at your arm, cock,' taking his cue from Vecchi.

Without opening his eyes Partridge said, 'It's going black. Have a look at it.'

Carefully, apprehensively, M'Bain unrolled the dirty bandage. What he saw shocked him. The forearm where the break was had swollen to disturbing size, and there was a black discoloration that wasn't a bruise and looked infinitely more painful. M'Bain wanted to draw away, shocked, but did not betray his feelings.

'That'll soon go, mate.' He put cheerfulness into his voice, but it deceived no one.

'Who're you kiddin'?' Partridge's eyes were wide open now, and fear was in them, terrible fear. 'It's gangrene. I'm goin' to lose my arm if I don't get attention.'

M'Bain said, 'Keep still and let me bandage you again.' When it was done he moved off with Vecchi and they squatted together in the shade, though there was no coolness there.

Vecchi said, 'He's right. He's got to have medical attention.' His own face was thin and fever bright, for all that M'Bain thought he looked stronger.

'You don't look so good yourself.'

Vecchi gestured impatiently. 'I'm just sore. Hurts like hell. Can't move without these ribs playing me up.' He did look bad, crouching to reduce the pain in his side. 'Sure I could do with a bed in a hospital, but I'm not like old Party there.' His eyes came round to meet M'Bain's and they were too bright and too widely distended, sharing Partridge's fear. 'He'll die. He's bound to die if we don't get a doc to him within a few hours.'

'Well, what can we do about it?' What could they do? This was war. Young men got hurt and died in wars, and Partridge looked as if he was going to be one of them.

Vecchi said, 'If we run close by an Italian camp, just go on and leave us. I'll stay with him; I can speak Italian, you know.' The old pride in his voice. 'I don't mind going in the bag. Anyway, I'm useless, no good any more for the patrol.'

M'Bain saw Lieutenant Fairlop stirring, crawling out from under a bush, then rising wearily to his feet and looking round as if in search of some cooler place. He was an optimist, thought M'Bain. To Vecchi he said, 'I'll have a word with Fairlop about what you say.'

Vecchi stopped him. His tone was venomous. 'Not that bastard. I want nothing to do with him. He only thinks of himself – he buggered off and left us.'

M'Bain wanted to say, 'The others didn't seem to notice it,' but he felt terribly tired, and the flies were eating him, and he didn't want to upset poor old Vecchi.

He said, 'I'll have a word with the captain.'

'Do it now,' said Vecchi. 'And tell him Antonio and Piero must be left with us, too.'

M'Bain whistled silently at that, knowing his captain, but he hauled himself on to legs that always felt weary in the heat of the day, and again went with dragging steps to find the patrol commander.

Yeats-Urley was awake this time, sweating it out under the bushes. 'You again, M'Bain,' said the officer, but in spite of the pressures upon him, and his own great tiredness, he did not speak with any impatience. 'Anything else you want?'

'Sir.' M'Bain squatted before him, the flies finding his bare skin and making him twitch. 'I've just been talking to Vecchi.'

'Yes? What's he got to say?'

M'Bain made the best of it for his comrade. 'Vecchi knows he and Partridge are drags upon you, sir.'

'But they're our men. We've got to look after them.' Yeats-Urley looked rather than expressed his surprise.

'Yes, sir. What Vecchi says is, couldn't you find some Italian camp and drop them off nearby, him and Partridge, sir? We could do it during the night. We're sure to find one across The Graveyard. Vecchi says he doesn't mind going in the bag, but old Party will die for sure if he doesn't get medical aid.'

The captain looked silently at the lance-corporal for a few seconds, weighing up the proposition. 'Vecchi really doesn't mind going in the bag?'

'No, sir. Not if it can save Party's life, sir.'

Yeats Urley gave more thought to the matter. It went against his instincts to leave any of his men to the mercy of the enemy, but he knew M'Bain was right. Partridge would die if his arm wasn't quickly attended to. Under the best of circumstances it would take them several days to reach their own lines, and 'days' were probably optimism. Unloading the two injured men would improve the rest's chances of making for safety – and Vecchi said he didn't mind. Probably would give anything to take his broken ribs out of this damned inferno and just rest in some bed in hospital, he thought, and didn't blame the driver.

'I'll talk to Mr Fairlop about it. Thank you for telling me.'

M'Bain rose and the flies attacked the flesh behind his legs, where it had creased in squatting and had accumulated a thin film of perspiration. The clinging little limbs crawled and made him want to dance, but he just batted behind him with his flat hand and obtained a second's relief.

'There's one thing more, sir.' Yeats-Urley waited for it. 'Vecchi wants the Italian prisoners to be left with him.'

Yeats-Urley gave a little laugh, genuinely amused at the thought. 'Hand our prisoners back to the enemy? I hardly think we can do that, corporal. Do you think so?'

M'Bain was silent. These are the sort of questions officers ask, but it is diplomatic not to make any reply unless you can agree. M'Bain couldn't care less about the blasted Eyties. Let the poor beggars go free, was his thought; it was wrong that civvies should have to suffer what they were going through. It was on the tip of his tongue to say, 'Leave me with Vecchi, too. I don't mind going into the bag, either.' Anything to get relief from this awful desert! But he said nothing.

Yeats-Urley's face set. 'When we go out, they go out with us.' Which could mean anything. Yeats-Urley wasn't a man to have obsessions, but having collared two important Italians he saw it as his duty to bring them back to the Allied line or in any other way deprive the enemy of their services. Yeats-Urley took the soldier's point of view that anything done to discomfit the enemy helped his side to win the war.

M'Bain trudged back to Vecchi. 'What's he say?' The eyes were eager now.

M'Bain struck out again at the flies. 'He says he'll have a word with Fairlop about it.'

'Fairlop!' The bitterness exploded from the injured man. 'Do you think he'll do anything for me after what I said against him?'

He raved on for quite a while, and M'Bain squatted there, just listening tiredly. No one was right in the head after weeks in the desert, but if your ribs were bust and you'd been bounced around in a truck for days on end – and nights, too – there wasn't much sanity left in a fellow. He thought poor old Vecchi was round the bend. Well, so was he. Again he began to think about staying behind when they dropped Vecchi. He couldn't stand much more of this scurrying and hiding, and all this terrible heat and too little water so that the thirst was always upon him, and the feeling of a relentless enemy determined to seek them out and end their lives with a spinning bullet. His mind, just as tormented as Vecchi's, kept on and on, spiralling miserably into depression though he never showed it.

He went and lay down but the heat was intolerable, rolling into the *ghot*, and his thoughts continued on and on, and all the time it was about getting out of this blasted desert, no matter how he managed it.

When Vecchi and poor old Party were dumped, he'd slip off and stay behind. He'd go into the bag and it would seem like heaven after this nightmare, he thought, no more being hunted like vermin, always plenty of water to drink and real shade and coolness, and no fear of death diving down from the sky or suddenly opening up on them from the surrounding cover. What was the difference between deserting here in the Sahara, and waiting to desert when they finally reached the Sweet Water Canal? Only that the agony of this tortured way of life would be ended quicker.

M'Bain talked to himself, arguing for and against, and always coming back to the determination that at the first opportunity he was going to scarper and the hell with the consequences.

He was not alone in his thoughts. Several others entertained something similar, the discomfort of their life momentarily too much for them. The thing was, with the cool of the evening for all but M'Bain there would be a change of mind. But M'Bain really was at the end of his tether.

Yeats-Urley suffered no less than his men. Sometimes his dreams went back to the gracious living in England, with a servant at home to do everything for him, baths and fresh linen, the ease and comfort of middle-class life, the wine at meals, the good fellowship in clubs, the hunt balls and the debs who went to them. And now this. But he mustn't show his weariness with the life, his own fears and depression. He had to keep the old upper lip stiff, and be hearty and set an example or morale would soon go. His class were born to lead, his father had always told him, and he felt he would be letting the side down if he failed to lead gallantly and well. But still it was hard agony, this miserable existence, and he too wished for the time when they got out and he could sit in the Continental or Shepheards and drink ice-cold beer, or dawdle in Groppis over coffee and rich cakes in company with some lush Italian or French *bint*, so easy to pop into bed at night.

As far as possible he stopped his thoughts when they escaped from the desert. That was no way to get on with the job. Now, lying there, too dehydrated to sweat, he thought of Vecchi's request and decided it was best to accede to it. Without the wounded they'd be able to move faster. But not the Italians, they must come with them, encumbrance and danger to their safety though they were.

He stopped thinking of Vecchi, and no longer even thought of Fairlop's warning when they first came into this *ghot* and he had filled the petrol tanks just in case they had to make a hurried departure. 'Alan, that's our lot. When that's done, we've no more juice left.' And those tankfuls would just about take them across The Graveyard. What then? He would meet that situation later, he told himself each time the question surfaced in his mind. At the moment he was too occupied in putting himself into the enemy's shoes.

All the time they had been travelling, and almost all the time he had lain there, dozing uncomfortably, he had been trying to divine the activities of the Germans back by the Junkers.

They'd drive across to the wrecked aircraft at dawn, as soon as they could see the way. Yeats-Urley pictured the scene on their arrival. The scout cars would halt, and probably with no great haste the men would alight. They would move round to the unloading doors, a working party all set to bring out the Opels inside.

Almost the only satisfaction Yeats-Urley got that day was in thinking of their consternation when they came round the side of the Junkers and saw the gaping hole and no cars within. They just wouldn't believe their eyes for a minute, and they'd probably run forward and clamber inside the hull, and look round as if to make sure someone hadn't hidden the cars round the corner.

Then they'd come out into the hot sunshine, all talking, unbelieving still, men suddenly apprehensive of military retribution; for this was their responsibility and they'd slept through the night with no guard on the aircraft.

What would they do then? the young captain kept asking himself.

They'd look round, of course – that would be the first instinct, as if hoping to see the missing cars standing there in full view on the desert. Some might even turn their glasses over the vastness, but the result would be the same – no Opels.

And then what? They'd be in quite a panic, horrified by their situation, Yeats-Urley thought, lying there, and once again he let his mind dwell on that fancied moment, the only thing of joy in a tedious day. He could imagine the way they would react, everyone too startled to think clearly for the moment, and being even more shaken when they thought to look for tyre marks and found none.

That would really put them in a tizzy, the officer thought, and smiled inwardly at their consternation. Someone would think to look on the ground, and seeing no treads would exclaim and draw attention to the further mystery, and then all those German soldiers would go running round the Junkers trying to find tyre marks and solve at lest part of the conundrum. When they found none anywhere, there would be bewilderment, real astonishment. Two Opels had vanished in the night, not even leaving traces of their going on the soft sand. They must have thought for a fleeting moment that there had been Divine Intervention, or at least a helicopter had been employed.

They'd sober quite quickly, of course; these Germans were a hard-headed and practical people, quickly losing any thoughts of the supernatural. There'd be an officer in command, and he'd soon start to bark out orders. Which would be, thought Yeats-Urley, having been on the spot more times than he liked to say in his army life, to radio an immediate confession to higher command that he had been negligent but was doing everything in his power to make good the situation.

The radio message would have to go out immediately. If there wasn't a radio on one of the scout cars that had come to the Junkers the officer would send one scudding back to the German camp, where for certain there would be one. And the message? It could only take one form, Yeats-Urley decided. 'Regret to report loss of two Opel scout cars believed taken by S.A.S.' What an awful admission to have to make, and how the officer must have hated sending it, knowing the wrath soon to fall upon him as a consequence. So he would quickly add a further sentence. 'Taking all steps to recover vehicles.'

Having sent the signal, ending on the note of optimism, how would the German officer, perhaps a *Hauptmann* like himself, set about finding them? And that was the important point of all Yeats-Urley's thoughts.

Of course aircraft would be summoned, but the immediate initiative would be in the hands of the officer. Logically he would beat about for tracks, but where was he likely to start looking for them? At the most he had four scout cars for the purpose of search, but he wouldn't send them scudding off singly – with two carloads of unpleasant S.A.S. maybe lurking in ambush for them? No, he'd most likely send them out in pairs, to give them massive firepower in case of attack. He would send them west and south of the Junkers, Yeats-Urley kept reassuring himself, because that was roughly the original line of flight, as Fairlop had pointed out. A big area to cover, and growing wider with each minute that failed to find Opel tracks mysteriously beginning in the sand. They could waste an hour or so just beating around the desert until finally coming together at the German camp, baffled and wondering where to search next. By which time there'd be aircraft taking up the search and reporting negative success over an even wider area.

Those were the hopes in Yeats-Urley's mind all that day, that clever Freddie Fairlop had out-thought the enemy and given them a chance to escape from the area of intensive search. Perhaps they would go on searching ever farther south and westward, taking the hunt farther and farther away from them, lying up in this God-awful *ghot*. That would be too good to be true, he thought, yet clung to it while keeping an ear open all the time for the ominous drone of an aircraft's propellers.

An intelligent officer, however, would not fall for the trick too long. Cars simply do not take off on a soft sandy desert and leave no marks over a territory miles in extent. Somewhere they had to start, and that meant quite close to the Junkers; for no one could carry Opels very far on that sand. Soon the German would suspect that the cars had gone and that a following party had obliterated the tracks, reducing mystery to simplicity, as a consequence, by this thought process.

At that he would probably order his men to cast about for tyre-marks, and sooner or later someone would come to where the Chev's treads had ended and would spot the overlying, narrower Opel tyres. There'd be a shout – it would be like a view on the hunting field, thought Yeats-Urley – and everyone would stream across, cursing at the simplicity of the ruse and damning themselves for not seeing through it before.

Instant radio messages, of course, up to the patrolling aircraft. 'Opel tracks found travelling east . . .' From that moment the hunt would be on again. The only thing that could save the S.A.S. now was how well they had sought hard ground and left no tyre impressions. Aircraft would continue to follow the Chev tracks, not able to distinguish between them and German tyre marks. Only the land force, tearing along in their Opels, would see where the scout cars had stopped running over the Chev marks, and that would put them hours behind, baffled by hard ground and little or no trace of the S.A.S.

But the aircraft would be called back, like hounds brought to heel by the master, to be sent off in a widening circle over the new area of search. All this would be taking up hours of time though, and for the moment time was welcome.

'Give us a few hours to rest up, then it will be dark and we'll be inside The Graveyard,' Yeats-Urley told himself, and as the hours dragged by it seemed that his wish was going to be granted. What happened when they reached The Graveyard was another matter; for neither vehicle had enough petrol to take it completely across the old battlefield.

Almost dead on three that torrid afternoon, the aerial search switched into the area where the S.A.S. lay up. They saw a plane distantly on the horizon, flying very low and probably ten miles away. Twenty minutes later it was closer, flying a parallel course but in a reverse direction. A third time it made the run, no more than two hundred feet above the desert, and now it was four or five miles south of them. They were able to predict, with fair accuracy, when the aircraft – a Breda again – would come looking into their *ghot*. Around four-ten, guessed Yeats-Urley, and he was only a few minutes out.

It came roaring overhead, so close it stirred the dust of the desert with its fanning propellers, and they knew sharp eyes sought to see them in their hiding. They lay close under cover, no man stirring a muscle. They lay face down, because faces glisten and reflect light and draw attention, and they even lay with their hands clasping the glass-and-metal faces of their canvas-strapped watches to prevent shine that would catch a vigilant eye. And no one was fool enough to blaze off with a gun, though the Breda was well within firing range; for that *would* have brought attention upon them.

It went skimming away into the distance, then returned on a course two miles north of them. The aerial search now embraced their territory. From now on they would have to move with caution. Fortunately the ground forces were still nowhere in sight, and Yeats-Urley was pretty sure they were lost far away, baffled by the cunning S.A.S.

Two more aircraft were sighted later that afternoon, but they were reccying other ground and did not come close enough to their *ghot* to worry them.

With the approach of darkness, the hunted stirred themselves and crept gratefully out of their shelter. It had been an unrewarding day, too stiflingly hot for them to feel any benefit from the halt, and poor Partridge was delirious now, and moaning constantly and it upset the men.

They had a welcome brew-up, and Medman, acting cook for the moment, incautiously opened a can of fish but no one wanted that. They ended up chewing on hard biscuit, and eating any odds and ends of food each man carried in his own kit. But not fish, not this sickeningly hot day.

Keeping a sharp watch out, the two vehicles risked setting off while the sun was still above the horizon. Luck was with them – they saw no aircraft and made excellent progress before darkness closed over them. After that they drove by headlight, the risk worth taking because they had to make a lot of ground that night.

Around four o'clock, the moon helping them and a vast starlit sky making its contribution to visibility, they began to move through the familiar Graveyard. With dawn coming to warm them, they were well inside the battle area, the twisted big guns, the burnt-out tanks and battered soft transport, monuments to destructive war, littering the land right up to the horizon like so many Easter Island statues. That, again, was M'Bain's unexpected impression of what he saw in the warm dawn sunlight.

On they drove, halting for breakfast before it got too hot to stand around. Fairlop peered into his petrol tank, then came over to where his superior officer was carefully scanning the horizon with his glasses.

'We're almost empty, Alan. What do we do when we run dry?'

Yeats-Urley lowered his glasses. 'What I was doing just then.' He shoved back the peaked hat that he always wore, even up the desert. 'If we have the most enormous luck we might run into an enemy recovery party and shoot them up and get petrol, food and drink.'

'So that's the plan,' Fairlop thought. Aloud – 'It's a thin hope.'

'Then give me something more substantial.'

Fairlop gave a shrug, that shrug which always seemed to convey insolence, Yeats-Urley thought. When it came to the point, though, this time Fairlop couldn't think of anything brilliant. Working parties recovering material from the wrecked guns and vehicles, or burying the dead, *were* their only hope. But how much hope could they reasonably entertain? Fairlop was pessimistic. Not much.

The certainty was that there would be several recovery parties in the old battle area – perhaps many. But The Graveyard was vast, and the problem was spotting them.

They'd be there, all right, Fairlop admitted to himself, scanning the terrain through his glasses. Might be right there within a few hundred yards of them, inconspicuously working, and they would pass by and never know. This damned refracting hot air, distorting vision, didn't help, either.

Yeats-Urley seemed to divine his thoughts. 'They've got to come in and go out of The Graveyard sometime, Freddie. That's my big hope. When someone raises the dust, we'll be after them.'

'Make sure it isn't a ground patrol looking for us.'

'Catch a tiger by the tail?' Yeats-Urley grinned at the thought. 'We'll have to take the risk.'

It meant moving by daylight, of course, though normally unless a hunt was on they took risks, crossing The Graveyard while it was light. There was plenty of cover in the form of wrecks, and for searchers, from the air or on the ground, it was always baffling, trying to detect which vehicles were wrecked and which were pretending to be. Anyway, they had no alternative; dust clouds don't show up in darkness.

They drove with very great care, partly because of Partridge, whose condition was worsening, raving in delirium, but also because they had to conserve the last of their fuel. So they travelled for several hours, stopping twice only to give the gunner shots of morphia. Fullalove administered it, their handyman. Fullalove could tackle anything mechanical, and took first aid in his stride, too.

As they drove, everyone scanned the area carefully, the two officers standing and using their glasses, but hour followed bleak hour and they saw no sign of life. The worst of it was, in that heat all vision was undependable, objects dancing and swaying and catching the eye with apparent movement where there was none. It meant that men in the two vehicles spent a lot of time intently watching where they thought they had seen human activity, only to find, when the picture resolved, that it was some derelict field gun with its barrel forlornly in the air.

Around eleven o'clock that morning, though, their search was finally rewarded. Far away, Yeats-Urley's glasses picked up a dust cloud. For ten minutes he said nothing to anyone, wanting to make sure, but finally there was no doubt about it. Someone was moving across the desert. Someone who travelled the desert would have, though not necessarily in abundance, what they urgently needed – fuel and water, and maybe some food.

Yeats-Urley turned and called out the news, signalling it with his arm to Fairlop's vehicle behind, and everyone roused themselves and tried to stand and look, indefatigable Hill even cheering but also saying, 'Bet them buggers are looking for us. You watch out, sir, it's probably a panzer division.'

But Yeats-Urley knew it wasn't. By now he was sure the dust was raised by a small party. How small, though? He didn't bother to waste time in speculating, because at that moment they had no alternative. Whatever its size it had to be tackled if they were to continue to escape. . . .

Of course while they were eagerly moving into the kill, the first of the day's aircraft began to cover this part of the battlefield. It cost them time, and they grew anxious, thinking they would lose their quarry while they hid. But with a Messerschmitt 109E this time flitting low over the desert, they had no alternative but to halt and get into disguise.

That was easy. Both vehicles were driven a few hundred yards apart, Yeats-Urley's almost up against a rusting Crusader tank, the other where gun-pits and some 2-pounders lay mangled following heavy shelling. Other real wrecks diverted attention, they had long ago learned. Bonnets up added to the illusion of abandoned vehicles. The men simply hid in the gun pits or abandoned vehicles, taking their wounded and prisoners with them.

When the Messerschmitt finally disappeared over the horizon, everyone came quickly out of hiding. Yeats-Urley had his glasses up immediately. The dust cloud had gone. When the others, crowding round, heard the news, they set up a train of blasphemy that shook even the hardened captain.

'That soddin' rotten, flamin' plane,' said Shiner, and went into details about the pilot's ancestry, and this was about the mildest that was said about German aviation.

Yeats-Urley, almost incapable of getting into a flap, just said, 'Okay, calm down, you chaps. Nothing's lost. I took a bearing on it before we took cover.'

The others looked at him with admiration and relief. 'You clever old captain,' crooned big Maurice Hill. 'We'll put you up for a Naafi medal for that, sir.' It made everyone laugh, but relief always makes people want to laugh away their recent fears.

Yeats-Urley told them – 'We know the bearing, but we don't know how far. So we're likely to come on them unexpectedly. Be ready, you chaps. Ready with your guns.' He knew they would be.

Five minutes later Fairlop's Opel ran out of petrol. To men, nerves keyed up for battle, this seemed a disaster. In Yeats-Urley's vehicle, Shiner saw the other scout car halt and recede behind them. 'Sir,' he called, 'Mr Fairlop's stopped.'

Yeats-Urley told Medman to halt. They waited. Fairlop did not resume his way. So Yeats-Urley got down and trudged the few hundred yards of burning sand back to the second Opel. He guessed the trouble, and walked instead of using his own vehicle to go back because he didn't also want to run out of petrol at this critical time. Even so, it would be a blow, having only one scout car in a time of need.

Fairlop said, 'Out of juice, Alan. What do we do now?'

'We leave you and go ahead and when we get petrol we'll return.' Captain Yeats-Urley was very calm and assured. He gave orders that the prisoners, who were in his car, should be brought back and left with Fairlop. All he wanted for this action was Fullalove, his best machine-gunner, Private Hill and his driver, Medman. Too many beds in a fighting vehicle got in the way, he told them. Anyway, he wasn't going into battle with a couple of Eytie prisoners to keep an eye on.

So Fairlop was left to keep his party comfortable the best way he could, Shiner marching the two Italians over to join them. Then Yeats-Urley checked his bearing and drove on.

They drove with great care, and all the time they listened to

171

the beat of the engine, expecting any moment to hear it die on them. But it kept going. Now they were almost indifferent to the possibility of another aircraft coming over and spotting them, and they might not even have halted if one had come hurtling towards them over the horizon. They were creeping forward to the kill, and had no thoughts for anything else.

They passed derelicts in the sand, scanning each one carefully on approach, but before reaching them eliminating them as their quarry. Too derelict. They also passed a lot of charred bodies, still unburied, alongside a blackened tank that had gone up in flames. The crew, no doubt, just getting out and dying. But the gruesome sight had no effect upon them. They wanted to live and for this they were prepared to kill – they had to, in fact, because those were now the rules of the desert.

They saw them suddenly. The dancing air currents seemed to freeze for a moment. Right in front of them were two vehicles – two good vehicles, they knew immediately. One was backed right up against a German 88mm gun. They drove up quietly, expecting any moment to hear a sentry's cry, but none came. So far behind the front line – at least three hundred as the crow or bomber flew – no one expected enemy trouble. So keeping watch was not performed with any great alertness.

Yeats-Urley, down on his seat now so as not to arouse suspicion, got the picture as they came quietly, rather slowly, over the bumpy sand. A German truck backed against the big gun, lifting-tackle around the barrel. Doubtless it was a recovery party salvaging precious gun barrels, the rest of the gun being too damaged to move. With all his losses in trying to ship supplies through Italy, Rommel would be anxious to use any spares he could get out of the desert wrecks.

The other vehicle – something like a Bedford with a canvas hood – turned out to be a Lancia on closer inspection. A German truck and an Italian. What nationality were these . . . and how many men were there? He felt pretty sure they would be Germans, in spite of the Italian Lancia, because Germans were most likely to be interested in an 88mm gun. But where were they, the working party?

For the moment there was absolutely no sign of life around the two vehicles and the Opel crept to within fifty yards before they saw their first enemy soldier.

They were running quietly, machine-guns ready, Fulla-love standing behind the Vickers which he had mounted in place of the German Spandau – the corporal felt more sure of the old Vickers than the German gun. But inevitably they made some sound and it must have attracted attention. From between the two parked vehicles a head peered round. There was a peaked baseball-type cap on it – a German. The face seemed to look at them with little surprise or interest, and then the German stepped into full view. He was without shirt, his muscular body beautifully tanned, as were the big legs that showed beneath the brief shorts he wore. He had a rifle slung over his shoulder – the sentry. Yet for the moment he was entirely unsuspicious. Just one small car was bumping towards him, and a German car at that. No reason to be suspicious. . . .

They came nearer, into sight of the space between the two vehicles. By the look of it they had broken off work to have a drink – ersatz coffee, it would be, being Germans. Four bared-bodied, fine-looking young men were squatting in the shadow from the Lancia, mugs in hand. They looked across at the approaching S.A.S. and there was never a suspicion in their minds that death was on its way to them.

But all at once the sentry took alarm. Perhaps he was alerted by sight of their bearded, ragged appearance. Perhaps into his mind clicked the warning he must have received before leaving their regiment – the S.A.S. are in the neighbourhood, watch out. Perhaps he had even been told they were in purloined Opel cars, only if so he would have been looking for two and not one, and maybe running out of petrol back there had given Yeats-Urley a surprise advantage he never suspected.

The captain saw the sentry freeze, then unsling his rifle

with a quick movement. He saw the mouth open, and a harsh German command rang out. '*Halt!*'

But Yeats-Urley had beaten him to it with another order. 'Let 'em have it!'

Fullalove got his Vickers going before the rifle could be lifted and fired. Both Yeats-Urley and Maurice Hill had their tommies spraying heavy bullets in almost the same instant. The sound was deafening after the silence of the vast desert.

They saw the men scrambling to their feet, one of them leaping up on to the back of the Lancia, as if to get a weapon. The hail of bullets got him across the middle and brought him tumbling back again, and the others went spinning away as they died, falling and only feebly moving for a second or so until the last life drained out of them. It was butchery. They had no chance at all.

Hill and Yeats-Urley immediately leapt from their Opel, leaving Fullalove standing there, covering them, Medman keeping the engine running in case they had to make a swift departure. Officer and man went through the correct drill. There might be others beyond these five. Each took a truck and looked swiftly inside, guns ready to burst into action. Empty – no one there. They ran swiftly round them, ducking and looking under them because that way legs can be seen beyond. No one. There were only these five.

They came together, captain and trusted private, and the tension went instantly. They laughed, for they had given themselves life with that brief but murderous foray. Here would be the fuel and the water their lives depended on. They slapped each others' backs in mutual self-congratulation, then came back to where the killing had occurred.

They were used to death, and the sight of those bloodied young bodies did not move them any more than it moves a surgeon when patients die under them. This was war, they always told themselves, us or them. This time it was them. Another time it could be us.

Yeats-Urley didn't examine the bodies closely. 'All dead,'

he pronounced, and with those heavy bullets inside them it was difficult to imagine anyone lingering on.

So they set about the several tasks they urgently had to perform before the next plane came over. First, petrol to bring Fairlop and party in. Medman was sent off with a jerrican salvaged from the Lancia truck. There was a lot more petrol there.

Between them, working swiftly, they took stock of the situation. They found they had about sixty gallons of petrol in the enemy trucks, that is, when they also siphoned the German recovery vehicle's tank dry. The Lancia's they did not touch. Yeats-Urley had decided they could do with such a vehicle. As it was, with Partridge having to lie down and occupy a whole seat, their scout cars were uncomfortably crowded. The canvas top would be better for the injured, too, he thought, for they badly needed shade from this awful sun, and when they left Vecchi and Partridge, as they must do soon, the injured men could have one of the vehicles. For the moment Yeats-Urley was not sure which, a Lancia or an Opel. The Opel was nippier, but the bigger Lancia had some advantages. They would see how the new vehicle behaved.

They found they had got themselves some forty-odd gallons of water, not a great deal, but welcome, and a lot of food, probably rations for five men for five or six days. Some of it was various forms of German sausage, but to the half-starved S.A.S. it looked a feast. What surprised them was to find some white loaves with the Germans' rations. Evidently they were making good use of the field-bakery captured in Tobruk, and the tons of white flour that went with it.

When finally the two Opels returned with Fairlop and party, everyone jubilant, Yeats-Urley announced, 'We're going to have a feast. As much as you like to drink, and all the food you can scoff.' It was good to relax just occasionally, and he'd put them on short rations again when they'd had their blow-out.

The men cheered, and heedless of the corpses so close to them, drank and ate their fill. But there was no idleness for them, all the same. Yeats-Urley kept them working in between eating and drinking. Softer beds were made for the two injured men on camouflage nets found in the German truck. Supplies were divided among the three vehicles. Then the German truck was immobilised so as to make it useless to the enemy if ever it were found again.

In all they were fifteen minutes – no more – working fast to get them on the trail again. Time was still important. The more miles they put behind them, the safer they felt themselves to be. Finally, in better spirits than when they arrived, the two Opels and the Lancia drove off. They had petrol enough to get them to the coast road now, out of this arid desert. There they must take their chances, getting more fuel and food by raids on isolated camps, or sticking up vehicles as they had just done. And then? Well, they must simply hide away, not all that difficult – it was when you were on the move that you were vulnerable – and the S.A.S. and L.R.D.G. often lay hidden for weeks on end without the enemy knowing they were close by.

The big push, too, was due any time from Alamein. All they need do, Yeats-Urley argued, was keep their heads down until the Eighth Army romped up the coast once again and brought safety to them. It was not an argument which all others might have taken to without criticism. There were too many imponderables about the plan to appeal to the cautious. The break-out mightn't occur for weeks. And Rommel might bloody their noses again and send them reeling back. An awkward man, the field-marshal. But one had to retain one's optimism in the S.A.S. What else was there to keep them going?

When the three vehicles took off across the desert again, the man who had tried to climb into the Lancia and had been shot down, lifted his head. He was in great pain, and in fact could not stand, his spine shattered. But he could crawl, and this he did, dragging his way through the dust, leaving blood behind. He crawled to the big German truck still with its sling around the 88mm gun barrel, and without the use of his legs he somehow dragged himself up into the driver's seat. If the truck door hadn't been left swinging open following a hurried search by the S.A.S. he would never have managed the feat.

As it was, when he was inside the cab, he rested on his face for a time, lying across the seats. He was dying and probably knew it, but there was one thing he had to do before he became unconscious again.

When he felt strong enough, he pulled down the passenger's seat. Behind it, cleverly built into the wood of the cabin, was a radio transmitter. It had been made near Cambridge, in England, and had been quietly looted on one trip in the desert and fitted in so that they could receive news and music from distant Germany. It was a good set and ought by rights to have been handed over to the German Signals, but men of all armies like to 'win' things and keep them for themselves. A super-radio receiver like this British-made set wasn't something to hand to a technical branch of their army, where probably it would never be used. A set capable of picking up their home stations was of inestimable value when they had to go for days on end into the desert.

Besides, they got fun out of it. On the quiet they had used it as a transmitter, too, chatting with their regimental operators to keep away the boredom inseparable with a desert existence. The survivor of the S.A.S.'s slaughtering guns, in fact, happened to be the ham who normally operated the transmitter.

Now he operated it for the last time. He called through to regiment. He told them what had happened. Then he lay down and died, no one to give him help for too many hours. He did his final act of duty, and cooked the S.A.S.'s goose into the bargain.

From being lost somewhere in the Sahara, that radio call pinned their presence to a very few square miles. Within an hour of their jubilant departure from the recovery vehicle and 88mm anti-aircraft gun, planes were taking off, intent on reaching The Graveyard in the shortest possible time.

Ground troops were again being sent out from various units, Italian and German, and in greater numbers than ever before. The S.A.S. *had* to be found and exterminated. Those were Rommel's orders now. The Axis Higher Command had had enough of the S.A.S. effrontery and destructive ways.

They were caught in the open two hours before sunset. They'd been making good pace, leaving the battleground quite soon after shooting up the German recovery party, and for the first time in days were feeling reasonably happy men. They had satisfied their thirst, had eaten unusual food which still lingered as a pleasant memory on their taste buds, and now they could ride comfortably, four men to each Opel, and five in the Lancia truck. It wasn't everybody's idea of comfort, the powerful rays of the sun hot upon them, the dust churning up, and every so often a halt or at least a slow-down to negotiate some awkward passage before them. Still, it was an improvement on previous journeying.

What really lifted their spirits, though, was the feeling that they had thrown off the pursuit. Even though they had had Messerschmitts over The Graveyard looking for them, that didn't say their presence was suspected there. And the pilots hadn't spotted them, so they weren't having any bother from aircraft. Each hour, they told themselves, put them still further from possible trouble. Soon they might have chance to hole up for a few days, to get in a good rest after five days being hunted with remorseless energy.

But how about poor old Partridge? They couldn't rest up until he had been put where medical attention could be given him. Already they had accepted that idea, that soon Vecchi should take Partridge in and surrender to the enemy. But where were the enemy camps, and how near dare they approach them to leave the two injured men behind? Of course now the injured would have a vehicle, and if Vecchi felt capable of driving again – he kept saying he'd be all right, but they were doubtful, for his ribs gave him hell when he tried to exert himself – if Vecchi could drive he could take the pair of them into a camp. But they couldn't be left to fend for themselves yet, not here, in the middle of the trackless desert. Vecchi mightn't have the strength to keep driving, and then the two men would die miserably alone.

The trouble was, the patrol was lost. They had had to do so much twisting and turning that navigation with the accuracy demanded by their situation had been impossible. It didn't worry Yeats-Urley too much, though, now that they had abandoned the idea of finding the L.R.D.G. in some rendezvous. With his tanks full of petrol, he knew that simply by travelling north – and while the sun shone he could do that without even looking at his compass – he must, sooner or later, hit the north coast of Africa. After all, there was several thousand miles of it.

In fact the patrol captain was now pursuing a course east of north, with the idea of coming on to the coast road somewhere east of Tobruk, and was tolerably certain he wouldn't be more than a hundred miles out. That would be near enough for his purpose.

He had an idea that they weren't too far from El Badim, anyway, the airfield they had shot up nearly a week ago. If so, that wasn't over far from Tobruk. It was a wry thought, though, that after all their travels and hardships in the desert, they were almost back where they started. It had been a long run round to Tobruk, he told himself, and then they saw another Messerschmitt.

They were in open ground, without cover, the wrecks which could have camouflaged them a few miles back. Yeats-Urley ought, perhaps, to have remained within The Graveyard, with its opportunity for cover, but elated by their good fortune in replenishing their stocks, and anxious to make the escarpment before dark, he had pressed on in daylight. Now, seeing that distant aircraft, he wondered if he was going to regret it.

He halted the little convoy, and hoped that the dust cloud would soon settle. It did, but not quickly enough. Some alert eye in that distant plane must have seen the lingering dust and promptly came across to investigate. They saw the plane heading for them. Yeats-Urley decided on bluff. He ordered the convoy to re-start. After all, they were two German vehicles and one Italian, and in his ignorance Yeats-Urley didn't think the enemy would be looking for them. Three or four miles away, also, was the beginning of the hills that led up to the escarpment – cover there, if they could make it.

For a little while it did look as if the Messerschmitt pilot was deceived. He came round in a big circle, viewing them from all angles, and to keep up the illusion of friendliness they waved to him, too. The patrol captain wondered, though, if the pilot was viewing them through glasses. If so and he saw their wild appearance it might set him thinking. Still, after making a wide sweep around them, the pilot took off in a southerly direction, climbing. They all heaved a sigh of relief, and the vehicles trundled on, getting nearer to the broken country.

Fullalove, sitting beside his beloved Vickers, suddenly yelled out, 'The bastard!' and scrambled to his feet. The Messerschmitt had turned and was coming in a dive towards them, his intention plain. They were in for a strafing.

They could have halted, the men leaping out and dispersing, but Yeats-Urley knew if they did they'd have no transport left within minutes, the Messerschmitt shooting up their vehicles at leisure. Besides, how could they get the unconscious Partridge into safe cover in the minute left to them before the attack began? Impossible.

Tantalisingly close, only three miles on was hilly country and a chance to find cover. If they could make it, they stood a chance of staying alive until dark set in – always it seemed they were struggling to live until night came to help them slip away from peril.

Yeats-Urley did the best he could under the circumstances. He gave the signal to the other vehicles to scatter, and they took off in all directions instantly. At least that gave some of them a chance to survive.

The Messerschmitt took on Yeats-Urley's Opel, perhaps

because it was the middle one of the three vehicles. It came in, machine-guns flaming on the wings, the noise of firing preceding the arrival of the aircraft. Driver Medman knew the drill. As the plane came in low he flung their vehicle all over the desert in an effort to evade the Messerschmitt fire. As so often happened on the initial run, none of the bullets hit them, though they ploughed up the sand to their right.

Yeats-Urley gave the order to halt. He was buying time for the other vehicles. Let them get into the hills with some chance of finding cover for a couple of hours, while he attracted the enemy attention. They would think their bullets had hit, seeing them stop, and that might even make them incautious. Corporal Fullalove crouched behind his Vickers, jeering nastily at the oncoming pilot and telling him what he intended to do with him. Medman got ready to leap into speed at the right moment.

It came, that swift dive to give all speed, the opening up of the machine-guns, and Medman, a few seconds before, getting a racing start and going away in a big curve which suddenly turned into a skid which had them going the reverse way before the Messerschmitt pilot knew what they were up to. Fullalove belted off with the Vickers, and missed the plane by a mile.

The aircraft pulled up and away, and circled for another attack, but that manoeuvre had bought a few minutes' time for their comrades. The other Opel – Fairlop's – and the canvas-hooded Lancia were a mile ahead now, and throwing up big clouds of dust as they raced for the foothills. Medman set off after them.

For some reason the Messerschmitt pilot took some time before mounting the next attack. Perhaps he was having to use his radio, reporting back to HQ. It brought the fleeing vehicles quite close to the broken ground now, and Yeats-Urley thought if he could dodge the next attack, they might yet escape with their skins.

This time Medman went at speed over the desert, reckless of stones or holes in the ground. Speed might save them, in his skilled hands.

As the Messerschmitt came in for its third attack, Medman dodged and swung across the line of flight, never keeping a straight course for a moment. Fullalove fired furiously, to intimidate the pilot as far as possible – nowhere near again, but it would have the usual effect of making the pilot take him into account.

This time the bullets hit the Opel but didn't stop it. The spare wheel, screwed on to the sloping bonnet, had its tyre ripped unpleasantly, and that probably gave protection to the engine. Splinters of metal flew up and stung, but did no serious damage. Fullalove came out of the fight looking in astonishment at blood spurting from a wound on his right arm. He had never felt a thing, but there he was, wounded, hit most likely by a flying metal splinter.

'Look!' he cried in delight. 'I'll be able to wear a wound stripe!'

Hill told him, 'You'll wear a bloody coffin if we don't get out of here jildy.' The Messerschmitt was circling for another attack.

They were entering the hills, eroded rocky ranges, shining dark red in the slanting rays of the late afternoon sun. The leading trucks had disappeared, and the others wondered where they had gone. Yeats-Urley saw they themselves had no time in which to find cover, but he did see a way of thwarting the German pilot.

In the wadi ahead, isolated as if it had been scoured round by rushing water, was a rugged pile of rocks. It stood up almost sheer, an island of stone rising some forty or fifty feet, with flat land round its base. Medman took evasive action which the S.A.S. had employed before.

He shot round the rock pile, then came to a halt with a scream of brakes. The Messerschmitt came in, banking to pull him round and in sight of the Opel. As he did so, Medman shoved in the gear and raced back round the rock mass, keeping the towering pile between them and the aircraft. The Messerschmitt never even got a bullet in at them, but Fullalove, dripping blood on to the Vickers, raked the aircraft as it sped away. He shouted that he had hit, but Fullalove was constantly shouting that he had hit his target, only to be disconcerted by another attack from his 'victim'.

This Messerschmitt came back into the fray again. It dived and circled the rocky island in the middle of the wadi, the pilot throwing himself into the tightest of turns to rout out the S.A.S. But Medman was a cunning man, and always he raced round the rock mass, keeping it between him and danger. The Messerschmitt this time did open fire, but it was temper rather than with any chance of hitting the Opel.

In the vehicle, Fullalove and Hill were cheering Medman on, thoroughly enjoying themselves. Another attack came, and again they went racing round the rocky island. Another miss for the aircraft pilot. He must have sensed the futility of trying to catch them out, for now he pulled away up the wadi, doubtless looking for the other targets.

From the security of their protective rocks, Yeats-Urley and his men watched the search. After a few minutes they began to realise that time had been bought sufficiently for the other S.A.S. to tuck their vehicles out of sight up some gully. Almost they could feel the bafflement of the Messerschmitt pilot as he kept making low runs up the wadi, doubtless searching and failing to find his quarry.

In Yeats-Urley's Opel they felt so relaxed and confident now that they anticipated their evening ration by half a pint of water, and chewed on hard biscuits. If they ate and drank now, they wouldn't have to eat and drink later, their captain opined, and was pretty sure the other vehicles wouldn't be wasting time while hiding, either.

'I just hope Vecchi knows how to give poor old Party his morphia,' Fullalove said once. And his sulphonamide, too, he added to himself; must get that miracle stuff inside him. But Fullalove, remembering the awful smell around the gunner the last time he doped him, was pretty sure no sulphonamide in the world was going to save that arm now. At the best, they might be in time to save Partridge's life.

The Messerschmitt came at them twice more, probably fed up of hunting for vehicles which had cleverly hidden themselves amid the rocks and camel thorn. It could not have improved his morale. Each time he attacked, Driver Medman tore round the rocky island and kept them out of harm's way. Finally, the German pilot flew off, no doubt running low on petrol. Before he cleared the area, though he came across the wadi at about five hundred feet and dipped his wings in parting salute. It was a gesture they all appreciated.

'You know,' said Maurice Hill, carefully picking broken biscuit out of his beard, 'that's what I call a nice fellow. I could really get on with that guy.' And he stood up and saluted the receding aircraft which had been trying to kill him and his mates for the past half-hour.

Yeats-Urley wasted no time. Still well over an hour to dark. Radio would have other planes over to seek them out before nightfall, and when they came he wanted all his vehicles to be safely hidden. They went climbing up the wadi, rough going because it was littered with small boulders. A quarter of a mile up, they spotted the other vehicles. There was an overhang, and they had driven under it and had quickly piled up camel thorn against their vehicles to hide them. It must have been swiftly done, but it had been sufficient to hide their presence from the Messerschmitt pilot.

All the same, Yeats-Urley thought the place wasn't sufficiently safe for them. If they were spotted they were open to enemy fire. What he wanted was camouflage but also solid rock to shield them from any bullets. He waved to the other vehicles to follow him, and they crawled closely up the bumpy wadi.

Before the next attack came, they found good hiding places. In a land where Nature had twisted rocks into all manner of fantastic shapes, it was usually not difficult to find good cover. There were two side entrants to the main wadi, and Yeats-Urley directed the other Opel and the Lancia into one, and tucked their own Opel into the other. All three vehicles would be difficult to hit now, with steep rock walls rising almost sheer on either side of them. Even ombers would have to lay their eggs very accurately. Only mortar fire was to be feared, and Yeats-Urley was pretty sure there was no one with a mortar within fifty miles.

They went through the usual uncomfortable routine of chopping through roots with their sand shovels and dragging sizeable bushes to throw over their vehicles. They had completed the job to Yeats-Urley's satisfaction, when the next aircraft came over looking for them. They just sat quietly there, not moving while it was nearby, and relaxing and finishing their evening meal when it went out of sight.

Yeats-Urley had no fears for their safety now, not that night, anyway. Once again they had escaped disaster by the skin of their teeth. They were alive, and in the night could slip away into new country, and by the following morning they ought to be so close to the coast road that they could lie up until the hunt died down and could then go on their way, wherever that was.

. . . it was a pity, though, the enemy had found them, he thought ruefully. They'd seemed to be making such good ground out of hostile territory, and he wondered why the Germans had abruptly switched the hunt right over the path of their attempted escape.

Two Messerschmitts came over them this time. Yeats-Urley thought it was a good job they hadn't stuck to that rocky island down the wadi, for two Messerschmitts, concerting their attack, would have blown the daylights out of them in short time.

The Luftwaffe kept up the search almost until darkness, a matter of regret for the S.A.S. captain, who wanted as much daylight as possible in that rocky wadi. There was always the possibility that the way would grow too steep, and they would be unable to gain the escarpment top, in which event they would have to retrace their steps most laboriously and find a new way up. Yeats-Urley didn't want that to happen. He wanted to be as far away as possible from this hunting ground. It had become too hot for them.

It was hard going, and they took much of the precious light in getting out of the wadi and on top of the escarpment.

Much of the way all three vehicles had to be manhandled, hauled to the top as much by muscle power as by engines they began to think. It was not work for tired men, and by this time they were very tired.

The elation of earlier in the day, which had come with the successful attack on the German recovery party, then later giving the slip to the Luftwaffe, drained away as the hour passed and they seemed no nearer the escarpment top. What made matters worse was to hear Partridge moaning in agony, massive doses of morphia no longer providing the sedation his tortured nerves demanded.

All during those hours up the hill Gunner Partridge was tended by the two Italian civilians. It was they who had administered the sulphonamide and morphia while Fullalove was on other work, not Vecchi. They who nursed the pain wracked ex-artilleryman and held him when the going was rough and threatened to throw his unconscious form around the bare metal floor of the Lancia. They who gave him water when he called for it, and kept his good hand from clawing at his bloody bandage.

The air was foul with the odour from the gangrene, so that Vecchi, who stayed on with his comrade, and Private Mack who didn't, wanted to vomit. Yet the two scientists seemed not to heed it, never once complaining.

Vecchi, at a halt, when the Italians were cleaning poor Partridge, said fiercely, 'Look at them! Ever seen two better blokes in your life? And that creep of a Fairlop, that whore's son, wants to kill them. Do hear that? He wants to kill them so as to get rid of them. And he's a soddin' rotten runaway and they're two wonderful blokes!'

He cried. He was recovering, but he was very weak, He'd never be able to drive the big Lancia over the rough desert they all knew.

Then he said, 'He's not going to do it. Not going to, I tell you. You've got to stand by me and say no harm's to come to them.'

He stopped talking. His audience consisted of Franki Mack and Tommy Shiner. Good lads, but they didn't feel

:eply. They just looked at him, not understanding. A
'op was a Wop. If Fairlop said the Eyties had to be topped,
ey'd do as they were ordered.

Vecchi, blood calling to compatriots, stopped his weak
ying and instead looked cunning. They were his friends.
hey weren't going to die at British hands, not if he could
·lp it. He began to build plans. The trouble was, he hadn't
e strength to go through with them, interesting though
ey were.

Just when the moon came up to help them, they dragged
e first Opel over the edge of the escarpment. It still looked
gged going, but at least they were through that dreadful
adi and would be able to make progress. They got the other
·hicles through the gap, then discovered that Fairlop's
pel had developed a puncture and no one had noticed it.
) more time was wasted as they stood around, torches
rected on to the wheel, while it was changed.

They got moving not much before three o'clock, and kept
) a steady ten miles in the hour, which wasn't bad going.
hen Fairlop's vehicle had another puncture, and when that
as mended they came upon another range of hills in the
oonlight, and with them Yeats-Urley guessed where they
ere. It was an escarpment upon an escarpment. The only one
e knew like that was within fifty miles of Tobruk. So they
eren't far off course, after all. Yeats-Urley decided to
ving farther east still, to keep away from the Axis-occupied
ort. But first they had to climb the hill, and that presented
s much difficulty as the last wadi.

Going became slower and slower, though they strained
·ery muscle to get on to the escarpment before daylight.
hat was another race they lost. Tired following their long
ight's struggle, they worked slower as each physical
ostacle had to be tackled. Exhausted, weary men struggled
) bring three loaded vehicles almost up the side of a
recipice. They almost did it, too, but it beat them in the end.

They had followed the course of a wadi, as usual when they
anted to gain the top of an escarpment, but they could

have picked a better one. Near to the summit it narrowed and wound disconcertingly, and was very steep, while the floor was littered with loose rocks that slipped away when their vehicles tried to get traction. It meant that each car, head-lights blazing to reveal the next difficulties, engine roaring futilely, had to be almost lifted up the face of the hill, every available hand concentrating in turn on each car or the truck.

A raw-cold wind kept blowing too, lifting in swift nasty gushes over the edge of the escarpment, showering sand on to their sweaty bodies, stinging their naked flesh if they had doffed their shirts, and clinging like sandy mud to sodden clothing and bodies. Those gusts never lasted long, but while they blew they held back progress, men crouching down and protecting their faces until it died away. It neither helped them in their efforts nor improved their lowering morale.

The sound of Partridge crying or moaning with pain on that moonlit escarpment face, like some tortured scene from the moon, did not improve their spirits, either. They had been on the run too long. They must have rest, Yeats-Urley knew, very quickly, or some of the men would crack. He said that, yet looking round he wondered if any of his iron men would ever crack. Not the massive Fullalove, so long as he ad his Vickers. Lumbering Oily Hoyle from Birmingham? He hadn't the imagination even to feel this night's discomfort. Hill? Impossible. Shiner, Medman and Mack? Hard as the rocks around them. And M'Bain, cool bastard just walking out there with a grin on his face and calmly tossing a grenade into an armoured car – he'd never go under. Yet whatever he said, he knew one of them would collapse when the strain grew too unbearable, and after the first one, others would go.

But rest, when could they look forward to it? Not until they were on the escarpment and miles away. If he was even approximate in his bearings, Yeats-Urley knew where he would find a good hiding place, overlooking the Tobruk-Mersa road. But they had to get there first, and he doubted now if they would do it during daylight. The hunt was still on for them.

Their luck ran finally, completely out when the Opels were no more than a hundred yards from the top, and probably could make the last fierce gradient under their own steam. The Lancia stuck and couldn't make it.

The eastern sky was paling. Twenty minutes or so and there would be light. An hour and the Messerschmitts would be hurtling down upon them, he guessed. And they were stuck.

Medman called out the news. 'Sir, I think the Lancia's jammed. It isn't moving.'

Sir turned wearily from propping rocks under the rear wheels of the leading Opel, and went scrambling in the light from the second Opel's headlamps down to where men worked around the Italian truck. He came through the beam of the Lancia's headlights, blinded by them, and had to stand for a second before his eyes adjusted to the darkness beyond. He saw the trouble.

He remembered this part, recently negotiated. An awkward needle of rock reared up from the wadi floor, narrowing the way. The two smaller Opels had got through, and Yeats-Urley, perhaps too tired to think clearly, hadn't given a thought to the wider Lancia following. Now he must do. It was stuck.

Mack was holding a torch while Shiner belted into the rock with a long steel bar. He was making little progress. He looked round, hearing someone moving towards him, recognised his officer and said in a very tired voice, 'Sir, this is a real cow's son.' He raised the bar and struck again. Yeats-Urley recognised the growing weakness in the stroke, almost Shiner was letting the weight of the bar carry it down to the rock.

He took charge. They were working foolishly, under cramped conditions. They'd save no time doing it that way. Yeats-Urley said, 'Get her out of here. Run her back a bit.' He'd get the big men, Hoyle and Hill, on this job, but they would need room in which to swing at the rock.

Mack got into the cab and released the handbrake. Under guidance from the officer and Shiner they ran the vehicle back a few yards. Then Yeats-Urley shouted up the hill to the two big men, who came down within a few minutes. The officer showed them the problem.

'It's the rear wheels. They stick when it tries to go through. But it only needs another inch or so and if you take hefty swings at it you'll chip away enough to get us by.'

Hoyle took the bar for the first swipe. Yeats-Urley said, 'This'll do your bowels a lot of good, Hoyle.'

Hoyle, the thick man, said hoarsely, 'I've got no bowels now, sir, I'm suffering from constipation.'

'Silly sod,' said Hill good-humouredly. 'You've got nothing left in you.' They began to attack the rock, each in turn swinging that heavy steel bar.

The light was brightening over the escarpment. Yeats-Urley wanted to get over the top and start running again, but this was holding them up. Sand showered on to their miserable forms again, the wind howling nastily over the escarpment edge. It kept on for several minutes, and Yeats-Urley thought, 'There's that sand-storm blowing up again.' It was the time of the year when the *Khamsin* wind brought sand-storms almost daily.

But it wasn't going to be a quick job, chipping away into this obstructing rock. The bar seemed to bounce off it, stinging their hands so that the men had to keep taking turns at frequent intervals. Mere flecks of rock fell off to reward herculean labours.

The light was very bright. All in one second Yeats-Urley knew it was no good. This race they had also lost – unless they could hide up for the day without detection in this wadi. He doubted it. They were too near the last place of attack, and this area would be combed with a thoroughness that wouldn't permit three vehicles to remain long unobserved.

He let them swing for another few minutes, always hoping that their efforts would find reward, and they would see a great slice of rock fall off. It didn't. Anyway, could they risk getting on to the open escarpment now, with all this light to reveal them? No. Only if the sand-storm blew up to cover them, as it looked as if it might do.

Almost full daylight seemed to flood the valley at once, and at that Yeats-Urley abandoned the exercise. No good trying any longer. He gave the order to find good places of hiding for the three vehicles. That was all they could do now. He had a feeling it wasn't sufficient.

So they worked the Lancia back a good hundred yards down the wadi to where it widened and it could be turned round. Then they coasted another couple of hundred yards and drew it into a crack in the hillside that looked tailor-made for it. That one, Yeats-Urley was pretty sure, wasn't going to be spotted easily.

They climbed laboriously back up the wadi to find a problem. There was no hiding place for them up this narrow gully, and no time to manhandle the vehicles back down the hill to join the Lancia. Yeats-Urley thought of taking to the escarpment on foot, and getting out of this wadi – something of a trap, he was beginning to feel – but what was the good of that? And he certainly couldn't shove off and leave the Lancia and the prisoners and wounded, as well as Shiner and Mack, down below for the enemy to get at.

They would have to hole up here for the day and try to survive all attacks from the air, he thought, then make a break for it under cover of the next night's darkness. They would have to abandon the Lancia, carry the unconscious Partridge up the hillside, then move off in the two Opels – very crowded, but what else was there they could do, and anyway they'd done it once before.

He set about ordering a state of defence. A stone sangar was built under a projecting ledge above the leading Opel, and all weapons, ammunition, food and water brought there. The Spandau machine-guns were dismounted, and with the Vickers this gave them three formidable weapons. They would be able to put up a concentrated firepower if the enemy did come in to the attack. In fact Yeats-Urley thought that fighters would never winkle them out. So long as they didn't bring bombers, or men with mortars. But men would be far away. . . .

Then they piled rocks all round the vehicles, even putting a layer of flat ones over the top of them, to render the scout cars invulnerable to bullets from the air. By which time it was fully light, and the first of the day's planes had been seen scouting south of them.

They had a brew up, and never been so thankful in their lives for those mugs of steaming tea. Medman ground up the hard biscuit, added sugar and water to it and boiled it up to make a palatable porridge. That was their breakfast. Then they went off to sleep, men dead on their feet, leaving a tired Yeats-Urley to take his customary first watch.

Glasses up, he watched the distant plane. In fact there were either two or three of them, working their way up from the slope to the first escarpment, systematically quartering the ground, like foxhounds, was all that the huntin' Yeats-Urley could think of.

By the end of his watch, two hours later, the aircraft – Messerschmitts, some 109Es, others 110s – were searching this escarpment face, and now there were five of them always somewhere in sight. It was a most resolute and intensive search. Nothing was going to be held back if it could end the activities of this destructive party of S.A.S. Rommel had said so again in the night.

Yeats-Urley got his head down at eight o'clock, still without the Messerschmitts having spotted them. Corporal Fullalove took second watch, with instructions to waken his commanding officer if the situation took a turn for the worse. The corporal gave his big grin and without saying a word, patted his Vickers as if looking forward to a deterioration in their situation.

The hunt seemed to go away for a time, and Fullalove finally handed over to his relief saying, 'I think we've given 'em the slip again. They've been over a few times, but seen nothing.'

At ten-thirty a Messerschmitt 109E seemed to come floating up the wadi, the pilot really giving the ground a

thorough scrutiny. He missed the Lancia, naturally camouflaged, but finally his attention was attracted by the
unnatural rock formation at the head of the gully. The
sangar wall wasn't quite as Nature built things, and perhaps
he discerned the lines of the Opels under their protective
disguise, too.

He went lifting over the top of the escarpment, came round
in a wide circle, and the next thing the sleeping men knew
was that bullets were raking their sangar.

The noise was tremendous. They had slept through the
sounds of aircraft cruising overhead, but this one, coming
in hard, throttle wide open, guns roaring in the confines of
the wadi, rock walls echoing and re-echoing the sounds, was
too much even for the heaviest sleepers. They came rolling
on to their feet, hands grabbing for weapons and slipping
off the safety catches. Then they crouched behind the rough
sangar wall and peered cautiously out.

They saw nothing. The Messerschmitt was a thing of
dying noise behind them.

That Messerschmitt called up the other aircraft; a
radio message flashed to Rommel in Tobruk – 'Found!'

The five Messerschmitts came in line astern into the
attack. Yeats-Urley thought, 'No good pretending we're
not here and they'll go away,' and gave the order to fire on
the enemy.

Hell broke loose up the wadi, a very noisy hell. It filled with
the sound of aircraft roaring full out, guns chattering,
head-on for the sangar, only to lift at seemingly the last
minute and flash above the escarpment. Six machine-guns
on each plane added to the deafening row, while inside the
sangar two Spandaus and a Vickers deafened the men
crouching under that overhang.

Each plane in turn flashed over their defence position.
Each hurled spinning hot lead at them, to shatter against the
rocks around the sangar and flatten all too often against the
sangar wall. Some even hit the back of the overhang and
dropped spent and flattened to the ground, a warning to all
to keep their thick heads down. But they were S.A.S., and

trained, and did not need this reminder to keep them alive.

And each plane was savaged by raking fire from three machine-guns, a daunting barrage that soon put off those daring fighter pilots. Probably some of the bullets landed on target, though for a time seemingly without doing much damage, but to a pilot, watching holes chewing into his wings or bits grouted out of the fuselage around him, it must have been unnerving. They changed their tactics.

Frontal attacks were likely to lead more to casualties for the Luftwaffe than for the obstinate S.A.S. behind their solidly constructed defence wall. Some observant pilot worked out that the sangar had two blind spots. Because of the shape of the overhang, almost a cave, the defenders could not cover the face of the hillside on either side of them.

He tried out a new tactic. He came in fast along the face of the escarpment, then at the last second or so swung in, got in a swift burst at the S.A.S., then shot up out of harm's way before the defenders could bring their guns to bear upon him. And those were the tactics for the next half-hour.

The flying was brilliant, impressive even to the hard-pressed British soldiers, huddled behind their thick stone wall. They never knew from which angle the attack would come next. Sometimes a Messerschmitt would dive upon them from the right, sometimes from the left, and sometimes another would come head-on for them up the wadi while they were distracted by aircraft attacking on their flank.

It was terrifying, noise, dust and drifting cordite smoke, and those flashing aircraft bodies hurtling so close above their heads. Yet as Yeats-Urley pointed out, they'd picked a good place for their sangar, and not a man had been hurt as yet in spite of the thousands of rounds poured at them.

A little while later Fullalove became their first casualty. By coincidence he stopped another missile on the same arm as his first, much-prized war wound. This time it was more severe, a ricochet that took a lump out of the hairy forearm, but again he didn't seem to feel it, and after a bit of crude bandaging he took over his old Vickers again and went cheerfully into action when another plane came at them.

Then the Stukas arrived, at which the Messerschmitts flitted back to El Adem thwarted, to fill their tanks for another sortie. A squadron of Ju87s came half an hour after the aerial attack began. By this time the sand was pouring down upon them from the top of the escarpment, telling them of the sandstorm beginning to rage there.

They came, flying high, at first in echelon, and then the Stukas began to peel off and come screaming down at terrifying speed towards the sangar. They carried sirens attached to their wings, which made unearthly sounds, morale-destroying even without those Stukas diving straight at one.

Each in turn, swiftly upon the heels of the other, came down in that steep dive. Each in turn released his bombs, then somehow pulled up and away in time to avert disaster against the rocky escarpment. Then they came wheeling back for another run and dive.

The earth shook as the bombs exploded, and bits of rock and dirt were shaken from the roof of the overhang. Yeats-Urley even got to worrying in case it collapsed on them, but it held. The bombs missed their target. In fairness to the daring Stuka pilots the target was difficult to pin-point. Up a narrow wadi, dug into an overhang, with the harsh rock face of the escarpment suicidally close? It could have been easier for the Luftwaffe!

Nothing was hit in that first run, though the explosions were uncomfortably close, the bombs bouncing off the solid rock and often bursting in mid-air. Yeats-Urley kept a cautious eye on the two hidden Opels. Protective rock or no protective rock, if they suffered a direct hit they'd be put out of action. Without transport they could abandon their ideas of escaping from the enemy. But the scout cars survived every raid.

He looked down, too, far below into the wadi where the Lancia was tucked away. Sensible men, Shiner and Mack hadn't drawn attention to their position by opening fire with a rifle and tommy-gun on the aircraft. Best thing for them was to put their heads down and sleep comfortably through this action.

Again the Stukas came in on a dive, and again the earth tremored to the explosive effect of their bombs along the escarpment. And again they survived. But the Stukas were more dangerous than the fighter aircraft.

Then the mortars arrived. Rommel had promised everything to teach these S.A.S. a lesson, and now he threw in his most formidable fighting men to do battle with the desert raiders.

Big Maurice Hill, his face a black mask from smoke and dust, saw them first. He could see the sky from his position crouching behind the sangar wall. He had taken time off 'to have a swaller', and was nursing the tab end of a Blighty Wood in his massive palm.

He suddenly said, 'Hello, now what does this mean?' Knowing it meant no good for the S.A.S.

They followed his gaze. Three aircraft were droning high from the south – two or three thousand feet up, anyway, but high after the low-level runs of the Messerschmitts and Stukas – and would cross the edge of the escarpment directly above their wadi.

Fullalove said, 'They're Ju52s,' but probably all the others had identified them, too. Harmless aircraft, used by the Germans to carry supplies and troops. Now, thought Yeats-Urley, what are *you* doing here? For their presence above the tiny battle area could not be ascribed to coincidence, the young captain was sure.

They passed out of sight above them. The wind was howling again, the dust flying, their misery about complete. But they had stayed alive another few hours, and that was all that counted. A look-out said there were more Messerschmitts on the horizon, and some time later said they were just cruising around, not coming closer. Puzzling.

And then the look-out, Driver Medman, started to shout and point as if he had gone mad. 'Christ, come and look at this!'

They all hauled themselves to their feet and peered

cautiously over the wall of the sangar. Not quarter of a mile away, but being hurried along by the strong wind, were parachutists. They could see the dark, helmeted forms swinging under canopies of red, green and yellow, huge chutes that billowed and changed shape as the parachutists spilled air from them, to control their descent.

Yeats-Urley thought, 'This is the end.' Not often did he allow himself this feeling that they'd done all they could have done and now there was nothing else left for them to do. But seeing those men swinging down on their chutes – men who had last been in action in the capture of Crete and had earned a big reputation by their reckless courage there – his heart sank.

The circling Messerschmitts effectively prevented any attempt at a break-out over the top and across the escarpment. They'd never get their Opels out of this wadi with those machine-guns waiting for them. And the longer they stayed here, the more certain he was that the paratroopers would soon blast them from out of their sangar. These men would bring mortars with them, he knew. Under covering fire from their automatic weapons the mortars would be brought into, say, the next wadi, from which they would plaster their hide-out. It was only a question of time before they got the range. Then the paratroopers would come leaping up to finish off the attack, machine-guns stammering, and grenades exploding.

Yeats-Urley thought, 'I don't like it. No, I really don't like it.' He gave no sign of his unhappiness to his men, but with as much battle experience as he they would hold views not too different from his own, he felt certain.

Hill was first to use his rifle on the swinging targets, and undoubtedly killed or wounded at least two paratroopers. Others took up the fire, but little damage was done because the strong wind had the swinging targets well out of range within seconds.

. . . Yeats-Urley, who had to analyse every significant fact of battle, thought, 'Why are they dropping below us?' Because that meant the paratroopers would have to labour back up the slope. They ought to have been dropped on the escarpment top, so that they could, more comfortably, work their way down. At which moment the wind came howling into their sangar, filling it with sand and choking dust, and Yeats-Urley thought he knew the answer to his own question. They hadn't made sufficient allowance for the wind, and it had carried the paratroopers over the edge instead of letting them land above. Ah, well, that might give them another hour's respite.

When the last of the parachutes had collapsed far down the valley, the Messerschmitts came in on cue, once again raking their position. That was to keep them occupied while the paratroopers worked their way into position.

By two in the afternoon the paras were within range of the sangar, and now the Stukas came back for another turn, and the bombs dropped, shaking the earth, and accurate fire from the hidden paras began to hit the roof of the sangar and drop down upon them. Taking big risks, leaving the machine-guns to open up and try to daunt the Stukas, Yeats-Urley, Fairlop, M'Bain and Hill kept up a steady rifle fire on the advancing paras. Unhappily they had only four rifles with them, and only precision-made rifles were any good for this type of job.

Their fire was not sufficient to keep the paras from advancing. Quick glimpses over the sangar wall revealed helmeted figures climbing all up the face of the escarpment, beginning to close in on them, but still several hundred yards away, still with a slow hard climb under fire before they were within grenade-throwing distance. But where were the mortars? That was what made Yeats-Urley worry most. One mortar-shell exploding in the confined space under the rocky overhang would do for the lot of them.

The men with the rifles were doing some damage. Fairlop said he thought he had hit at least two paratroopers, and maybe more. He was very calm under heavy fire, giving no sense of panic. He *wasn't* the sort of man to run away, Yeats-Urley thought approvingly. Not quite his sort, but a good fellow in an emergency. Vecchi must have been mistaken in his accusations, probably his sore ribs making impressions jaundiced. No, he wouldn't believe anything against Fairlop after seeing him in action. . . .

Fullalove got one of the Stukas. He had claimed hits several times before, but the others had jeered and he hadn't been able to prove anything. This time he got a full burst into the Stuka just as it was peeling away after dropping its bombs. It was Fullalove's victim, they all knew, for both other Spandaus were out of action, reloading, for the moment.

'His arse!' chanted Fullalove gleefully, turning a gargoyle-like face, caked and sweat-lined, towards the others. 'Right up his jaxie! Knocked the shit out of his tail feathers – Look, look!'

Fullalove *had* hit the Stuka. It had gone winging away erratically west along the face of the escarpment, but now it was turning, beginning to somersault slowly, a dead pilot at the controls. It went over and over in the air, the sirens dying suddenly, and then it landed below with a great crump! and a huge pyre of black smoke rose off the plain.

It didn't end the battle. The Stukas kept coming back for more. The paratroopers were getting closer. A mortar shell did explode but well away from them. The noise, the pressure, was almost unbearable. Casualties began to occur. Fairlop had his cheek blown away and lost most of his teeth in the process. Medman took a bullet in the throat and died gasping for breath and going blue in the face. Fullalove, who took more risks than anyone, was hit twice more, both times in the flesh of his right arm, but still went on firing. Big Maurice Hill had his rifle shattered and got his face full of wood splinters, which hurt him a lot.

M'Bain knew he couldn't stand much more of it. He had neither rifle nor machine-gun now to help him through this moment, Oily Hoyle having relieved him of his Lee-Enfield some time back. A gun in his hand might have helped him under that heavy fire. It was all he could do to hold himself back when the Stukas with their terrifying sirens came swooping at them. He kept saying to himself, 'I'm not staying. I'm getting out of here.' But still he kept with the others.

Not helping them now was the increasing fury of the storm raging overhead. It brought sand pouring down upon them, and filled the air down the wadi. It reduced visibility and gave the paras a chance to advance with safety up the steep mountainside. Fairlop, speaking with difficulty, said, 'Alan, we could get away when the dust blows up like that.' A few minutes dragging the stones away from their vehicles. A few frantic minutes getting the cars to the top. Then away again, the sand-storm hiding them from circling planes. On the escarpment the dust would be a few hundred feet high now, though in the wadi it would clear considerably when the wind died, as it so often did. The Stukas weren't taking any chances now, and didn't make their dangerous runs unless visibility was clear. At any time Yeats-Urley expected them to pull out and go home, as the Messerschmitts had done, leaving the battle to the paras . . . who would win, they all knew. Too many of them to hold off forever.

'Yes, we could.' The thought was tempting. But there was the responsibility of the men in the Lancia below. Then he shook his head. There'd be dust enough to hide them on the escarpment, but he didn't think it had got thick enough yet quite to disguise movement at the head of the wadi. Those paras, picked marksmen, would do a lot of damage before they got their scout cars over the top.

He expressed his feelings to the lieutenant who grudgingly admitted he was right. 'What we need is a diversion, Alan. Something to draw their attention away for a few minutes.'

'We're not likely to get that.' Yeats-Urley had no doubts on that score. The paras were getting uncomfortably close now, the fire more concentrated and accurate. Then the dust and sand really swirled about them. It was getting thicker. In time it might be dense enough for them to get away. But before then the paras would have their guts for garters.

M'Bain, crouching behind the sangar wall, heard them talking yet never heard a word. He was on the point of breaking. He had to get out of here. He had a horror of being trapped in a confined space like this; it built up a panic within him and made him feel desperate. Like in the slit trench on the edge of The Graveyard. He had cracked then, when they talked of flame-throwers, and he'd had those pictures of great gouts of flame hurtling in on them and burning them, screaming with agony, alive. Now he cracked because of the remorseless advance of the German paras, conveying with their deliberate movements the certainty that in time they would be lobbing stick-bombs at them and that was a horrible way to die.

M'Bain remembered the legless body that was dragged from the half-track. Perhaps *he* had blown the poor sod's legs off. He looked down at his own. He didn't want to see bleeding stumps. He was getting out of here!

Panic brought him rearing to his feet. The hell with everything, he was leaving, deserting, doing the thing called cowardly. It meant nothing to him in his terror. All he could think of was the vague plan he had worked out a while ago, when he was comparatively sane. Now he wasn't right in his head. Germans, he thought; pity Vecchi couldn't speak German. And he went over the sangar wall, and by coincidence the sand and dust blew thick at that moment and no one spotted him as he crawled out and down the wadi.

The mortar shells were getting closer. It was only a question of time. But the Stukas had drawn away. Too dangerous now for them to fly into that thickening dust storm. That was some relief.

Fairlop said calmly, through broken teeth, 'I'm not going to die here, Alan, defending nothing. I'm going on the run — on foot.'

The others had heard. Yeats-Urley said, 'What about it, chaps?'

Hill said, 'Too tired, sir. Done all the running I'm going to do. If there's no vehicle, I'm going to stay here until the ammo runs out, then they can put me in the bag.'

The other men seemed of a similar sentiment. They'd had enough of running. Just for the hell of it they'd go on fighting until they could fight no more.

Fairlop said, 'Is it okay by you, Alan?'

Yeats-Urley said, 'Why not? Sure, you try to get away, and if you make it, drink our health in Shepheards.' He wasn't going. He couldn't leave his men.

So Fairlop stood up, and cautiously scanned the steep-sloping ground below. He saw movement. The paras were coming in very steadily. He thought, 'They're no more than four hundred yards away.' He thought some of them must have passed the Lancia in its hide-out without noticing it. But they wouldn't be looking for another enemy vehicle down there, so that wasn't surprising.

The stray thought made him look to where they had seen the Lancia tuck itself out of sight. He gasped with astonishment. 'Alan! Look!'

The startled cry brought them all peering over the edge of the sangar. They found themselves looking between dust clouds, settling down the wadi. Below a vehicle was trundling out where the dried-up watercourse widened on to the lower escarpment. It was their Lancia. And white cloths – towels, probably – were waving energetically from the windows of the cab.

Yeats-Urley said, 'Christ!' and then the wind came roaring over the escarpment again and the world was more full of dust and sand than it had been at any time. And the captain didn't know what to do.

Fairlop, the man who looked after himself, did. He shouted, his face spitting gore, unrecognisable now in his blood and muck, 'Don't fire, any of you!' Mustn't attract any attention now.

'Alan, don't you see? Here's our chance. That's the diversion we talked about. They'll all be looking at the Lancia. Alan, we've got two or three minutes only. . . .'

Every man there got it immediately. Leaving the dead Medman, they went scrambling over the sangar wall. In seconds they were at their precious vehicles; in two minutes all rocks had been removed. The dust cloud began to settle as the wind changed course above. They began to shove the Opels even before drivers could start engines. The noise echoed and re-echoed down the wadi, sudden, startling, surprising. For half a minute no lead came after them, though. Perhaps they weren't as easy to see as they thought.

Then the firing opened up, a few shots only for the moment. The first scout car was shoved over the top, and the men went scrambling after it. The second car couldn't seem to get going. Wheelspin. And not as many men to shove. Just Yeats-Urley and the faithful Hill, but Hill was wounded. And then two more came panting up and shoved and the Opel went over the top without anyone getting hurt.

When they'd driven a few hundred yards into the murk of the sandstorm on top, and found Fairlop with the other Opel, Yeats-Urley stopped heaving the wind into his tortured lungs and calmed down. It was then he noticed the two men who had come to help them. Shiner and Mack.

When he could speak he said, 'Good God, where did you come from? I thought you'd gone off with the Lancia.'

'You sent for us, sir.' That was Frankie Mack, innocently.

'I sent for you?' Yeats-Urley was incredulous.

'Yes, sir. Corporal M'Bain told us. He came down and said you wanted us in the sangar.'

'But M'Bain's here –' Yeats-Urley's words halted. He was looking at the other car. M'Bain wasn't there. M'Bain wasn't with the party.

'M'Bain said you'd said the Lancia had to give itself up. The only thing for Partridge. He was going to drive it out. But we had to come back to you, sir.'

'He said that, did he?' Yeats-Urley was stunned with astonishment. And when they'd gone M'Bain had driven off to surrender to the enemy, waving white towels.

They all talked about it that night, and every night later while they holed up and rested and finally made contact with the Eighth Army as it came up from Alamein.

Yeats-Urley said, thoughtfully, 'With any other man I might think of cowardice. But not M'Bain.'

Fairlop, talking through an awkward bandage, said, 'Not M'Bain. A man who takes on an armoured car like he did doesn't run away.' And then, in a later conversation, he said, 'Alan, remember we were talking in the sangar just before the end – about needing some diversion, something to draw the attention of the paras for a few minutes? Remember? M'Bain was there at the time, because I remember seeing him. I think he heard and he went down and gave himself up to the enemy so as to create a diversion so that we could get away.'

Yeats-Urley's eyes shone. No man wants to believe something bad about a favourite, and M'Bain had stood high in the captain's favour. It was consistent with the opinion he had held of the man, and he was going to cling to it.

So when he went down to Alexandria to rejoin his squadron, he wrote a report which spoke highly of M'Bain and his gallantry. 'Not only did he wipe out an enemy armoured car at a time when it was unlikely that my patrol would otherwise have survived, but in the end he gave himself up to the enemy so as to enable his other comrades to escape.' And M'Bain became a legend in the S.A.S. though he never knew it, being with Vecchi and a one-armed Partridge in an Italian prison camp.

And when he came out of the P.O.W. camp on the collapse of Italy, an astonished M'Bain found he had been awarded the Military Medal for devotion to duty beyond that of other men.

It still didn't encourage him to go back with the S.A.S., now operating in Italy. Not bloody likely, he said, and got himself a cushy billet in a Q store.

THE BEST
IN WAR BOOKS!

_____The Franklin Comes Home
A.A. Hoeling   12422 ★ $1.25

_____Patton's Third U.S. Army/Lucky Forward
Col. Robert S. Allen   17115 ★ $1.75

_____The Untold Story of Douglas MacArthur
Frazier Hunt   25101 ★ $2.50

_____The Flight of the Phoenix
Elleston Trevor   15234 ★ $1.50

_____The Glasshouse Gang
Gordon Landsborough   15255 ★ $1.50

_____Desert Marauders
Gordon Landsborough   15261 ★ $1.50

_____Pass the Ammunition
Stan Smith   12394 ★ $1.25

_____Assignment: Devil's Playground
Joseph Decker   12486 ★ $1.25

_____Operation Damascus
Joseph Levy   17149 ★ $1.75

_____The Champagne Spy
Wolfgang Lotz   15109 ★ $1.50

_____The Nazi Who Lived As A Jew
Edgar Hilsenrath   19145 ★ $1.95

_____Squadron Airborn
Elleston Trevor   15270 ★ $1.50.

A MAJOR BOOK CLUB SELECTION!

ESCAPE

JAMES PURVIS

THE DRAMATIC
TRUE STORY OF
THE MAN
NO CONCENTRATION CAMP
COULD HOLD!

⌐ ★

THE GLASSHOUSE GANG
IN 4 OF THE MOST
STARTLING WAR STORIES
EVER WRITTEN!
by Gordon Landsborough

☐**THE GLASSHOUSE GANG** 15255 ★ $1.50
☐**DESERT MARAUDERS** 15261 ★ $1.50
☐**BENGHAZI BREAKOUT** 15271 ★ $1.50
☐**THE DEAD COMMANDO** 15279 ★ $1.50

★★★★★★★★★★★★★★★★★★★★★

Manor Books Inc.
432 Park Avenue South
New York, New York 10016

Please send me the MB books I have checked above.
I am enclosing $ _____ Check or money order, (no
currency or C.O.D. s). Enclose price listed for
each title plus 35¢ per copy ordered to cover cost
of postage and handling.

☐ Send me a free list of all your books in print.

Name _____

Address _____

City _____ State _____ Zip _____

PATTON'S THIRD U.S. ARMY

LUCKY

★★★★★★ ────── ★★★★★★

FORWARD

BY COLONEL ROBERT S. ALLEN

This spectacular book not only explodes with the action and drama of men at war but also reveals a fascinating portrait of George S. Patton, the most dynamic and controversial general of World War II.